Praise for Donna Leon's Internationally Bestselling Commissario Guido Brunetti Mysteries

"The appeal of Guido Brunetti, the hero of Donna Leon's long-running Venetian crime series, comes not from his shrewdness, though he is plenty shrewd, nor from his quick wit. It comes, instead, from his role as an everyman . . . not so different from our own days at the office or nights around the dinner table. Crime fiction for those willing to grapple with, rather than escape, the uncertainties of daily life."
—Bill Ott, *Booklist* (starred review)

"The evocative Venetian setting and the warmth and humanity of the Brunetti family add considerable pleasure to this nuanced, intelligent mystery; another winner from the Venice-based Leon. Highly recommended."
—Michele Laber, *Library Journal* (starred review)

"Another of her fabulous Italian mysteries. . . . She has her finger on the pulse."   —*Bookseller*

"Gives the reader a feel for life in Venice. . . . The story is filled with the average citizen's cynicism, knowledge of corruption, and deep distrust and fear of government and police. Characters are brilliantly portrayed. Even bit players become real and individual and Brunetti and his family are multifaceted and layered."   —Sally Fellows, *Mystery News*

"In her classy, literate, atmospheric Commissario Guido Brunetti series, Donna Leon takes readers . . . to a Venice that tourists rarely see."   —*Bookpage*

"If you're heading to Venice, take along a few of [Leon's] books to use for both entertainment and travel directions."
—*The Pittsburgh Post-Gazette*

"Venice provides a beautifully rendered backdrop for this operatic story of fathers and sons, and Leon's writing trembles with true feeling."   —*The Star-Tribune* (Minneapolis)

"One of the best international crime writers is Donna Leon, and her Commissario Guido Brunetti tales set in Venice are at the apex of continental thrillers. . . . The author has written a pitch-perfect tale where all the characters are three-dimensional, breathing entities, and the lives they live, while by turns sweet and horrific, are always believable. Let Leon be your travel agent and tour guide to Venice. It's an unforgettable trip."   —*Rocky Mountain News*

"Events are powered by Leon's compelling portraits."
    —*The Oregonian* (Portland)

"The plot is silky and complex, and the main appeal is the protagonist, Brunetti."   —*The Cleveland Plain Dealer*

"Leon, a wonderfully literate writer, sets forth her plot clearly and succinctly. . . . The ending of *Uniform Justice* is not a neat wrap-up of the case with justice prevailing. It is rather the ending that one would expect in real life. Leon says that 'the murder mystery is a craft, not an art,' but I say that murder mystery in her hands is an art."   —*The Roanoke Times*

Donna Leon

Fatal Remedies

A PENGUIN / GROVE PRESS BOOK

PENGUIN BOOKS

Published by the Penguin Group

Penguin Group (USA) Inc., 375 Hudson Street, New York, New York 10014, U.S.A.
Penguin Group (Canada), 90 Eglinton Avenue East, Suite 700, Toronto,
Ontario, Canada M4P 2Y3 (a division of Pearson Penguin Canada Inc.)
Penguin Books Ltd, 80 Strand, London WC2R 0RL, England
Penguin Ireland, 25 St Stephen's Green, Dublin 2, Ireland (a division of Penguin Books Ltd)
Penguin Group (Australia), 250 Camberwell Road, Camberwell,
Victoria 3124, Australia (a division of Pearson Australia Group Pty Ltd)
Penguin Books India Pvt Ltd, 11 Community Centre,
Panchsheel Park, New Delhi – 110 017, India
Penguin Group (NZ), 67 Apollo Drive, Rosedale, North Shore 0632,
New Zealand (a division of Pearson New Zealand Ltd)
Penguin Books (South Africa) (Pty) Ltd, 24 Sturdee Avenue,
Rosebank, Johannesburg 2196, South Africa

Penguin Books Ltd, Registered Offices:
80 Strand, London WC2R 0RL, England

First published in Great Britain by William Heinemann 1999
Reprinted by arrangement with Grove/Atlantic, Inc.
Published in Penguin Books 2007

5 7 9 10 8 6

PUBLISHER'S NOTE
This is a work of fiction. Names, characters, places, and incidents are either the product
of the author's imagination or are used fictitiously, and any resemblance to actual persons,
living or dead, business establishments, events, or locales is entirely coincidental.

LIBRARY OF CONGRESS CATALOGING IN PUBLICATION DATA
Leon, Donna.
Fatal remedies / Donna Leon.
p. cm.
ISBN 978-0-14-311242-6
1. Brunetti, Guido (Fictitious character)—Fiction.
2. Police—Italy—Venice—Fiction.   3. Venice (Italy)—Fiction.   I. Title.
PS3562.E534F38 2007
813'.54—dc22   2007019725

Printed in the United States of America

for William Douglas

Di questo tradimento
Chi mai sarà l'autor?

Of this treachery,
Who could be the author?

La Clemenza di Tito
Mozart

1

The woman walked quietly into the empty *campo*. To her left stood the grill-covered windows of a bank, empty and sleeping the well-protected sleep that comes in the early hours of the morning. She crossed to the centre of the *campo* and stood beside the low-hung iron chains enclosing the monument to Daniele Manin, who had sacrificed himself for the freedom of the city. How fitting, she thought.

She heard a noise to her left and turned towards it, but it was nothing more than one of the Guardia di San Marco and his German shepherd, a gap-mouthed dog that looked too young and too friendly to present any real threat to thieves. If the guard thought it strange to see a middle-aged woman standing still in the middle of Campo Manin at three fifteen in the morning, he gave no sign of it and went about his business of wedging orange paper rectangles into the frames of doors and near the locks of the shops, proof that he had made his rounds and found their premises undisturbed.

When the guard and his dog left, the woman moved away from the low chain and went to stand in front of a large glass display window on the far side of the square. In the dim light from inside she studied the posters, read the prices listed for the various special offers, saw that MasterCard, Visa, and American Express were all accepted. Over her left shoulder, she carried a blue canvas beach bag. She pivoted her body and the weight of what was in the bag swung it round to the front. She set it on the ground, glanced down into it, and reached in with her right hand.

Before she could remove anything, she was so startled by footsteps from behind her that she yanked her hand from the bag and stood upright. But it was nothing more than four men and a woman, just off the number 1 boat that stopped at Rialto at three fourteen, now crossing the *campo* on their way to some other part of the city. None of them paid any attention to the woman. Their footsteps died away as they walked up, then down the bridge that led into Calle della Mandola.

Again, she bent and reached into the bag and this time her hand came out with a large rock, one that had stood for years on the desk in her study. She'd brought it back from a vacation on a beach in Maine more than ten years before. The size of a grapefruit, it fitted perfectly into her gloved palm.

She looked down at it, raised her hand, even tossed the stone up and down a few times, as if it were a tennis ball and her turn to serve. She looked from the rock to the window and again to the rock.

She stepped back from the window until she was about two metres from it and turned until she stood sideways, but still looking at the window. She pulled her right hand back level with her head and raised her left arm as counterweight, just as her son had taught her to do one summer when he had tried to teach her to throw like a boy, not a girl. For an instant it occurred to her that her life, at least part of it, would perhaps be divided in half by her next action, but she dismissed the idea as melodramatic self-importance.

In one sweeping motion she brought her hand forward with all her strength. At the full extension of her arm she released the rock, then staggered forward a half-step, powerless to resist the momentum of her own motion. Because the step pulled her head down, the fragments of glass that exploded from the shattering window landed in her hair and did her no injury.

The stone must have found some inherent fault line in the glass, for instead of punching out a small hole its own size, it shattered open a triangle two metres high and almost as wide. She waited until there was no more sound of falling glass, but that had no sooner stopped than from the back room of the office in front of her the sharp double-wail of a burglar alarm blared out into the silent morning. She stood upright and plucked absently at the shards of glass that stuck to the front of her coat, then shook her head wildly, as if just rising up from under a wave, to free it of the glass she could feel trapped there. She stepped back, picked up her bag and placed the straps over her shoulder, then, suddenly aware of how weak her knees had become, went and sat on one of the low pillars that anchored the metal chains.

She hadn't really considered what the hole would be like, but she was surprised to see it was so big, large enough for a man to walk through. Cobwebs in the shattered glass ran from the hole towards the four corners; the glass around the hole was milky and opaque, but the sharp shards that pointed inward were no less dangerous for that.

Behind her, in the top-floor apartment to the left of the bank, lights went on, then in the one that stood directly above the still wailing alarm. Time passed, but she was curiously uninterested in it: whatever was going to happen would happen, no matter how long or short a time it took for the police to get there. The noise bothered her, however. Its sharp double bleat destroyed the peace of the night. But then, she thought, that's what all this is about, the destruction of peace.

Shutters were flung out, three heads appeared and as quickly disappeared, more lights came on. Sleep was impossible so long as the alarm continued to scream out that crime was afoot in the city. After about ten minutes two policemen came running into the *campo*, one with his pistol in his hand. He went to the hole in the shattered window and called out, 'Whoever's in there, come out. This is the police.'

4

Nothing happened. The alarm continued.

He called out again, but when there was still no response he turned to his partner, who shrugged and shook his head. The first one put his pistol back into its holster and moved a step closer to the shattered window. Above him, a window opened and someone called out, 'Can't you turn that damn thing off?' Then another angry voice called down, 'I want to get some sleep.'

The second policeman approached his partner and they peered in together, then the first raised a foot and kicked away the tall stalagmites of glass that rose up dangerously from the base of the frame. Together they climbed inside and disappeared into the back. Minutes passed and nothing happened. Then, in the same instant, the lights in the office went out and the alarm stopped.

They came back into the main room, one of them now leading the way with a flashlight. They looked around to see if anything appeared to be missing or destroyed, then stepped back through the hole in the window into the *campo*. It was then that they noticed the woman sitting on the stone pillar.

The one who had pulled out his pistol went towards her. 'Signora, did you see what happened?'

'Yes.'

'What? Who was it?' Hearing his questions, the other policeman came up and joined them, pleased that they had so easily found a witness. That would speed things up, prevent their having to ring doorbells and ask questions, get them a

5

description and out of this damp autumn cold, back to the warmth of the Questura to write up the report.

'Who was it?' the first one asked.

'Someone threw a rock through the window,' the woman said.

'What did he look like?'

'It wasn't a man,' she answered.

'A woman?' the second one interrupted and she stopped herself from asking if there were perhaps some other alternative she didn't know about. No jokes. No jokes. There were not going to be any more jokes, not until all this was over.

'Yes, a woman.'

With a sharp look at his partner, the first one resumed his questions. 'What did she look like?'

'She was in her early forties, blonde hair, shoulder-length.'

The woman's hair was tucked inside a scarf, so at first the policemen didn't get it. 'What was she wearing?' he asked.

'A tan coat, brown boots.'

He noticed the colour of her coat, then looked down at her feet. 'This isn't a joke, Signora. We want to know what she looked like.'

She looked straight at him and in the light cast down from the street lamps, he saw the glint of some secret passion in her eyes. 'No jokes, officer. I've told you what she was wearing.'

'But you're describing yourself, Signora.' Again, her own inner alarm against melodrama prevented her from saying 'Thou sayest it'. Instead, she nodded.

'You did it?' the first one asked, unable to disguise his astonishment.

She nodded again.

The other one clarified, 'You threw a stone through that window?'

Once more she nodded.

With unspoken agreement the two men backed away from her until they were out of earshot, though they both kept their eyes on her. They put their heads together and spoke in lowered voices for a moment, then one of them pulled out his cellular and punched in the number of the Questura. Above them, a window was flung open, a head popped out, only to disappear immediately. The window slammed shut.

The policeman spoke for several minutes, giving what information he had and saying they'd already apprehended the person responsible. When the night sergeant told them to bring him in, the policeman didn't bother to correct him. He folded the mouthpiece back into place and slipped the phone into the pocket of his jacket. 'Danieli told me to take her in,' he told his partner.

'And that means I get to stay here?' the other one asked, making no attempt to disguise his irritation at having been finessed into staying there in the cold.

'You can wait inside. Danieli's calling the owner. I think he lives around here somewhere.' He handed his partner the phone. 'Call in if he doesn't show up.'

With an attempt at good grace the second officer took the phone with a smile. 'I'll stay until he shows up. But next time I get to take the suspect in.'

His partner smiled and nodded. Good feelings restored, they approached the woman who, during their long conversation, had remained exactly where she was, seated on the pillar, eyes studying the damaged window and the shards of glass that spread out in a monochrome rainbow in front of it.

'Come with me,' the first policeman said.

Silently she pushed herself away from the pillar and started towards the entrance to a narrow *calle* to the left of the destroyed window. Neither policeman made note of the fact that she knew the way to begin the shortest route to the Questura.

It took them ten minutes to walk there, during which time neither the woman nor the policeman spoke. Had any of the very few people who saw them bothered to pay attention to them as they walked across the sleeping expanse of Piazza San Marco and down the narrow *calle* that led towards San Lorenzo and the Questura, they would have seen an attractive, well-dressed woman walking in company with a uniformed policeman. Strange to see at four in the morning, but perhaps her house had been burgled or she'd been called in to identify a wayward child.

There was no one waiting to let them in, so the policeman had to ring repeatedly before the sleep-dulled face of a young policeman popped out from the guard room to the right of the door. When he saw them, he ducked back and re-emerged seconds later, pulling on his jacket. He opened the door with a muttered apology. 'No one told me you were coming, Ruberti,' he said. The other dismissed his apology, but then waved him back towards his bed, remembering what it was to be new to the force and dead with heavy sleep.

He led the woman to the steps on the left and up to the first floor, where the officers had their room. He opened the door for her and held it politely while she came in, following her into the room and taking a seat at his desk. Opening the right drawer, he pulled out a heavy block of printed forms, slapped it down on the desk in front of them, looked up to the woman and motioned with one hand that she should take the seat in front of him.

While she sat and unbuttoned her coat, he filled out the top of the form, giving the date, the time, his name and rank. When it came to, 'Crime', he paused for a moment, then wrote 'Vandalism' in the empty rectangle.

He glanced up at her then and, for the first time, saw her clearly. He was struck by something that made no sense to him at all, by how much everything about her – her clothing, her hair, even the way she sat – gave off the self-assurance that comes only from money, great amounts of it. Please let her not be a crazy, he prayed silently.

'Do you have your *carta d'identità*, Signora?'

She nodded and reached into her bag. At no time did it occur to him that there was any danger in letting a woman he had just arrested for a crime of some violence reach into a large bag to pull something out.

Her hand emerged holding a leather wallet. She

opened it and took out the beige identity card, pulled it open, reversed it and placed it on the desk in front of him.

He glanced down at the photo, saw that it must have been taken some time ago, when she was still a real beauty. Then he looked down at the name. 'Paola Brunetti?' he asked, unable to disguise his astonishment.

She nodded.

'Jesus Christ, you're Brunetti's wife.'

2

Brunetti was lying on the beach when the phone rang, his arm placed across his eyes to protect them from the sand stirred up by the dancing hippos. That is, inside the world of his dreams, Brunetti lay on a beach, his location no doubt the result of a fierce argument with Paola some days before, the hippos a hold-over from the escape he had chosen from that argument, joining Chiara in the living-room to watch the second half of *Fantasia*.

The phone rang six times before Brunetti recognized it for what it was and moved to the side of the bed to reach for it.

'*Sì?*' he asked, stupid with the restless sleep that always followed unresolved conflict with Paola.

'Commissario Brunetti?' a man's voice asked.

'*Un momento*,' Brunetti said. He put down the receiver and switched on the light. He lay back in bed and pulled the covers up over his right shoulder, then looked towards Paola to see that he hadn't pulled them away from her. Her side of the bed was empty. No doubt she was in the bathroom or had gone down to the kitchen for a drink of water or, if the argument still lingered with her as it did with him, perhaps for a glass of hot milk and honey. He'd apologize when she came back, apologize for what he'd said and for this phone call, even though it hadn't woken her.

He reached over and picked up the phone. 'Yes, what is it?' he asked, sinking down low in the pillows and hoping this wasn't the Questura, calling him from his bed to go to the scene of some new crime.

'We've got your wife, sir.'

His mind went white at the juxtaposition of the opening remark, certainly the sort of thing every kidnapper has ever said, with the use of 'sir'.

'What?' he asked when thought returned.

'We've got your wife, sir,' the voice repeated.

'Who is this?' he asked, anger surging into his voice.

'It's Ruberti, sir. I'm at the Questura.' There was a long pause, then the man added, 'I have night duty, sir, me and Bellini.'

'What are you saying about my wife?' Brunetti demanded, not at all concerned with where they were or who had night duty.

'We do, sir. Well, I do. Bellini's still in Campo Manin.'

Brunetti closed his eyes and listened for noises from some other part of the house. Nothing. 'What's she doing there, Ruberti?'

There was a long pause, after which Ruberti said, 'We've arrested her, sir.' When Brunetti didn't say anything, he added, 'That is, I've brought her down here, sir. She hasn't been arrested yet.'

'Let me talk to her,' Brunetti demanded.

After a long pause he heard Paola's voice. '*Ciao*, Guido.'

'You're there, at the Questura?' he asked.

'Yes.'

'Then you did it?'

'I told you I was going to,' Paola said.

Brunetti closed his eyes again and held the receiver at arm's length. After a while, he pulled it back and said, 'Tell him I'll be there in fifteen minutes. Don't say anything and don't sign anything.' Without waiting for her response, he put down the phone and got out of bed.

He dressed quickly, went into the kitchen and scribbled a note for the children, saying that he and Paola had had to go out, but would be back soon. He left the house, careful to close the door quietly behind him, and crept down the stairs as though he were a thief.

He turned right outside the door, walking quickly now, almost running, body inflamed with anger and fear. He hurried through the abandoned market and over the Rialto Bridge without seeing anything or anyone he passed, eyes on the ground in front of him, blind to all sensation. He remembered only her rage, the passion with which she had slammed her hand on to the table, shaking the plates and knocking over a glass of red wine. He remembered watching it soak into the table-cloth and wondering that this issue could so madden her. For he had, at the time and even now – sure that whatever she had done was provoked by that same rage – marvelled that she could become so angry at this far-off injustice. In the decades of their marriage he had become familiar with her anger, had learned that civil, political, social injustices could catapult her over the edge and into a kind of gasping outrage, but he had never learned to predict with any accuracy just what it was that could push her that extra distance until she was beyond all possibility of restraint.

As he walked across Campo Santa Maria Formosa, he remembered some of the things she'd said, deaf to his reminder that the children were there, blind to his surprise at her response. 'It's because you're a man,' she'd hissed in a tight, angry voice. And later, 'It's got to be made to cost them more to do it than to stop. Until then, nothing will happen.' And finally, 'I don't care if it's not illegal. It's wrong and someone's going to have to stop them.'

As was so often the case, Brunetti had dismissed her anger, then her promise – or had it been a threat – to do something on her own. And now, here he was, three days later, turning on to the embankment of San Lorenzo and approaching the Questura, where Paola sat, arrested for a crime she'd told him she was going to commit.

The same young officer let Brunetti in, saluting him as he entered. Brunetti ignored him and headed for the steps, ran up them two at a time and into the officers' room, where he found Ruberti at his desk, Paola sitting quietly in front of him.

Ruberti stood up and saluted when his superior entered.

Brunetti nodded. He glanced at Paola, who met his eyes, but he had nothing to say to her.

He motioned Ruberti to sit down and when the officer did, Brunetti said, 'Tell me what happened.'

'We had a call about an hour ago, sir. A burglar alarm went off in Campo Manin, so Bellini and I went to answer the call.'

'On foot?'

'Yes, sir.'

When Ruberti didn't continue, Brunetti nodded to him and he went on, 'When we got there we found the window broken. The alarm was going off like crazy.'

'Where was it coming from?' Brunetti asked, though he knew.

'The back room, sir.'

'Yes, yes. But from what place?'

'The travel agency, sir.'

Seeing Brunetti's response, Ruberti subsided into silence again until Brunetti prodded him by asking, 'And then?'

'I went in, sir, and turned off the electricity. To stop the alarm,' he explained unnecessarily. 'Then, when we came out, we saw a woman in the *campo*, like she was waiting for us, and we asked her if she had seen what happened.' Ruberti looked down at his desk, up at Brunetti, across at Paola and when neither of them said anything, he continued, 'She said she'd seen who did it and when we asked her to describe him, she said it was a woman.'

Again, he stopped and looked at each of them and again neither said anything. 'Then, when we asked her to describe the woman she described herself and, when I pointed that out to her, she said she'd done it. Broken the window, sir. That's what happened.' He thought for a moment, then added, 'Well, she didn't say it, sir. But she nodded when I asked her if she'd done it.'

Brunetti lowered himself into a chair on Paola's right and folded his hands on the surface of Ruberti's desk.

'Where's Bellini?' he asked.

'Still there, sir. He's waiting for the owner to show up.'

'How long ago did you leave him?' Brunetti asked.

Ruberti glanced down at his watch. 'More than a half-hour, sir.'

'Does he have a phone?'

'Yes, sir.'

'Call him,' Brunetti said.

Ruberti reached forward and pulled the phone towards him, but before he could begin to dial they heard footsteps on the stairs and a moment later Bellini came into the office. When he saw Brunetti he saluted, though he was unable to show his surprise at finding the commissario there at that hour.

'*Buon dì*, Bellini,' Brunetti said.

'*Buon dì*, Commissario,' the officer responded

and looked towards Ruberti for some hint about what was going on.

Ruberti gave the barest of shrugs.

Brunetti reached across the desk and pulled the stack of crime reports towards him. He saw Ruberti's neat printing, read the time and date, the officer's name, the name Ruberti had chosen to give the crime. Nothing else was written on the report, no name was listed under 'Arrested', not even under 'Questioned'.

'What has my wife said?'

'As I told you, sir, she hasn't actually really said anything. Just nodded when I asked her if she did it,' Ruberti said. To cover the rush of air that sneaked through his partner's lips he added, 'Sir.'

'I think you might have misunderstood what she meant, Ruberti,' Brunetti said. Paola leaned forward as if about to speak, but Brunetti suddenly slapped his outstretched palm on the crime report form and crushed it together in a tight ball.

Ruberti remembered, again, times when he had been a young officer, weary with sleep and once wet with fear, and he recalled that the commissario had once or twice turned a blind eye to the terrors or errors of youth. 'Yes, sir, I'm sure I could have misunderstood what she meant,' he answered seamlessly. Ruberti looked up at Bellini, who nodded, not really understanding but knowing what he had to do.

'Good,' Brunetti said and got to his feet. The crime report was now a crushed ball in his hand. He stuffed it into the pocket of his overcoat. 'I'll take my wife home now.'

Ruberti got to his feet and went to stand beside Bellini, who said, 'The owner's there now, sir.'

'Did you tell him anything?'

'No, sir, only that Ruberti had come back to the Questura.'

Brunetti nodded. He leaned down towards Paola but did not touch her. She pushed herself up by the arms of her chair and stood, but she did not stand beside her husband.

'I'll say good-night, then, officers. I'll see you later this morning.' Both men saluted, Brunetti waved a hand towards them, then stood back to allow Paola to walk in front of him to the door. She went through it first, Brunetti following behind. He closed the door and, one behind the other, they walked down the stairs. The young officer was there to hold the door open for them. He nodded to Paola, though he had no idea who she was. As was only proper, he saluted his superior as he walked through the door and out into the chill Venetian dawn.

3

Outside the door of the Questura, Brunetti set off to the left and made for the first turning. There he paused and waited for Paola to join him. Still neither of them spoke. Side by side, they continued through the deserted *calli*, their feet automatically piloting them towards home.

When they turned into Salizzada San Lio, Brunetti could finally bring himself to speak, but not to say anything of substance. 'I left a note for the kids. In case they woke up.'

Paola nodded, but he was carefully not looking at her, so he didn't notice. 'I didn't want Chiara to worry,' he said, and when he realized how much this must have sounded like an attempt to make her feel guilt, he recognized that he didn't much care if it did.

'I forgot,' Paola said.

They entered the underpass and were quickly out into Campo San Bartolomeo, where the cheerful smile on the statue of Goldoni seemed wildly out of place. Brunetti glanced up at the clock. Venetian, he knew to add an hour: almost five, not early enough to bother to go back to bed, yet how to fill the hours between now and the time when he could legitimately leave for work? He looked to his left, but none of the bars was open. He wanted coffee; far more desperately, he needed the diversion it would provide.

On the other side of the Rialto, they both turned to the left, then right into the underpass that ran alongside Ruga degli Orefici. Halfway along, a bar was just opening and by silent consent they turned into it. An immense pile of fresh brioches lay on the counter, still enveloped in the white paper of the *pasticceria*. Brunetti ordered two espressos but ignored the pastries. Paola didn't even notice them.

When the barman set the coffee in front of them, Brunetti spooned sugar into both cups and slid Paola's along the bar to her. The barman moved off towards the end of the counter and began to place the brioches, one by one, into a glass display case.

'Well?' Brunetti asked.

Paola sipped at the coffee, added another half spoonful of sugar and said, 'I told you I was going to do it.'

'It didn't sound like that.'

'Then what did it sound like?'

'It sounded like you were saying that everyone should do it.'

'Everyone should do it,' Paola said, but her voice held none of the rage that had filled it the first time she had uttered those words.

'I didn't think you meant this.' Brunetti gestured with a hand that encompassed, not the bar, but all that had happened before they reached it.

Paola put her cup down into the saucer and looked at him directly for the first time. 'Guido, can we talk?'

His impulse was to say that this was exactly what they were doing, but he knew her well enough to understand what she meant, so he nodded instead.

'I told you, three nights ago, what they were doing.' Before he could interrupt, she went on, 'And you told me there was nothing at all illegal about it, that it was their right as travel agents.'

Brunetti nodded and when the barman approached he signalled with a wave of his hand for more coffee. After the man had moved back towards the machine, Paola continued, 'But it's wrong. You know it and I know it. It's disgusting to arrange sex-tours so that rich – and not so rich – men can go off to Thailand and the Philippines and rape ten-year-olds.' Before he could speak, she held up a hand to stop him. 'I know it's illegal now. But has anyone been arrested? Convicted? You know as well as I, all they have to do is change the language in the ads and it's business as usual. "Tolerant hotel reception. Friendly local companions." Don't tell me you don't know what that means. It's business as usual, Guido. And it disgusts me.'

Still Brunetti said nothing. The waiter brought them two fresh cups of coffee and removed the used ones. The door opened and two burly men followed a gust of damp air into the bar. The waiter moved off towards them.

'I told you then', Paola resumed, 'that it was wrong and that they had to be stopped.'

'Do you think you can stop them?' he asked.

'Yes,' she answered and before he could question or contradict, she continued, 'Not me alone, not here in Venice, breaking a window in a travel agency in Campo Manin. But if all the women in Italy went out at night with stones and broke the windows of every travel agency that organized sex-tours, then, after a very short time, there wouldn't be any sex-tours organized in Italy, would there?'

'Is that a rhetorical question or a real question?' he asked.

'I think it's a real one,' she said. This time, it was Paola who put the sugar into their coffee.

Brunetti drank his before he said anything. 'You can't do it, Paola. You can't go breaking the windows of offices or stores that do things you don't want them to do or sell things you don't think they should sell.' Before she could say anything he asked her, 'Remember when the Church tried to ban the sale of contraceptives? Remember your reaction to that? Well, if you don't, I do, and it was the same thing: off on a crusade against what you decided was evil. But that time you were on the other side, against people who were doing what you say now you have the right to do, stopping people from doing what you think is wrong. No, the obligation.' He felt himself giving in to the anger that had filled him since he had got out of bed, that had walked through the streets with him and that stood beside him now, in this quiet, early-morning bar.

'It's the same thing,' he continued. 'You decide, all by yourself and for yourself, that something's wrong, then you make yourself so important that you're the only one who can stop it, the only one who sees the perfect truth.'

He thought she'd say something here, but when she didn't he went on irresistibly, 'This is a perfect example. What do you want, your picture on the front page of the *Gazzettino*, you the great defender of little children?' By a conscious act of will he stopped himself from going on. He reached into his pocket, walked over to the barman and paid for the coffee. He opened the door to the bar and held it for her.

Outside, she turned to the left, went a few steps, stopped and waited for him to come up to her. 'Is that how you really see it? That all I want from this is attention, that I want people to see me as being important?'

He walked past her, ignoring the question.

From behind him he heard her voice, raised for the first time. 'Is that it, Guido?'

He stopped and turned back to face her. A man came from behind her, wheeling a dolly covered with bound stacks of newspapers and magazines.

He waited for him to pass them and answered, 'Yes. Partly.'

'How much a part?' she shot back.

'I don't know. You can't divide something like that.'

'Do you think it's the reason I'm doing this?'

His exasperation urged him to answer, 'Why does everything have to be such a *cause* for you, Paola? Why does everything you do, or read or say – or wear and eat, for the love of God – why does everything have to be filled with such *meaning*?'

For a long time she looked at him without saying anything, then she lowered her head and walked away from him, heading for home.

He caught up with her. 'What's that supposed to mean?'

'What's what supposed to mean?'

'That look.'

She stopped again and gazed up at him. 'Sometimes I wonder where the man I married went.'

'And what's *that* supposed to mean?'

'It means that when I married you, Guido, you believed in all those things that you make fun of now.' Before he could ask her what they were, she answered him, 'Things like justice and what's right, and how to decide to do what's right.'

'I still believe in those things,' he insisted.

'You believe in the law now, Guido,' she said, but gently, as though she were speaking to a child.

'That's exactly what I mean,' he said, raising his voice, deaf and blind to the people who hurried past them in increasing numbers, now that it was closer to the time when the first stalls would open.

'You make what I do sound stupid or dirty. I'm a policeman, for God's sake. What do you want me to do except obey the law? And enforce it?' He felt his entire body blaze with hot rage as he saw, or thought he saw, how she had for years belittled and dismissed what he did.

'Then why did you lie to Ruberti?' she asked.

His rage fled. 'I didn't lie.'

'You told him there was some confusion, that he didn't understand what I meant. But he knows, and you do, and I do, and so did that other policeman, exactly what I meant and what I did.' When he said nothing she moved closer to him. 'I broke the law, Guido. I broke their window and I'd do it again. And I'll go on breaking their windows until your law, this precious law you're so proud of, until your law does something – either to me or to them. Because I won't let them go on doing what they're doing.'

His hands shot out before he could stop himself and grabbed her by the elbows. But he didn't pull her to him. Instead, he stepped towards her, then wrapped his arms round her back, one hand pressing her face into the angle of his neck. He kissed the top of her head and sank his face into her hair. Suddenly he pulled himself back, hand clasped to his mouth.

'What is it?' she asked, frightened for the first time.

Brunetti pulled away his hand and saw that there was blood on it. He raised a finger to his lip and felt something hard, sharp.

'No, let me,' Paola said, placing her right hand

25

on his cheek and moving his face down to hers. She removed her glove and touched his lip with two fingers.

'What?' he asked.

'A piece of glass.'

A sudden tweak of pain, then she kissed him on the lower lip, but gently.

4

On the way home they stopped in a *pasticceria* and bought a large tray of brioches, telling one another it was for the children but knowing it was a sort of celebratory offering to their peace, no matter how precarious its restoration. The first thing Brunetti did when they got home was remove the note he'd left on the kitchen table and stuff it deep into the plastic bag of garbage under the sink. Then he went down the corridor, quietly because of the still-sleeping children, and into the bathroom, where he took a long shower, hoping to steam away the troubles that had come to him so unexpectedly and so early this morning.

By the time he was shaved and dressed and back in the kitchen, Paola had changed into her pyjamas and dressing-gown, an old flannel tartan thing she'd worn for so long that they'd both forgotten where she had got it. She sat at the table, reading a magazine and dunking a brioche into a large cup of *caffè latte*, as though she'd just now got up from a long and restful night's sleep.

'Am I supposed to come in, kiss you on the cheek and say, "*Buon giorno, cara*, did you sleep well?"' he asked when he saw her, but there was no hint of sarcasm, either in his voice or in his intention. If anything, he hoped to distance them from the events of the night, though he well knew how impossible that was. Delay, then, the inevitable consequence of Paola's actions, even if those consequences would be no more than their facing off verbally again, each doomed to the impossibility of accepting the other's position.

She looked up, considered his words and smiled, suggesting that she, too, would be happy to wait. 'Will you be home for lunch today?' she asked, getting up to go to the stove and pour coffee into a wide-mouthed cup. She added heated milk and placed it on the table at his usual place.

As he sat, Brunetti thought how strange the situation was, how even stranger the fact that they both so readily accepted it. He'd read about the spontaneous Christmas truce that had broken out in the trenches on the Western Front during the Great War; Germans crossing over to light the cigarettes they'd just given to the Tommies; the British waving and smiling at the Huns. Massive bombardments had put an end to that: Brunetti saw no brighter possibility of a prolonged truce with his wife. But he'd enjoy it while he could, so he added sugar to his coffee, picked up a brioche and answered, 'No, I've got to go up to Treviso to talk to one of the witnesses to the bank robbery in Campo San Luca last week.'

Because a bank robbery in Venice was such an unusual event, it served to divert them and Brunetti told Paola – even though everyone in the city was sure to have read about it in the paper – the little that was known: a young man with a gun had walked into a bank three days before, demanded money, walked out with it in one hand, the pistol in the other, and had calmly disappeared in the direction of Rialto. The camera hidden in the ceiling of the bank had provided the police with a fuzzy picture, but it had allowed the police to make a tentative identification of the brother of a local man said to have powerful connections to the Mafia. The robber had pulled a scarf up over his mouth and nose as he entered the bank, but he'd removed it as he left, providing a man on the way in with a clear view of his face.

The witness, a *pizzaiolo* from Treviso who had been going into the bank to make a mortgage payment, had had a good look at the robber and Brunetti hoped he would be able to pick him out from among the photos of suspects the police had assembled. That would be enough to make an arrest and it might be sufficient to win a conviction. So that was where Brunetti was headed that morning.

From the back part of the apartment they heard the sound of an opening door and the unmistakable heavy tread of Raffi, sleep-sodden, on his way towards the bathroom and, they hoped, consciousness.

Brunetti took another brioche, surprised to find himself so hungry at this hour: breakfast was something for which normally he had little understanding and less sympathy. While they awaited further sounds of life from the back of the apartment, they kept themselves very busy with their coffee and their brioches.

Brunetti was just finishing when another door opened. A few moments later Chiara stumbled down the hallway and came into the kitchen, one hand prodding at her eyes, as if to help them with the complicated business of opening. Saying nothing, she shuffled barefoot across the kitchen and lowered herself into Brunetti's lap. She wrapped one arm round his back and planted her head on his shoulder.

Brunetti put both arms round her and kissed the top of her head. 'You going to school like this today?' he asked in an entirely conversational voice, studying the pattern on her pyjamas. 'Nice. I'm sure your classmates will like the look. Balloons. Very tasteful, balloons. Chic, I'd even say. A fashion statement every twelve-year-old will envy.'

Paola lowered her head and returned her attention to her magazine.

Chiara shifted around in his lap, then pushed herself away from him to look down at her pyjamas. Before she could say anything, Raffi came into the kitchen, bent down to kiss his mother and went to the stove to pour himself a cup of coffee from the six-cup moka express. He added hot milk, came back to the table, sat down and said, 'I hope you don't mind that I used your razor, Papà.'

'To do what?' Chiara asked, 'trim your fingernails? There's certainly nothing growing on that face of yours that needs a razor.' That said, she moved out of Raffi's range and closer to Brunetti, who gave her a reproving squeeze through the thick flannel of her pyjamas.

Raffi leaned towards her across the table, but his heart wasn't in it and he stopped his hand over the pile of brioches and picked one up. He dunked one end into the coffee and took an enormous bite. 'How come there's brioches?' he wanted to know. When no one answered he turned to Brunetti and asked, 'You go out?'

Brunetti nodded and took his arms from around Chiara. He slipped out from under her and got to his feet.

'You get the papers, too?' Raffi asked from around another mouthful of brioche.

'No,' Brunetti said, moving to the door.

'How come?'

'I forgot,' he lied to his only son, went into the hall, put on his coat and left the apartment.

Outside, he turned towards Rialto and the decades-long familiar route to the Questura. Most mornings he found delight in some small element of the walk: a particularly absurd headline on one of the national papers, some new misspelling on the front of the cheap sweat-shirts that filled the booths on both sides of the market, the first arrival of some longed-for fruit or vegetable. But this morning he saw little and noticed nothing as he made his way through the market, over the bridge and into the first of the narrow streets that would take him to the Questura and to work.

Much of the time it took him to walk to his office he spent thinking about Ruberti and Bellini, wondering if their personal loyalty to a superior who had treated them with a certain measure of humanity would prove sufficient motive for them to betray their oath of loyalty to the State. He assumed it would, but when he realized how suspiciously close this was to the scale of values that had animated Paola's behaviour, he forced his mind away from them and, instead, contemplated the day's immediate trial: the ninth of the *'convocations du personnel'* which his immediate supervisor, Vice-Questore Giuseppe Patta, had instituted at the Questura after the recent training course he'd attended at Interpol headquarters in Lyon.

There, in Lyon, Patta had exposed himself to the elements of the various nations which now made up united Europe: champagne and truffles from France, Danish ham, English beer and some very old Spanish brandy. At the same time he had sampled the various managerial styles on offer by bureaucrats of the different nations. At the end of the course he'd returned to Italy, suitcases filled with smoked salmon and Irish butter, head bursting with new, progressive ideas about how to handle the people who worked for him. The first of these, and the only one so far to be revealed to the members of the Questura, was the now weekly '*convocations du personnel*', an interminable meeting at which matters of surpassing triviality were presented to the entire staff, there to be discussed, dissected and ultimately disregarded by everyone present.

When the meetings had first begun two months ago, Brunetti had joined the majority in the opinion that they would not last more than a week or two, but here they were, after eight of them, with no end in sight. After the second Brunetti had started to bring his newspaper, but that had been stopped by Lieutenant Scarpa, Patta's personal assistant, who had repeatedly asked if Brunetti were so little interested in what happened in the city that he would read a paper during the meetings. He had then tried a book, but he could never find one small enough to hold in his cupped hands.

His salvation had come, as had often been the case in the last years, from Signorina Elettra. On the morning of the fifth meeting she had come into his office ten minutes before it was due to begin and asked Brunetti, with no explanation, for ten thousand lire.

He had handed it over and, in return, she'd given him twenty brass-centred five-hundred-lire coins. In response to his questioning look she'd handed him a small card, little bigger than the box that held compact discs.

He'd looked down at the card, seen that it was

divided into twenty-five equally sized squares, each of which contained a word or phrase, printed in tiny letters. He'd had to hold it close to his eyes to read some of them: 'Maximize', 'prioritize', 'outsource', 'liaison', 'interface', 'issue' and a host of the newest, emptiest buzz-words to have slipped into the language in recent years.

'What's this?' he'd asked.

'Bingo,' was Signorina Elettra's simple answer. Before he could ask, she'd explained, 'My mother used to play it. All you have to do is wait for someone to use one of the words on your card – all the cards are different – and when you hear it, you cover it with a coin. The first one to cover five words in a straight line wins.'

'Wins what?'

'The money of all the other players.'

'What other players?'

'You'll see,' was all she'd had time to say before they were summoned to the meeting.

And since that day the meetings had been tolerable, at least for those provided with the small cards. That first day there had been only Brunetti, Signorina Elettra and one of the other commissari, a woman just returned from maternity leave. Since then, however, the cards had appeared on the laps or within the notebooks of an ever expanding number of people and each week Brunetti felt as much interest in seeing who had a card as in actually winning the game. Each week, too, the words changed, usually in conformity with the changing patterns or enthusiasms of Patta's speech: they sometimes reflected the Vice-Questore's attempts at urbanity and 'multiculturalism' – a word which had also appeared – as well as his occasional attempt to use the vocabulary of languages he did not speak; hence, 'voodoo economics', 'pyramid scheme' and *'Wirtschaftlicher Aufschwung'*.

Brunetti arrived at the Questura half an hour before the meeting was scheduled to begin. Neither Ruberti nor Bellini was on duty when he got there, so it was a different officer who handed him the previous night's crime log when he asked to see it. He glanced with every appearance of lack of interest at the pages: a burglary in Dorsoduro at the home of people away on vacation; a fight in a bar in Santa Marta between sailors from a Turkish freighter and two crewmen from a Greek cruise ship. Three of them had been taken to Pronto Soccorso at the Giustinian Hospital, one with a broken arm, but no charges had been pressed as both boats were to sail that afternoon. The window of a travel agency in Campo Manin had been shattered by a rock, but no one had been arrested, nor had there been any witnesses. And the all-night machine that sold prophylactics in front of a pharmacy in Cannaregio had been prised open, probably with a screwdriver and, according to the calculations of the owner of the pharmacy, seventeen thousand lire had been taken. And sixteen packages of prophylactics.

The meeting, when it finally convened, brought no surprises. At the beginning of the second hour, Vice-Questore Patta announced that, in order to assure that they were not being used to launder money, the various non-profit organizations in the city would have to be asked to allow their files to be 'accessed' by the computers of the police, at which point Signorina Elettra made a small motion with her right hand, looked across at Vianello, smiled and said, but very softly, 'Bingo.'

'Excuse me, Signorina?' Vice-Questore Patta was aware that something had been going on for some time but ignorant of what it could be.

She looked at the Vice-Questore, repeated her smile and said, 'Dingo, sir.'

'Dingo?' he enquired, peering at her over the tops of the half-glasses he affected for these meetings.

'The animal protection people, sir, the ones who put the canisters in the shops to collect money to take care of strays. They're a non-profit organization. So we should contact them as well.'

'Indeed?' Patta asked, not certain that this was what he had heard, or what he had expected.

'I wouldn't want anyone to forget them,' she explained.

Patta turned his attention back to the papers in front of him and the meeting continued. Brunetti, chin propped on his hand, watched as six other people made small stacks of coins in front of themselves. Lieutenant Scarpa watched them carefully, but the cards, previously shielded by hands, notebooks and coffee cups, had all disappeared. Only the coins remained – and the meeting, which dragged itself tiredly along for yet another half-hour.

Just at the moment when insurrection – and

most of the people in the room carried weapons – was about to break out, Patta removed his glasses and set them tiredly on the papers in front of him. 'Has anyone anything else to say?' he asked.

Anyone who might have spoken did not, no doubt deterred by the thought of all those weapons, so the meeting ended. Patta left, followed by Scarpa. Small piles of coins were slid down two sides of the table until they stood either in front of or directly across from Signorina Elettra. With a croupier's grace she swept them all off the side of the table into one cupped hand and got to her feet, signalling that the meeting really was over.

Brunetti went back upstairs with her, strangely cheered by the sound of coins jingling in the pocket of the grey silk jacket she wore. 'Accessed?' he repeated, using the English word but making it, this time, sound like an English word.

'It's computer speak, sir,' she said.

'To access?' he asked. 'It's a verb now?'

'Yes, sir, I believe it is.'

'But it didn't used to be,' Brunetti said, remembering when it had been a noun.

'I think Americans are allowed to do that to their words, sir.'

'Make them verbs? Or nouns? If they feel like it?'

'Yes, sir.'

'Ah,' Brunetti breathed.

He nodded to her at the top of the first flight of stairs, and she went towards the front of the building and her small office, just outside Patta's.

Brunetti continued up to his own, thinking about the liberties some people thought they could take with language. Just like the liberties Paola thought she could take with the law.

Brunetti went into his office and closed the door. Everything, he realized when he tried to read the papers on his desk, would pull his thoughts back to Paola and the events of the early morning. There would be no resolution and they would not be free of it until they could talk about it, but the memory of what she had dared to do launched him into a state of anger so consuming that he knew he was still incapable of discussing it with her.

He looked out of the window, seeing nothing, and tried to discover the real reason for his rage. Her behaviour, had he failed to stamp out evidence of it, would have put his job and his career in jeopardy. Had it not been for Ruberti's and Bellini's presence and quiet complicity, the newspapers would soon have been full of the story. And there were many journalists – Brunetti busied himself for some minutes making a list of them – who would delight in telling the story of the criminal wife of the commissario. He rethought the phrase, turning it into a headline in capital letters.

But she had been stopped, at least for the present. He remembered taking her in his arms, recalled the current of raw fear running through her. Perhaps her exposure to real violence, even though it was no more than violence against property, would have been a sufficient gesture against injustice. And perhaps she would have time to realize that Brunetti's career would be put at risk by her action. He glanced down at his watch and saw that he had just enough time to get to the station for the train to Treviso. At the thought of being able to deal with something as straightforward as a bank robbery, Brunetti felt himself filled with a sense of happy relief.

5

During the journey back from Treviso late in the afternoon, Brunetti felt no sense of success, even though the witness had identified a photo of the man the police believed was the one who appeared on the video and said he would be willing to testify against him. Feeling he had to do it, Brunetti explained who the suspect was, as well as the possible dangers of identifying and testifying against him. Much to his surprise, Signor Iacovantuono, who worked as a cook in a *pizzeria*, hadn't been worried about that, indeed, did not seem to be at all interested. He had seen a crime committed. He recognized photos of the man accused of it. And so to him it was his duty as a citizen to testify against the criminal, regardless of the risk to himself or his family. He had seemed, if anything, puzzled at Brunetti's continued assurances that they would be provided with police protection.

More unsettling, Signor Iacovantuono was from Salerno and hence one of those criminally disposed southerners whose presence here in the north was said to be destroying the social fabric of the nation. 'But, Commissario,' he had insisted in his heavily accented voice, 'if we don't do something about these people, what life will our children have?'

Brunetti was unable to free himself from the echo of these words and began to fear that his days were now to be haunted by the baying of the moral hounds that had been unleashed in his conscience by Paola's actions of the night before. It had all seemed so simple to the dark-haired *pizzaiolo* from Salerno: wrong had been done; it was his duty to see that it was punished. Even when warned of the potential danger, he had remained adamant in his need to do what he thought to be right.

As the sleeping fields on the outskirts of Venice swept past the window of the train, Brunetti wondered how it could seem so simple to Signor Iacovantuono and yet so complicated to him. Perhaps the fact that it was illegal to rob banks made it easier. After all, society was in general agreement about that. And no law said it was wrong to sell a ticket to Thailand or the Philippines; nor that it was illegal to buy one. Nor, for that matter, did the law concern itself with what a person chose to do when he got there, at least not laws that had ever been applied in Italy.

Rather like those against blasphemy, they existed in a kind of juridical limbo for the existence of which no real proof had ever been seen.

For the last few months, even longer than that, articles had been appearing in national newspapers and magazines in which various experts analyzed the international traffic in sex-tourism statistically, psychologically, sociologically – in any of those ways the press loved to chew up a hot topic. Brunetti could remember some of them, even recalled a photo of prepubescent girls, said to be working in a brothel in Cambodia, their budding breasts an offence to his eyes, their small faces blotted out by some sort of visual computer static.

He had read the Interpol reports on the subject, seen how the estimates of the numbers involved, both as clients and as – he could find no other word – victims varied by as much as half a million. He had read the numbers and part of him had always chosen to believe the lowest numbers given: his humanity would be soiled were he to accept the highest.

It was the most recent article – he thought it had appeared in *Panorama* – which had provoked Paola to incendiary rage. He had heard the first salvo two weeks before in Paola's voice, which had shouted from the back of the apartment '*Bastardi*', a sound which had shattered the peace of a Sunday afternoon and, Brunetti now feared, far more than that.

He had not had to go back to her study, for she had stormed into the living-room, the magazine a clenched cylinder in her right hand. There had been no preamble. 'Listen to this, Guido.'

Paola had unrolled the magazine, flattened the page against her knee and straightened up to read, '"A paedophile, as the word says, is one who doubtlessly loves children."' She stopped there and looked across the room at him.

'And rapists, presumably, love women?' Brunetti had asked.

'Do you believe this?' Paola had demanded, ignoring his remark. 'One of the most popular magazines in the country – and only God knows how that can be – and they can print this shit?' She glanced down at the page and added, 'And he teaches sociology. God, have these people no conscience? When is someone in this disgusting country going to say that we're responsible for our behaviour instead of blaming it on society or, for God's sake, the victim?'

Because Brunetti could never answer questions like this, he had made no attempt to do so. Instead, he asked her what else the article said.

She'd told him then, her rage not at all diminished by her having to become lucid to do so. Like any good tour, the article touched all the by now famous sites: Phnom Penh, Bangkok, Manila, then brought things closer to home by regurgitating the most recent cases in Belgium and Italy. But it was the tone which had enraged her and, he had to admit, disgusted Brunetti: starting from the astonishing premise that paedophiles loved children, the magazine's resident sociologist had gone on to explain how a permissive society induced men to do these things. Part of the reason, this sage opined, was the tremendous seductiveness of children. Rage had stopped Paola from reading further.

'Sex-tourism,' Paola had muttered between teeth clenched so hard that Brunetti could see the tendons in her neck pulled out from the skin. 'God, to think that they can do it, that they can buy a ticket, sign up for a tour, and go and rape ten-year-olds.' She had thrown the magazine to the back of the sofa and returned to her study, but it was that night after dinner that she had first proposed the idea of stopping the industry.

Brunetti had at first thought she was joking and now, in retrospect, he feared that his refusal to take her seriously might have upped the ante and driven her that fatal step from outrage to action. He remembered asking her, his voice in memory arch and condescending, if she planned to stop the traffic all by herself.

'And the fact that it's illegal?'

'What's illegal?'

'To throw rocks through windows, Paola.'

'And it's not illegal to rape ten-year-olds?'

Brunetti had stopped the conversation then, and in retrospect he had to admit it had been because he had no answer to give her. No, it seemed, in some places in the world it was not illegal to rape ten-year-olds. But it *was* illegal, here in Venice, in Italy, to throw rocks through windows, and that was his job: to see that people did not do it or, if they did, that they were arrested.

The train pulled into the station and came to a

slow stop. Many of the passengers getting down on to the platform carried paper-wrapped cones of flowers, reminding Brunetti that today was the first of November, the day of the dead, when most citizens would go out to the cemetery to lay flowers on the tombs of their departed. It was a sign of his misery that he welcomed the thought of dead relatives as a comfortable distraction. He wouldn't go; he seldom did.

Brunetti decided to walk home rather than go back to the Questura. Eyes that see not, ears that hear not; he walked through the city blind and deaf to its charms, playing and replaying the conversations and confrontations that had resulted from Paola's original explosion.

One of her many peculiarities was that she was a peripatetic tooth-brusher, would often walk around the apartment or into their bedroom while she cleaned her teeth. So it had seemed entirely natural to him that she had been standing at the door of their bedroom three nights ago, toothbrush in hand, when she had said, entirely without prelude, 'I'm going to do it.'

Brunetti had known what she meant, but had not believed her, so he had done no more than glance up at her and nod. And that had been the end of it, at least until the call had come from Ruberti to disturb his sleep and now his peace.

He stopped in the *pasticceria* below their house and bought a little bag of *fave*, the small round almond cakes that were found only at this time of year. Chiara loved them. Following fast upon that thought, he found himself considering how this could be said to be true of virtually every edible substance in existence, and with that memory came the first release from tension that Brunetti had experienced since the night before.

Inside the apartment all was calm, but in the current climate that didn't mean much. Paola's coat hung on a hook beside the door, Chiara's beside it, her red wool scarf on the floor below. He picked it up and draped it over her coat, removing his own and hanging it to the right of Chiara's. Just like the three bears, he thought: *Mamma*, *Papà* and baby.

He pulled open the paper bag and dropped a few *fave* into his open palm. He tossed one into his mouth, then another, and finally two more. With a sudden flash of memory he remembered, decades ago, buying some for Paola when they were university students and still caught up in the first glow of love.

'Aren't you tired of people talking about Proust every time they eat a cake or biscuit?' he'd asked as if he were graced with some open window to her mind.

A voice from behind startled him and brought him back from reverie. 'Can I have some, *Papà*?'

'I got them for you, angel,' he answered, reaching down and handing the bag to Chiara.

'Do you mind if I eat just the chocolate ones?'

He shook his head. 'Is your mother in her study?'

'Are you going to have an argument?' she enquired, hand poised above the neck of the open bag.

'Why do you say that?' he asked.

'You always call *Mamma* "your mother" when you're going to have an argument with her.'

'Yes, I suppose I do,' he agreed. 'Is she there?'

'Uh huh,' she answered. 'Is it going to be a big one?'

He shrugged. He had no idea.

'I'd better eat all of these, then. In case it's going to be.'

'Why?'

'Because dinner will be late. It always is.'

He reached into the bag and took a few *fave*, careful to leave her the chocolate ones. 'I'll try not to make it be an argument, then.'

'Good.' She turned and went down the corridor to her room, taking the bag with her. Brunetti followed a few moments later, stopping in front of the door to Paola's study. He knocked.

'*Avanti*,' she called.

When he went in he found her, as he usually did when he got home from work, sitting at her desk, a pile of papers in front of her, glasses low on her nose as she read through them. She looked up at him, smiled a real smile, removed her glasses and asked, 'What happened in Treviso?'

'Just what I thought wouldn't. Or couldn't,' Brunetti said and moved across the room to his usual place on a stout, middle-aged sofa that stood against the wall to her right.

'He'll testify?' Paola asked.

'He's eager to testify. He identified the photo instantly and he's coming down here tomorrow to have a look at him, but I'd say he's certain.' In

47

response to her evident surprise Brunetti added, 'And he's from Salerno.'

'And he's really willing?' She made no attempt to disguise her wonderment. When Brunetti nodded, she said, 'Tell me about him.'

'He's a little man, about forty, supporting a wife and two children by working in a *pizzeria* in Treviso. He's been up here for twenty years, but still goes down there every year for vacation. When they can.'

'Does his wife work?' Paola asked.

'She's a cleaning lady in an elementary school.'

'What was he doing in a bank in Venice?'

'He was paying the mortgage on his apartment in Treviso. The bank that gave the original mortgage was taken over by a bank here, so he comes down once a year to pay the mortgage himself. If he tries to do it through his bank in Treviso they charge him two hundred thousand lire, which is why he travelled to Venice on his day off to pay it.'

'And found himself in the middle of a robbery?'

Brunetti nodded.

Paola shook her head. 'It's remarkable that he'd be willing to testify. You said the man who was arrested is mixed up with the Mafia?'

'His brother is.' Brunetti kept to himself his belief that this meant they both were.

'And does the man in Treviso know this?'

'Yes. I told him.'

'And he's still willing?' When Brunetti nodded again, Paola said, 'Then perhaps there is hope for all of us.'

Brunetti shrugged, conscious that there was some dishonesty, perhaps a great deal of dishonesty, in his not telling Paola what Iacovantuono had said about having to behave bravely for our children's sake. He shifted himself lower on the sofa, stuck his feet out in front of him and crossed his ankles.

'Are you finished with it?' he asked, knowing she would understand.

'I don't think so, Guido,' she said, both hesitation and regret audible as she spoke.

'Why?'

'Because the newspapers, when they write about what happened, will call it a random act of vandalism, like someone who knocks over a garbage can or slashes the seat on a train.'

Brunetti, though tempted, said nothing, waiting for her to continue.

'It wasn't random, Guido, and it wasn't vandalism.' She put her face down into her open palms and slid her hands up until they were covering the top of her head. From below, her voice came to him. 'The public have got to understand why it was done, that these people are doing something that is both disgusting and immoral, and that they've got to be made not to do it.'

'Have you thought about the consequences?' Brunetti asked in a level voice.

She looked up at him. 'I couldn't be married to a policeman for twenty years and not have thought of the consequences.'

'To yourself?'

'Of course.'

'And to me?'

'Yes.'

'And you don't regret them?'

'Of course I regret them. I don't want to lose my job or have your career suffer.'

'But . . .?'

'I know you think I'm a terrible show-off, Guido,' she began and continued before he had the chance to say anything. 'And it's true, but only at times. This isn't like that, not at all. I'm not doing this to be in the newspapers. In fact, I can tell you honestly that I'm afraid of the trouble this is going to cause us all. But I have to do it.' Again, when she saw him about to interrupt, she amended that. 'I mean, someone has to do it, or, to use the passive voice you hate so much,' she said with a gentle smile, 'it has to be done.' Still smiling, she added, 'I'll listen to anything you have to say, but I don't think I can do anything different from what I've chosen to do.'

Brunetti changed the position of his feet, putting the left on top, and leaned a little to the right. 'The Germans have changed the law. They can now prosecute Germans for things they do in other countries.'

'I know. I read the article,' she said sharply.

'And?'

'And one man was sentenced to a few years in jail. As the Americans say, "Big fucking deal." Hundreds of thousands of men go there every year. Putting one of them in jail, in a well-lit German jail where he gets television and visits from his wife every week, is not going to stop men from going to Thailand as sex-tourists.'

'And what you want to do, that will?'

'If the planes don't go, if no one's willing to take the risk of organizing the tours, with hotel rooms and meals and guides to take them to the brothels, well, then fewer of them will go. I know it's not much, but it's something.'

'They'll go on their own.'

'Fewer of them.'

'But still some? But still a lot of them?'

'Probably.'

'Then why do it?'

She shook her head in annoyance. 'Maybe all of this is because you're a man,' she said.

For the first time since coming into her study Brunetti felt anger. 'What's that supposed to mean?'

'It means that men and women look at this differently. Always will.'

'Why?' His voice was level, though both of them knew that anger had slipped into the room and between them.

'Because, no matter how much you try to imagine what this means, it's always got to be an exercise in imagination. It can't happen to you, Guido. You're big and strong and, from the time you were a little boy, you've been accustomed to violence of some sort: soccer, rough-housing with other boys; in your case police training as well.'

She saw his attention drifting away. He'd heard this before and never believed it. She thought he didn't want to believe it, but she had not told him that. 'But it's different for us, for women,' she went on. 'We spend our lives being made afraid of violence, made to think always of avoiding it. But still every one of us knows that what happens to those kids in Cambodia or Thailand or the Philippines could just as easily have happened to us, could still happen to us. It's as simple as that, Guido: you're big and we're little.'

He gave no response, and so she went on, 'Guido, we've been talking about this for years and we've never really agreed. We don't now.' She paused for a moment, then asked, 'Will you listen to two more things, then I'll listen to you?'

Brunetti wanted to make his voice sound amiable, open and accepting; he wanted to say 'Of course', but the best he could manage was a tight 'Yes'.

'Think of that vile article, the one in the magazine. It's one of the major sources of information in this country and in it a sociologist – I don't know where he teaches, but it's certain to be at some important university, so he's considered an expert and people will believe what he writes – can say that paedophiles love children. And he can say that because it's convenient for men to have everyone believe it. And men run the country.'

She stopped for a moment, then added, 'I'm not sure if this has anything to do with what we're talking about, but I think another cause of the gulf that separates us on this – not just you and me, Guido, but all men from all women – is the fear that the idea that sex might sometimes be an unpleasant experience is real to all women and unthinkable to most men.' As she saw him beginning to protest, she said, 'Guido, the woman doesn't exist who thinks for an instant that paedophiles love children. They lust after them or want to dominate them, but those things have nothing to do with love.'

He kept his head lowered; she saw that as she looked across the room at him. 'That's the second thing I want to say, dear Guido whom I love with all my soul. That's how we look at it, most women, that love isn't lust and domination.' She stopped here and glanced down at her right hand, idly picking at a rough piece of cuticle on the nail of her thumb. 'That's all, I think. End of sermon.'

The silence between them stretched out until Brunetti broke it, but tentatively.

'Do you believe all men or just some men think like this?' he asked.

'Just some, I think. The good ones – like you're a good man – they don't.' But before he could say anything, she added, 'They don't think like us, either, like women. I don't think that the idea of love as lust and violence and the exercise of power – I don't think that idea is as entirely alien to them as it is to us.'

'To all women? Alien to all of you?'

'I wish. No, not to all of us.'

He looked up at her. 'Have we resolved anything, then?'

'I don't know. But I want you to know how serious I am about this.'

'And if I were to ask you to stop, not to do anything more?'

Her lips pressed together as she pulled her mouth closed, a gesture he'd watched for decades. She shook her head without saying anything.

'Does that mean you won't stop or you don't want me to ask you?'

'Both.'

'I will ask you and I do ask you.' But before she could give an answer, he raised a hand towards her and said, 'No, Paola, don't say anything because I know what you'll say and I don't want to hear it. But remember, please, that I've asked you not to do this. Not for me or my career, whatever that means. But because I believe that what you're doing and what you think should be done is wrong.'

'I know,' Paola said and pushed herself to her feet.

Before she moved away from the desk he added, 'And I too love you with all my soul. And always will.'

'Ah, that's good to hear, and know.' He heard the relief in her voice and from long experience he knew that some dismissive, joking remark would have to follow it. As had been the case for all the important years of his life, she did not disappoint. 'Then it's safe to put knives on the table for dinner.'

6

The next morning Brunetti did not take his usual route to the Questura but turned right after he crossed the Rialto Bridge. Rosa Salva, it was generally agreed, was one of the best bars in the city; Brunetti especially liked their small ricotta cakes. So he stopped there for coffee and a pastry, exchanged pleasantries with a few people he knew, nods with some he only recognized.

He left the bar, heading down Calle della Mandola towards Campo San Stefano, a route that would lead him eventually to Piazza San Marco. The first *campo* he crossed on his way was Campo Manin, where four workmen were lifting a large sheet of glass from a boat on to a wooden roller to transport it to the travel agency where it was to be installed.

Brunetti joined the other spectators who gathered to watch the men roll the plate of glass across the *campo*. The workmen had wadded towels between the glass and the wooden frame that held it upright. Two on either side, they rolled it towards the gaping hole that awaited it.

As the men crossed the *campo*, opinions rolled behind them from person to person. 'Gypsies did it.' 'No, someone who used to work there came back with a gun.' 'I heard it was the owner who did it to collect the insurance.' 'What stupidity; it was hit by lightning.' Typically, each of them was absolutely convinced of the truth of his version and had nothing but scorn for the alternatives.

When the wooden trolley reached the window, Brunetti pulled himself away from the small crowd and continued on his way.

Inside the Questura, he stopped at the large room where the uniformed officers worked and asked to see the crime reports of the previous night. Little had happened and none of it interested him in any way. Upstairs, he spent most of the morning in the seemingly endless process of moving papers from one part of his desk to another. His banker had told him, years ago, that all copies of any bank transactions, no matter how innocuous, had to be placed in an archive for ten years before they could be destroyed.

His eyes wandered away from the page, following his attention, and he found himself imagining an Italy entirely covered, to the height of a man's ankles, with papers, reports, photocopies, carbon copies, tiny receipts from the bars, shops and pharmacies. And in this sea of paper, it still took a letter two weeks to get to Rome.

He was distracted from this train of thought by the arrival of Sergeant Vianello, who came to tell him that he'd managed to arrange a meeting with one of the petty criminals who sometimes gave them information. The man had told Vianello he had something interesting to exchange; but because the thief was afraid of being seen with anyone from the police, Brunetti had to meet him in a bar in Mestre, which meant he had to take the train to Mestre after lunch and a bus to the bar. It was not the kind of place a person went to in a taxi.

It all came to nothing, as Brunetti had secretly known it would. Encouraged by newspaper reports of the millions the government was giving to those who had turned on the Mafia and were testifying against it, the young man wanted Brunetti to advance him five million lire. The idea was absurd, the afternoon a dead loss, but at least it kept him in motion until well after four, when he got back to his office to find an agitated Vianello waiting for him.

'What is it?' Brunetti asked when he saw the expression on Vianello's face.

'That man in Treviso.'

'Iacovantuono?'

'Yes.'

'What about him? Has he decided not to come?'

'His wife's been killed.'

57

'How?'

'She fell down the stairs in their apartment building and broke her neck.'

'How old was she?' Brunetti asked.

'Thirty-five.'

'Medical problems?'

'None.'

'Witnesses?'

Vianello shook his head.

'Who found her?'

'A neighbour. A man coming home for lunch.'

'Did he see anything?'

Again, Vianello shook his head.

'When did it happen?'

'The man said he thinks she might still have been alive when he found her, a little before one. But he isn't sure.'

'Did she say anything?'

'He called 113, but by the time the ambulance got there she was dead.'

'Have they spoken to the neighbours?'

'Who?' Vianello asked.

'The Treviso police.'

'They haven't spoken to anyone. I don't think they're going to speak to anyone.'

'Why not, for the love of God?'

'They're treating it as an accident.'

'Of course it would look like an accident,' Brunetti exploded. When Vianello said nothing, Brunetti asked, 'Has anyone spoken to the husband?'

'He was at work when it happened.'

'But has anyone spoken to him?'

'I don't think so, sir. Other than to tell him what happened.'

'Can we get a car?' Brunetti asked.

Vianello picked up the phone, punched in a number and talked for a moment. After he hung up he said, 'There'll be one waiting for us in Piazzale Roma at five thirty.'

'Let me call my wife,' Brunetti said. Paola wasn't home, so he told Chiara to tell her that he had to go to Treviso and would probably be home late.

During his more than two decades as a policeman, Brunetti had developed an instinct that very often proved accurate and that allowed him to sense failure well before he encountered it. Even before he and Vianello set foot outside the Questura, he knew that the trip to Treviso was doomed and that any chance they had ever had of getting Iacovantuono to testify had died with his wife.

It was seven before they got there, eight before they persuaded Iacovantuono to speak to them, ten before they finally accepted his refusal to have anything further to do with the police. The only thing in the entire evening's doings that made Brunetti feel at all relieved or satisfied was his own refusal to pose the rhetorical question to Iacovantuono of what would happen to all their children if he failed to testify. It was too evident, at least it was evident from Brunetti's reading of events, what would happen in that case: he and his children would remain alive. Feeling every kind of fool, he gave the red-eyed *pizzaiolo* one of his cards before he and Vianello went out to the car.

The driver was ill-tempered from having had to sit idly for so long, so Brunetti suggested the three of them stop and eat on the way back, though he knew it would delay his arrival at home until well after midnight. The chauffeur finally left him and Vianello at Piazzale Roma a little before one and an exhausted Brunetti decided to take a vaporetto rather than walk home. He and Vianello made desultory conversation while waiting for the boat and inside the cabin as it made its majestic way up the most beautiful waterway in the world.

Brunetti got out at San Silvestro, blind to the beauty of the moonlit night. He wanted nothing more than to find his wife and his bed, and to lose the memory of Iacovantuono's sad, knowing eyes. Inside the apartment, he hung up his coat and went down the corridor towards their bedroom. No light came from either of the children's rooms, but nevertheless he opened their doors and checked that they were both asleep.

He opened the door of their bedroom quietly, hoping to undress in the light that filtered in from the corridor and not to disturb Paola. But it was a vain courtesy: the bed was empty. Even though there was no gleam coming from under the door of her study, he checked to confirm his certainty that it was empty. No lights burned in any other part of the apartment, but he went into the living-room, half hoping, yet knowing how vain the hope was, that he would find her asleep on the sofa.

The only light in that part of the house flickered red from the answering machine. There were three messages. The first was his own phone call, made from Treviso at about ten, telling Paola that he would be delayed even longer. The second was a hang-up and the third, as he had both known and feared it would be, was from the Questura, Officer Pucetti asking the commissario to call as soon as he got home.

He did so, using the direct number to the officers' room. It was answered on the second ring.

'Pucetti, this is Commissario Brunetti. What is it?'

'I think you'd better come down here, Commissario.'

'What is it, Pucetti?' Brunetti repeated, but his voice was tired, not at all brusque or imperative.

'Your wife, sir.'

'What's happened?'

'We've arrested her, sir.'

'I see. Can you tell me more about it?'

'I think it would be better if you came over, sir.'

'May I speak to her?' Brunetti asked.

'Of course,' Pucetti answered, relief flooding his voice.

After a moment, Paola asked, 'Yes?'

Sudden rage swept him. She gets herself arrested and all she can do is act the prima donna. 'I'm on my way down there, Paola. Did you do it again?'

'Yes, I did.' Nothing more.

He put down the phone, went into the kitchen and left a note, and the light burning, for the children. He headed towards the Questura, his heart heavier than his feet.

A light shower had begun to fall, really more a liquefaction of air than anything as distinct as rain. Automatically he pulled up his collar as he walked.

After a quarter of an hour he arrived at the Questura. A very worried-looking uniformed officer stood at the door and opened it for him with a salute so crisp it seemed out of place at this hour. Brunetti nodded at the young man – he couldn't remember his name, though he knew he knew it – and took the steps up to the first floor.

Pucetti stood and saluted when he came in. Paola looked up at him from where she sat facing Pucetti, but she didn't smile.

Brunetti took a chair on Paola's side of the desk and pulled the arrest form that lay in front of his colleague towards him. He read it slowly.

'You found her there, in Campo Manin?' Brunetti asked the officer.

'Yes, sir,' Pucetti answered, still standing.

Brunetti motioned to the young man to sit down, which he did with obvious timidity. 'Was anyone with you?'

'Yes, sir. Landi.'

That cuts it, then, Brunetti thought and pushed the paper back across the desk. 'What did you do?'

'We came back here, sir, and we asked her, your wife, for her *carta d'identità*. When she gave it to us and we saw who she was, Landi called Lieutenant Scarpa.'

Landi was bound to do that, Brunetti knew. 'Why did you both come back here? Why didn't one of you stay there?'

'One of the Guardia di San Marco heard the alarm and came, so we left him there until the owner showed up.'

'I see, I see,' Brunetti said, then, 'Did Lieutenant Scarpa come in?'

'No, sir. He and Landi talked. But he didn't give any orders, just left it to us to do it the normal way.'

Brunetti almost said there probably was no normal way to arrest the wife of a commissario of police, but instead he stood and glanced down at Paola, addressing her for the first time. 'I think we can go now, Paola.'

She didn't answer, but immediately got to her feet.

'I'll take her home, Pucetti. We'll be back here in the morning. If Lieutenant Scarpa asks any questions, tell him that, would you?'

'Of course, sir,' Pucetti answered. He started to add something, but Brunetti cut him off with an upraised hand.

'It's all right, Pucetti. You had no choice.' He glanced at Paola and added, 'And besides, it would have happened sooner or later.' He tried to smile at the man.

When they got to the bottom of the stairs, they found the young policeman at the door, his hand already pulling it open. Brunetti let Paola pass in front of him, raised a hand without actually looking at him, and walked out into the night. The liquid air surrounded them, instantly turning their breath into soft clouds. They walked side by side, the sword of discord as palpable between them as their breath was visible in the air.

7

Neither of them spoke on the way home, nor did they sleep for the rest of the night, save for odd patches of troubled dreams. A few times, as they drifted between waking and moments of forgetting, their bodies rolled together, but there was none of the ease of long familiarity in the contact. Quite the opposite: the touch could have been that of a stranger and each responded by moving away. They had the grace not to make it a sudden move, not to start in shock and horror at the touch of this stranger who had invaded their marriage bed. Perhaps that would have been more honest, to let the flesh give voice to the mind and the spirit, but both of them managed to control that impulse, to beat it down out of some idea of loyalty due to memory or the love both of them feared had been damaged or somehow changed.

Brunetti forced himself to wait for the seven o'clock bells from San Polo, refused to let himself get out of bed until then, but they had not finished sounding before he was into the bathroom, where he stood under the shower for a long time, washing away the night and the thought of Landi and Scarpa, and what was bound to be waiting for him when he got to work that morning.

As he stood under the water, he told himself that he would have to say something to Paola before he left the house, but he had no idea what that would be. He decided to let it depend upon how she behaved when he went back into the bedroom, but when he did she was no longer there. He heard her in the kitchen, the familiar sounds of water, coffee pot, a chair scraping on the floor. Knotting his tie, he went along there and, as he saw her sitting at her regular place, noticed that two large cups were placed at their normal places on the table. He finished with his tie, bent and kissed the top of her head.

'Why do you do that?' she asked, reaching backwards with her right arm and wrapping it around his thigh. She pulled him towards her.

He leaned against her, but he did not touch her with his hand. 'Habit, I suppose.'

'Habit?' she asked, already on the way to being offended.

'The habit of loving you.'

'Ah,' she said, but anything further was cut off by the hiss of the coffee pot. She poured coffee,

66

added steaming milk and stirred sugar into both cups. He didn't sit, drank his standing.

'What will happen?' she asked after the first sip.

'As it's your first offence, I suppose there will be a fine.'

'That's all?'

'That's enough,' Brunetti said.

'And what about you?'

'That depends on how the papers play it. There are a few journalists who have waited years for something like this.'

Before he could list the possible headlines she said, 'I know. I know,' and so he spared them both that.

'But there's an equal chance that you'll be turned into a heroine, the Rosa Luxemburg of the sex industry.'

Both of them smiled, but there was no attempt at sarcasm.

'That's not what I'm after, Guido. You know that.' Before he could ask her what it *was* she was after she said, 'I just want them to stop it. I want them to be so shamed by what they do that they'll stop it.'

'Who, the travel agents?'

'Them, yes,' she said and returned to her coffee for a while. When it was almost gone she set down the cup and said, 'But I'd like them all to be shamed by what they do.'

'The men who go as sex-tourists?'

'Yes, all of them.'

'That's not going to happen, Paola, no matter what you do.'

'I know.' She finished her coffee and got up to make some more.

'No,' Brunetti said. 'I'll stop at a bar and get some on the way.'

'It's early.'

'There's always a bar,' he said.

'Yes.'

There was, and he stopped for more coffee, lingering over it so as to delay his arrival at the Questura. He bought the *Gazzettino*, even though he knew it was impossible that anything could appear until the next day. Still he looked at the first page of the first section, then at the second, the part dedicated to local news, but there was nothing.

There was a different officer at the front door of the Questura: because it was still before eight he had to unlock the door for Brunetti and saluted him as he walked past.

'Is Vianello here yet?' Brunetti asked.

'No, sir. I haven't seen him.'

'Tell him I'd like him to come up to my office when he gets in, would you?'

'Yes, sir,' he said and saluted again.

Brunetti took the back steps. Marinoni, the woman just returned from maternity leave, greeted him on the steps, but said only that she'd heard about the man in Treviso and was sorry.

In his office, he hung up his coat, sat at his desk, and opened the *Gazzettino*. There was the usual: magistrates investigating other magistrates, former ministers making accusations against other former ministers, riots in the capital of Albania, the Minister of Health asking for an investigation of the illegal manufacture of false pharmaceuticals for the Third World.

He turned to the second section and, on the third page, found the story about the death of Signora Iacovantuono. '*Casalinga muore cadendo per le scale* (Housewife dies by falling down the stairs).' Sure.

He'd heard it all the day before: she fell, the neighbour found her at the foot of the steps, the paramedics declared her dead. The funeral would take place tomorrow.

He had just finished reading the article when Vianello knocked on his door and came in. All Brunetti needed was a glance at his face. He asked, 'What are they saying?'

'Landi started talking about it as soon as people began to come in, but Ruberti and Bellini haven't said a word. And the papers haven't called.'

'Scarpa?' Brunetti asked.

'He's not in yet.'

'What's Landi saying?'

'That he brought your wife down here last night after she broke a window in the travel agency in Campo Manin. And that you came down and took her home without filling out the paperwork. He's turning into a jailhouse lawyer, saying she's technically a fugitive from justice.'

Brunetti folded the paper in half, then in half again. He recalled telling Pucetti that he would bring his wife with him that morning, but he hardly thought her absence was sufficient to turn her into a fugitive from justice. 'I see,' he said. He paused for a long time and finally asked, 'How many people know about the last time?'

Vianello considered the question for a moment and answered, 'Officially, no one knows. Officially, nothing happened.'

'That's not what I asked.'

'I don't think anyone knows who shouldn't know,' Vianello said, obviously unwilling to explain more than that.

Brunetti didn't know whether he should thank the sergeant, or thank Ruberti and Bellini. Instead, he asked, 'Has there been anything from the Treviso police this morning?'

'Iacovantuono went to their office to say he couldn't be certain about the identification he made last week. He thinks he was mistaken. Because he was so afraid. And now he's sure the robber had red hair. It seems he remembered that a few days ago, but never got around to telling the police.'

'Until his wife died?' Brunetti asked.

Vianello didn't answer at first. After a while, he asked, 'What would you do, sir?'

'If what?'

'If you were in his place.'

'I'd probably remember the red hair, too.'

Vianello stuffed his hands into the pockets of his uniform jacket and nodded. 'I suppose we all would, wouldn't we, especially if we had a family?'

Brunetti's intercom rang. 'Yes,' he said when he'd picked it up. He listened for a moment, then put the phone down and got to his feet. 'It's the Vice-Questore. He wants to see me.'

Vianello pushed back his sleeve and looked at his watch. 'Quarter past nine. I suppose that explains what Lieutenant Scarpa's been doing.'

Brunetti carefully centred the newspaper on his desk before he left the office. Outside Patta's door, Signorina Elettra sat at her computer, but the screen was blank. She looked up when Brunetti came in, caught her lower lip between her teeth and raised her eyebrows. It could have been surprise, but it could just as easily have been the sort of encouragement one student gives another who has been called to see the principal.

Brunetti closed his eyes for a moment and felt his lips pulling together. He didn't say anything to the secretary, but knocked at the door and opened it at the shouted,'*Avanti*'.

Brunetti had expected to find only the Vice-Questore in the office, so he failed to hide his surprise when he saw four persons: Vice-Questore Patta; Lieutenant Scarpa, seated to the left of his superior, the same as the seat always given to Judas in paintings of the Last Supper; and two men, one in his late fifties, the other about ten years younger. Brunetti had no time to study them, save to get the sense that the older man was somehow in command, though the younger was more attentive.

Patta began without preamble. 'Commissario Brunetti, this is Dottor Paolo Mitri.' He indicated the older man with a graceful wave of his hand. 'And his lawyer, Avvocato Giuliano Zambino. We've called you here to discuss the events of last night.'

There was a fifth chair, a bit to the left of the lawyer, but no one suggested Brunetti take it. He nodded to the two men.

'Perhaps the Commissario could join us?' suggested Dottor Mitri, motioning to the empty chair with his hand.

Patta nodded and Brunetti sat.

'You know why you're here, I suppose,' Patta said.

'I'd like to hear it stated clearly,' Brunetti answered.

Patta waved to his lieutenant, who began. 'Last night, at about midnight, I received a call from one of my men that the window of the travel agency in Campo Manin – the travel agency owned by Dottor Mitri,' he added, with a small inclination of his head in his direction, 'had again been destroyed by vandals. He told me that a suspect had been taken to the Questura and that the suspect was the wife of Commissario Brunetti.'

'Is this true?' Patta interrupted, speaking to Brunetti.

'I have no idea what Officer Landi said to the lieutenant last night,' was Brunetti's calm response.

'That's not what I mean,' Patta interrupted before the lieutenant could say anything. 'Was it your wife?'

'In the report which I read last night,' Brunetti began, his voice still calm, 'Officer Landi gave her name and address, and said she admitted breaking the window.'

'What about the other time?' Scarpa asked.

Brunetti didn't bother to ask what other time he meant. 'What about it?'

'Was it your wife?'

'You'll have to ask my wife that, Lieutenant.'

'I will,' he said. 'You can be sure I will.'

Dottor Mitri coughed once, hiding the sound behind a raised hand. 'Perhaps I could interrupt here, Pippo,' he said to Patta. The Vice-Questore, apparently honoured by the intimacy of address, nodded.

Mitri turned his attention to Brunetti. 'Commissario, I think it would be helpful if we could come to an understanding about this matter.' Brunetti turned towards him but said nothing. 'The damages to the agency have been considerable: the first window cost me almost four million lire to replace, and I assume this time it will be the same. There is also the matter of lost business during the time the agency was closed while we waited for the glass to be replaced.'

He paused, as if waiting for Brunetti to say or ask something, but when he did not, Mitri continued. 'Because no one was apprehended for the first crime, I assume my insurance company will pay for the original damages and perhaps even for some of the lost business. It will take a considerable time for this to be achieved, of course, but I'm certain we'll reach a settlement. In fact, I've already spoken to my agent and he assures me this is the case.'

Brunetti watched him as he spoke, listened to the confidence in his voice. This was a man accustomed to the full attention of the people he dealt with; his assurance and sense of self radiated from him in waves that were almost tangible. The rest of him gave the same impression: razor-cut hair worn shorter than was then the fashion, a light tan, skin and nails that were taken care of by someone else. He had light-brown eyes, almost the colour of amber, and a voice so pleasing as to be almost seductive. Because he was seated, Brunetti wasn't sure of his height, but he looked as if he'd be tall, with the long arms and legs of a runner.

During all this the lawyer sat silent, attentive, listening to his client, but he said nothing.

'Do I have your attention, Commissario?' Mitri asked, aware of Brunetti's scrutiny and perhaps not liking it.

'Yes.'

'The second case is, and will be, different. Since your wife has apparently admitted to breaking the window, it seems only just that she should pay for it. That's why I asked to speak to you.'

'Yes?' Brunetti asked.

'I thought you and I might come to an agreement about this.'

'I'm afraid I don't understand,' Brunetti said, wondering how far he could push this man and what would happen when he overdid it.

'What is it you don't understand, Commissario?'

'What it is you called me in here to talk about.'

Mitri's voice tightened, but it remained light. 'I want to resolve this matter. Between gentlemen.' He nodded in the direction of Patta. 'I have the honour of being a friend of the Vice-Questore, and

I would prefer not to cause the police any embarrassment in this matter.'

That, Brunetti thought, could explain the silence of the press.

'And so I thought we might settle this matter quietly, without causing unnecessary complications.'

Brunetti turned to Scarpa. 'Last night, did my wife say anything to Landi about why she did it?'

Scarpa was caught off guard by the question and glanced quickly at Mitri, who spoke before the lieutenant did. 'I'm sure that's of no consequence now. What's important is that she admitted the crime.' He turned his attention to Patta. 'I think it is in the best interests of us all that we settle this while we can. I'm sure you agree, Pippo.'

Patta permitted himself a sharp 'Of course'.

Mitri returned his attention to Brunetti. 'If you agree with me, then we can proceed. If not, then I'm afraid I'm wasting my time.'

'I'm still not sure what it is you want me to agree to, Dottor Mitri.'

'I want you to agree that your wife will pay me for the damage to my window and for the business lost by the agency while it's being repaired.'

'I can't do that,' Brunetti said.

'And why not?' Mitri demanded, not much patience left.

'It's none of my business. If you'd like to discuss the matter with my wife, you are certainly free to do so. But I can't make any decision, much less one like this, for her.' Brunetti thought his voice sounded as reasonable as what he had to say.

'What sort of man are you?' Mitri asked angrily.

Brunetti turned his attention to Patta. 'Is there any other way I can be helpful to you, Vice-Questore?' Patta seemed too surprised, or too angry, to answer, so Brunetti got to his feet and let himself quickly out of the office.

8

In response to Signorina Elettra's raised eyebrows and pursed mouth, Brunetti gave nothing more than a quick, inconclusive shake of his head signalling to her that he'd explain later. He went back up the stairs to his office, considering the real meaning of what had just happened.

Mitri, who boasted of his friendship with Patta, no doubt had sufficient influence to keep a story as potentially explosive as this out of the papers. It was a natural, had everything a reporter could want: sex, violence, police involvement. And if they managed to discover the way in which Paola's first attack had been covered up, that would provide their readers with even headier delights – police corruption and the abuse of power.

What editor would renounce a possibility like this? What newspaper could deny itself the pleasure of printing such an item? Paola, as well, was the daughter of Conte Orazio Falier, one of the most famous and certainly one of the wealthiest men in the city. It was all such remarkably good press that the newspaper which would deny itself such a coup did not exist.

That meant there had to be some greater recompense to the editor or editors who did not use it. Or, he added after a moment's reflection, to the authorities who managed to prevent the story from getting to the papers. There also existed the possibility that the story had been put off limits, dressed up in reasons of state and thus prohibited to the press. Mitri had not seemed a man to possess that much power, but that kind, Brunetti had to remind himself, was often invisible. He had but to think of a former politician, currently on trial for association with the Mafia, a man whose appearance had been the butt of cartoon humour for decades. One did not normally associate great power with a man who looked so thoroughly innocuous, yet Brunetti had no doubt that one wink of those pale-green eyes could bring about the destruction of anyone who opposed him in even the most insignificant way.

There had been as much bravado as truth in Brunetti's disclaimer that he could not make a decision for Paola, but on sober reflection he realized that he meant it.

Mitri had appeared at Patta's office with a

lawyer, one known to Brunetti, at least by reputation. Brunetti had a vague memory that Zambino usually concerned himself with business law, normally for large companies out on the mainland. He thought he might live in the city, but so few companies remained here that Zambino, at least professionally, had been forced to follow the exodus to the mainland in search of work.

Why bring a business lawyer to a meeting with the police? Why involve him in something that was or might become a criminal matter? Zambino had the reputation, he recalled, of being a forceful man, not without enemies, yet he hadn't said a word during the entire time Brunetti was in Patta's office.

He called down and asked Vianello to come up. When the sergeant came in some minutes later, Brunetti waved him to a seat. 'What do you know about a certain Dottor Paolo Mitri and Avvocato Giuliano Zambino?'

Vianello must have learned their names in some other way, for his answer was immediate. 'Zambino lives in Dorsoduro, not far from the Salute. Big place, must be three hundred metres. He specializes in corporate and business law. Most of his clients are out on the mainland: chemicals and petrochemicals, pharmaceuticals and one factory that manufactures heavy earth-moving equipment. One of the chemical companies he works for was caught dumping arsenic into the *laguna* three years ago: he got them off with a fine of three million lire and the promise not to do it again.'

Brunetti listened until the sergeant had finished, wondering if Signorina Elettra had been the source of this information. 'And Mitri?'

Brunetti sensed that Vianello was fighting hard to disguise his pride in having so swiftly gathered all of this information. He continued eagerly, 'He got his start in one of the pharmaceutical companies, began there when he got out of university. He's a chemist, but he doesn't work at that any more, not after he took over the first factory, then two more. He's branched out in the last few years and as well as a number of factories, he owns that travel agency, two estate agencies and is rumoured to be the major shareholder in the string of fast-food restaurants that opened last year.'

'Any trouble, either of them?'

'No,' Vianello said. 'Neither of them.'

'Could that be negligence?'

'On whose part?'

'Ours.'

The sergeant considered this for a moment. 'Possibly. There's a lot of that around.'

'We might take a look, eh?'

'Signorina Elettra is already talking to their banks.'

'Talking?'

Instead of answering, Vianello spread his hands flat on Brunetti's desk and aped typing into a computer.

'How long has he owned this travel agency?' Brunetti asked.

'Five or six years, I think.'

'I wonder how long they've been arranging

these tours,' Brunetti said.

'I can remember seeing the posters for them a few years ago, in the agency we use down in Castello,' Vianello said. 'I wondered how a week in Thailand could cost so little. I asked Nadia and she explained what it meant. So I've sort of kept an eye on the windows in travel agencies since then.' Vianello did not explain the motive for his curiosity and Brunetti did not ask.

'Where else do they go?'

'The tours?'

'Yes.'

'Usually Thailand, I think, but there are lots of them to the Philippines. And Cuba. And in the last couple of years they've started them to Burma and Cambodia.'

'What are the ads like?' asked Brunetti, who had never paid any attention to them.

'They used to say things overtly: "In the middle of the red light district, friendly companions, all dreams come true", that sort of thing. But now that the law's been changed, it's all in a sort of code: "Hotel staff very open-minded, near the night spots, friendly hostesses." It's all the same sort of thing, though, lots of whores for men too lazy to go out on the road and look for them.'

Brunetti had no idea how Paola had learned about this or how much she knew concerning Mitri's agency. 'Has Mitri's place got the same sort of ads?'

Vianello shrugged. 'I suppose so. The ones who do it all seem to use a similar coded language. You learn to read it after a while. But most of them also do a lot of legitimate booking: the Maldives, the Seychelles, wherever there's cheap fun and lots of sun.'

For a moment Brunetti feared that Vianello, who had had a pre-cancerous growth removed from his back some years ago and had militantly avoided the sun since then, would launch into his favourite topic, but instead Vianello said, 'I've asked about him. Downstairs. Just checking to see if the boys know anything.'

'And?'

Vianello shook his head. 'Nothing. Might as well not exist.'

'Well, it's not illegal, what he's doing,' Brunetti said.

'I know it's not illegal,' Vianello finally said. 'But it should be.' Then, before Brunetti could answer, he added, 'I know it's not our job to make the law. Probably not even our job to question it. But no one should be allowed to send grown men off to have sex with children.'

Put like that, Brunetti realized, there was little to be argued against it. But all the travel agency did, so far as the law was concerned, was arrange for the purchase of tickets so that people could travel to other places and arrange hotels for them when they arrived. What they did when they were there was entirely their own affair. Brunetti found himself remembering his university course in logic and how excited he had been by the all but mathematical simplicity of it. All men are mortal. Giovanni is a man. Therefore Giovanni is mortal. There had been rules, he remembered, for checking the validity of a syllogism, something about a major term and a middle term: they had to be in certain places and not too many of them could be negative.

The details seemed to have disappeared, flown off to join all those other facts, statistics, and first principles that had escaped his keeping in the decades since he had finished his exams and been accepted into the ranks of the doctors of law. He recalled, even at this remove, the tremendous sense of assurance that had come to him in learning that certain laws did apply and could be used to govern the validity of conclusions, that they could be demonstrated to be correct or arrived at truly.

The ensuing years had worn away that assurance. Now truth seemed to reside in the possession of those who could shout the loudest or hire the best lawyers. And there was no syllogism that could resist the argument of a gun or a knife, or any of the other forms of argumentation with which his professional life was filled.

He pulled himself away from these reflections and returned his attention to Vianello, caught him in mid-sentence: '. . . a lawyer?'

'Excuse me?' Brunetti said. 'I was thinking about something else.'

'I wondered if you'd thought of getting a lawyer for this.'

Ever since he had walked down from Patta's office, Brunetti had been thrusting away this idea. Just as he would not answer for his wife to the men in the upstairs office, he had not allowed himself to plan a strategy for dealing with the legal consequences of Paola's behaviour. Though he was acquainted with most of the criminal lawyers in the city and was on reasonably good terms with many of them, he knew them only in the most strictly professional way. He found himself going through their names, trying to recall that of the man who had made a successful defence in a murder case two years ago. He pulled his mind away. 'My wife will have to take care of that, I think.'

Vianello nodded and got to his feet. He didn't say anything further and left the office.

When he was gone, Brunetti pushed himself up and began to pace back and forth between the wardrobe and the window. Signorina Elettra was checking out the bank records of two men who had done nothing more than report a crime and suggest it be settled in a way that would give least trouble to the person who all but boasted of having committed it. They had gone to the trouble of coming to the Questura, where they had offered a compromise, which would save the culprit from the legal consequences of her behaviour. And Brunetti was going to sit idly by as *their* finances were investigated in a manner that was probably as illegal as was the original crime of which one of them was the victim.

He had no doubts whatsoever about the illegality of what Paola had done. He stopped walking and considered that she had never denied it was illegal. She simply didn't care. He spent his days and his life in defence of the concept of the law, and she could spit on it as though it were some stupid convention that was in no way binding on her, just because she didn't agree. He felt the pulse of his heart increase as his indignation mounted towards the anger that had lurked in his chest for days now. She answered a whim, following some self-constructed definition of right behaviour, and he was simply supposed to stand idly by, mouth agape at the nobility of her actions, while his career was destroyed.

Brunetti caught himself sinking into this mood and stopped himself before he began to lament the effect all this would have on his position among his peers at the Questura, the cost to his self-respect. So he was forced, here, to give himself much the same answer he had given Mitri: he was not responsible for his wife's behaviour.

The explanation, however, did little to calm his anger. He resumed pacing, but when that proved fruitless, he went downstairs to Signorina Elettra's office.

She smiled when he came in. 'The Vice-Questore has gone to lunch,' she offered but said nothing else, waiting to catch Brunetti's mood.

'Did they go with him?'

She nodded.

'Signorina,' he began, then paused as he thought how to phrase it. 'I don't think it's necessary that you ask any further questions about those men.'

He saw her begin to protest, and he spoke before she could make any sort of objection. 'There's no suspicion that either one of them has committed a crime, and I think it would be impolitic to begin investigations about them. Especially in these circumstances.' He left it to her imagination to supply just what those circumstances were.

She nodded. 'I understand, sir.'

'I didn't ask if you understood, Signorina. I'm saying that you are not to initiate an investigation of their finances.'

'Yes, sir,' she said, turning from him and flipping on the screen of her computer.

'Signorina,' he repeated, his voice level. When she looked up from the screen, he said, 'I'm serious about this, Signorina. I don't want any questions asked about them.'

'Then none will be asked, sir,' she said and smiled with radiant falseness. Like a soubrette in a cheap film comedy, she put her elbows on the table, laced her fingers together and propped her chin on their linked surface. 'Will that be all, Commissario, or do you have something you do want me to do?'

He turned away from her without answering, started towards the stairs, but instead turned and left the Questura. He walked up the embankment towards the Greek church, crossed the bridge, and went into the bar that stood facing him.

'*Buon giorno*, Commissario,' the barman greeted him. '*Cosa desidera*?'

Before knowing what to order, Brunetti looked down at his watch. He'd lost all sense of time and was surprised to see that it was almost noon. '*Un'ombra*,' he answered and, when it came, drank the small glass of white wine without bothering to sip or taste it. It didn't help at all, and he had sense enough to know that another would help even less. He dropped a thousand lire on the counter and went back to the Questura. He spoke to no one, merely went up to his office and got his coat, then left again and went home.

At lunch, it was clear that Paola had told the children about what had happened. Chiara looked at her mother with obvious confusion, but it seemed that Raffi looked at her with interest, perhaps even curiosity. No one brought up the subject, so the meal passed in relative calm. Ordinarily, Brunetti would have rejoiced in the fresh tagliatelle and porcini, but today he barely tasted them. Nor did he much enjoy the spezzatini and fried melanzane which followed. When they had finished, Chiara went to her piano lesson and Raffi to a friend's to study maths.

Alone, the table still littered with plates and serving bowls, Paola and Brunetti drank their coffee, his laced with grappa, hers black and sweet. 'You going to get a lawyer?' he asked.

'I spoke to my father this morning,' she said.

'What did he say?'

'Do you mean before or after he yelled at me?'

Brunetti was forced to smile. 'Yell' was not a verb he ever would, even in his wildest flights of imagination, have associated with his father-in-law. The incongruity amused him.

'After, I think.'

'He told me I was a fool.'

Brunetti recalled that this had been the Count's response to Paola's declaration, twenty years ago, that she was going to marry him. 'And after that?'

'He told me to hire Senno.'

Brunetti nodded at the name of the best criminal lawyer in the city. 'Perhaps a bit excessive.'

'Why?'

'Senno's good at defending rapists and murderers, rich kids who beat up their girlfriends, those same girlfriends caught selling heroin to pay for their habit. I hardly think you're in that class.'

'I'm not sure if that's a compliment or not.'

Brunetti shrugged. Neither was he.

When Paola volunteered nothing more, he asked, 'Are you?'

'I won't hire a man like him.'

Brunetti pulled the grappa bottle towards him and poured a bit more into his empty coffee cup. He swirled it around and drank it down in a single mouthful. Leaving her last remark to hang between them, he asked, 'Who are you going to hire?'

She shrugged. 'I'll wait to see what the charge is. Then I'll decide.'

He thought for a moment about drinking another grappa, but realized he didn't want it. Making no offer to help with the washing up or even with clearing the table, Brunetti stood and pushed his chair under the table. He glanced down at his watch, this time surprised to see that it was still so early, not yet two. 'I think I'll lie down for a while before I go back,' he said.

She nodded, stood, and began stacking the plates one on top of the other.

He went down the corridor to their room, removed his shoes and sat on the side of the bed, aware of how tired he was. He lay back, latched his hands behind his head, and closed his eyes. From the kitchen came the sound of running water, plates clicking against one another, the clang of a pan. He pulled one arm out from under his head and covered his eyes with his forearm. He thought about his schooldays, hiding in his room whenever he brought home a report card with bad marks, lying on his bed in fear of his father's anger, his mother's disappointment.

Memory sank its teeth into his spirit and took him away with it. At some point, at the same time that he became aware of motion beside him on the bed, he sensed pressure, then warmth across his chest. He smelled, then felt, her hair against his face, smelled that combination of soap and health that decades had seared into his memory. He lifted his arm from his eyes without bothering to open them. Moving it down across her shoulders, he brought the other arm out from under his head and latched his hands across her back.

After a while they both slept and, when they woke, nothing had changed.

9

The next day passed quietly, things as normal as they ever were in the Questura. Patta demanded that Iacovantuono be brought to Venice and questioned about his refusal to testify, and that was done. Brunetti passed him on the steps as he was being led up to Patta's office between two machine-gun carrying policemen. The *pizzaiolo* raised his eyes to Brunetti's but gave no sign that he recognized him, his face frozen into that mask of ignorance Italians learn to adopt with officialdom.

At the sight of his sad eyes, Brunetti wondered if knowing the truth about what had happened would make any difference. Whether the Mafia had murdered his wife or Iacovantuono merely believed they had – in either case, he perceived the

State and its agencies as helpless to protect him from the menace of a far greater power.

All these thoughts crowded into Brunetti's mind as he saw the small man coming up the steps towards him, but they were too confused for him to be able to express them, even to himself, in words, so all he could do was nod in recognition as they passed, the little man made even smaller by the two policemen who towered above him.

As he continued up the stairs, Brunetti found himself thinking of the myth of Orfeo and Eurydice, of the man who lost his wife by looking behind to assure himself that she was still there, disobeying the gods' command not to do so and thus condemning her to remain forever in Hades. The gods that govern Italy had commanded Iacovantuono not to look at something and when he did not obey, his wife had been taken from him for ever.

Luckily, Vianello was waiting at the top of the stairs, and Brunetti's reflections were driven from him. 'Commissario,' the sergeant began as he saw him arrive, 'we've had a phone call from a woman in Treviso. She said she lives in the same house as the Iacovantuonos, but from the way she spoke, I think she might live in the same building.'

Brunetti walked past the sergeant, signalling with his head that he was to follow and leading him down the corridor into his office. As he put his overcoat into the *armadio*, Brunetti asked, 'What did she say?'

'That they fought.'

Thinking of his own marriage, Brunetti answered, 'Lots of people fight.'

'He beat her.'

'How does the woman know that?' Brunetti asked with immediate curiosity.

'She said the wife used to come down to her apartment and cry about it.'

'Did she ever call the police?'

'Who?'

'The wife. Signora Iacovantuono.'

'I don't know. I just spoke to this woman,' Vianello began, looking down at a slip of paper in his hand, 'Signora Grassi, ten minutes ago. I was just hanging up when you came in. She said he's pretty well known in the area, in the building.'

'For what?'

'Causing trouble with the neighbours. Yelling at their children.'

'And the business with the wife?' Brunetti asked, going to sit behind his desk. As he spoke, he pulled a small pile of papers and envelopes towards him, but did not begin to look at them.

'I don't know. Not yet. There's been no time to talk to anyone.'

'It's not in our jurisdiction,' Brunetti said.

'I know. But Pucetti said they were bringing him in this morning to talk to the Vice-Questore about the bank robbery.'

'Yes. I saw him.' Brunetti looked down at the envelope on the top of the pile and stared at the stamp, so distracted by what Vianello had just told him that all he could perceive was a pale-green rectangle. Slowly, the pattern emerged: a Gaulish soldier, his expiring wife at his feet, the sword plunged deeply into his own body. 'Roma Museo Nazionale Romano' on one side, 'Galatea Suicida' on the other. And across the bottom, the number '750'.

'Insurance?' Brunetti finally asked.

'I don't know, sir. I just now took the call.'

Brunetti got to his feet. 'I'll go and ask him,' he said and left the office alone, heading for the stairs that would take him down to Vice-Questore Patta's office.

The outer room was empty and small toasters flew softly across the screen of Signorina Elettra's computer. Brunetti knocked on Patta's door and was told to enter.

Inside, there was a familiar enough scene: Patta sat behind his desk, its surface empty and all the more intimidating for that. Iacovantuono sat nervously on the edge of the chair that faced Patta, his hands wrapped around the sides of the seat and his elbows locked straight, propping up his weight.

Patta looked up at Brunetti, face impassive. 'Yes?' he asked. 'What is it?'

'I'd like to ask Signor Iacovantuono something,' Brunetti answered.

'I think you'll be wasting your time, Commissario,' Patta said. Then, voice rising, he added, 'Just as I've been wasting mine. Signor Iacovantuono seems to have forgotten what happened in the bank.' Patta leaned forward – loomed might be a more accurate word – across his desk and brought his fist down on its surface, not hard, but with enough force to break the fist open and leave four fingers pointing at Iacovantuono.

When the cook didn't respond at all, Patta glanced back at Brunetti. 'What is it you want to ask him, Commissario? Whether he remembers seeing Stefano Gentile in the bank? Whether he remembers the first description he gave us? Or remembers identifying Gentile's photo when he saw it?' Patta reared back in his chair, his hand in the air in front of him, fingers still pointing at Iacovantuono. 'No, I don't think he remembers any of that. So I suggest you don't waste your time asking him.'

'That's not what I wanted to ask him about, sir,' Brunetti said, his soft tone in strange dissonance to Patta's histrionic anger.

Iacovantuono turned to look at Brunetti.

'Well, what is it?' Patta demanded.

'I wanted to know', Brunetti began, addressing Iacovantuono and ignoring Patta completely, 'if your wife was insured.'

Iacovantuono's eyes widened in genuine surprise. 'Insured?' he asked.

Brunetti nodded. 'Life insurance.'

Iacovantuono looked back at Patta but, seeing no help there, he returned his attention to Brunetti. 'I don't know,' he said.

'Thank you.' Brunetti turned to leave.

'Is that all?' Patta asked angrily from behind him.

'Yes, sir,' Brunetti said, turning to Patta but looking at Iacovantuono. The man was still perched on the edge of his chair, but now his hands were clasped in his lap. His head was lowered and he seemed to be examining his hands.

Brunetti turned back to the door and let himself out. The toasters continued in their endless migration to the right, technological lemmings bent on their own destruction.

He went back up to his office and found Vianello waiting for him, standing at the window and looking out at the garden on the other side of the canal and to the façade of the church of San Lorenzo. The sergeant turned when he heard the door open. 'And?' he asked as Brunetti came in.

'I asked about the insurance.'

'And?' Vianello repeated.

'He didn't know.' Vianello made no comment, so Brunetti asked, 'Does Nadia have an insurance policy?'

'No.' Then, after a moment's pause, Vianello added, 'At least I don't think so.' Both considered this, then Vianello enquired, 'What will you do?'

'The only thing I can do is tell the people in Treviso.' It struck him then. 'Why would she call us?' he asked, suddenly turning to Vianello, one hand raised halfway to his mouth.

'What do you mean?'

'Why would the neighbour call the police in Venice? The woman died in Treviso.' Brunetti suddenly found himself blushing. Of course, of course. Iacovantuono's reputation needed to be blackened only in Venice: if he decided to testify, that's where he was going to do it. Were they watching him so closely that they knew when the police brought him in? Or, worse, did they know when the police were going to do it? *'Gesù bambino,'* he whispered. 'What did she say her name was?'

'Grassi,' Vianello answered.

Brunetti picked up the phone and asked to be connected to the police in Treviso. When he was put through, he identified himself and asked to talk to the person who was in charge of investigating the Iacovantuono case. It took a few minutes before the man he spoke to told him that it had been filed as an accidental death.

'Do you have the name of the man who reported finding the body?'

The phone was put down for a while, then the officer was back. 'Zanetti,' he said. 'Walter Zanetti.'

'Who else lives in the building?' Brunetti asked.

'Only the two families, sir. The Iacovantuonos live on the top floor, the Zanettis below.'

'Does anyone named Grassi live there?'

'No. Only those two families. Why do you ask?'

'It's nothing, nothing. We had a mix-up here with our records, couldn't find Zanetti's name. That's all we need. Thank you for your help.'

'Glad to do it, sir,' the policeman said and hung up.

Before Brunetti could explain, Vianello asked, 'She doesn't exist?'

'If she does, she doesn't live in that building.'

Vianello considered this for a while, then enquired, 'What do we do about it, sir?'

'Tell Treviso.'

'You think it happened there?'

'The leak?' Brunetti asked, though he knew Vianello couldn't mean anything else.

Vianello nodded.

'There or here. It doesn't matter where. It's enough that it happened.'

'It doesn't mean they knew he was coming in here today.'

'Then why call?' Brunetti demanded.

'Just to plant the idea. In case.'

Brunetti shook his head. 'No. The timing's too good. For God's sake, he was coming into the building when you got the call.' Brunetti hesitated for a moment, then he said, 'Who did they ask for?'

'The operator said they wanted to talk to the person who had gone up to Treviso to talk to him. I think he tried you and when you weren't there he put the call through to us. Pucetti gave it to me because I was the one who went to Treviso with you.'

'How did she sound?'

Vianello cast his mind back to the conversation. 'Worried, like she didn't want to cause him trouble. She said that once or twice, that he had suffered enough, but she had to tell us what she knew.'

'Very civic-minded.'

'Yes.'

Brunetti went over to the window and looked down at the canal and at the police boats nestling up against the dock in front of the Questura. He remembered the look on Iacovantuono's face when he'd asked him about the insurance and he felt his face grow red again. He'd reacted like a child with a new toy, running off at the first impulse, not pausing long enough to reflect or to check the information they did have available to them. He knew it was by now standard policy to suspect the spouse in any case of suspicious death, but he should have trusted his instinct about Iacovantuono, should have played his memory back across his halting voice, his palpitant fear for his children. He should have trusted that and not gone snapping wildly at the first accusation that came springing out of the quiet air.

There was no way he could apologize to the *pizzaiolo* because any explanation would only increase his own guilt and embarrassment. 'Any chance of tracing the call?' he asked.

'There was noise in the background. Sounded like street noise. I'd guess it was made from a phone booth,' Vianello said.

If they were smart enough to make the call – or well-informed enough, a cold voice added in Brunetti's mind – then they would be careful enough to make it from a public phone. 'Then that's all, I suppose.' He lowered himself into his chair, suddenly feeling very tired.

Without bothering to say anything, Vianello left the office and Brunetti addressed himself to the papers on his desk.

He began to read a fax from a colleague in Amsterdam, enquiring if there was any chance that Brunetti could speed up a request from the Dutch police for information about an Italian who had been arrested there for killing a prostitute. Because the man's passport gave his permanent address as Venice, the Dutch authorities had contacted the police of that city to learn if he had any previous convictions. The original request had been sent more than a month ago and so far no answer had been received.

Brunetti's hand was just reaching to call down to see if the man had a record when the phone rang . . . and it began.

He had, in a sense, known it was going to happen, had even tried to prepare himself for it by thinking of a strategy with which to deal with the press. But even though he had done this, he was still completely surprised by it when it came.

At the beginning, the journalist, one he knew, one who worked for *Il Gazzettino*, said that he was calling to check on a report that Commissario Brunetti had resigned from the police. When Brunetti said that this came as a complete surprise to him, that he had never thought of resigning, the journalist, Piero Lembo, asked how he planned, then, to deal with his wife's arrest and the conflicts it created between her situation and his position.

Brunetti answered that as he was in no way involved in the case, he saw no possibility of a conflict.

'But certainly you've got friends at the Questura,' Lembo said, though he managed at the same time to sound sceptical about the likelihood of that. 'Friends in the *magistratura*. Wouldn't that affect their judgement or the decisions they make?'

'I think that's unlikely,' Brunetti lied. 'Besides, there's no reason to believe there will be a trial.'

'Why not?' Lembo demanded.

'A trial usually attempts to determine guilt or innocence. That's not in question here. I think there will be a judicial hearing and a fine.'

'And then what?'

'I'm not sure I understand your question, Signor Lembo,' Brunetti said, looking out of the windows of his office, where a pigeon was just landing on the roof of the building across the canal.

'What will happen when the fine is imposed?'

'That's a question I cannot answer.'

'Why not?'

'Any fine will be imposed on my wife, not on me.' He wondered how many times he would have to make this same reply.

'And what is your opinion of her crime?'

'I have no opinion.' At least not one he was going to give to the press.

'I find that strange,' Lembo said and added, as if the use of his title would loosen Brunetti's tongue, 'Commissario.'

'As you will.' Then, in a louder voice, Brunetti said, 'If you have no further questions, Signor Lembo, I'll wish you a good afternoon,' and replaced the phone. He waited long enough for the line to be cut and picked it up, dialling the switchboard. 'No more calls for me today,' he said and hung up.

He called down to the clerk in the records office and gave the name of the man in Amsterdam, asking that they check to see if he had a file and, if so, to fax it to the Dutch police immediately. He expected to have to listen to a protest about the enormous load of work, but none came. Instead, he was told it would go out that afternoon, assuming, of course, that the man did prove to have a criminal record.

Brunetti spent the rest of the morning answering his mail and writing reports on two cases he was conducting at the moment, in neither of which he had achieved any great success.

A little past one, he got up from his desk and prepared to leave the office. He went downstairs and across the front hall. No guard stood at the door, but that wasn't at all strange during the lunch-break, when the offices were closed and no visitors were allowed into the building. Brunetti pressed the electric switch that released the large glass door, then pushed it open. The cold had seeped into the vestibule and he pulled up his collar in response, tucking his chin into the protection of the heavy cloth of his overcoat. Head lowered, he stepped outside and into the firestorm.

The first indication was a sudden glare of light, then another and another. His lowered eyes saw feet approach, five or six pairs of them, until his path was blocked and he had to stop and look up to see what confronted him.

He was surrounded by a tight ring of five men holding microphones. Behind them, in a looser ring, danced three men with video cameras aimed at him, their red lights aglow.

'Commissario. Is it true that you've had to arrest your wife?'

'Will there be a trial? Has your wife hired a lawyer?'

'What about divorce? Is that true?'

The microphones waved in front of him, but he stifled the impulse to brush them away with an angry hand. In the face of his obvious surprise, their voices mounted in a feeding frenzy and their questions drowned one another out. He heard only flashes of phrases: 'Father-in-law', 'Mitri', 'free enterprise', 'obstruction of justice'.

He put his hands in the pocket of his coat, lowered his head again, and started to walk away. His chest came up against a human body, but he kept walking, twice treading heavily upon someone else's feet. 'Can't just walk away', 'obligation', 'right to know . . .'

Another body placed itself in front of him, but he kept going, eyes on the ground, this time to avoid stepping on their feet. At the first corner he turned left and headed towards Santa Maria Formosa, walking steadily, giving no sign that he was fleeing. A hand grabbed his shoulder, but he shook it off, shook off as well the desire to rip the hand from his body and smash the reporter against the wall.

They followed him for a few minutes, but he neither slowed his pace nor acknowledged their presence. He turned suddenly right into a narrow *calle*. Strangers to Venice, some of the reporters must have been alarmed by how dark and cramped it was because none of them followed him. At the end, he turned left and along the canal, finally free of them.

From a phone in Campo Santa Marina he called home and learned from Paola that a camera crew was stationed in front of their apartment and three reporters had unsuccessfully tried to prevent her entering long enough to be able to interview her.

'I'll have lunch somewhere, then,' he said.

'I'm sorry, Guido,' she said. 'I didn't . . .' She stopped, but he had nothing to say into her silence.

No, he supposed she hadn't thought about the consequences of her actions. Strange, really, in a woman as intelligent as Paola.

'What will you do?' she asked.

'I'll go back this afternoon. You?'

'I don't have a class until the day after tomorrow.'

'You can't stay in the house all that time, Paola.'

'God, it's like being in prison, isn't it?' she asked.

'Prison's worse.'

'Will you come home? After work?'

'Of course.'

'You will?'

He was going to say that he had nowhere else to go, but he realized she'd misunderstand him if he said it like that. Instead, he said, 'There's no place else I want to go.'

'Oh, Guido,' she said, then, '*Ciao, amore*,' and put down the phone.

10

These sentiments, however, meant nothing in the face of the crowd that awaited his return to the Questura after lunch. Avian metaphors beat around him as he came down from Ponte dei Greci and walked towards the assembled members of the press: crows, vultures, harpies, crowding round the front of the Questura in a tight circle, they lacked only the putrefying corpse at their feet to make the picture complete.

One of them saw him and – traitor – giving no sign to his companions, slipped away from them and hurried towards Brunetti, his microphone jammed out before him like a cattle prod. 'Commissario,' he began, while still a metre from Brunetti, 'has Dottor Mitri decided to bring civil charges against your wife?'

Smiling, Brunetti stopped. 'You'll have to ask Dottor Mitri, I believe.' As he spoke, he saw the pack sense the absence of their colleague and turn in a kind of collective spasm towards the voices behind them. Instantly, they broke up and ran at him, microphones pressed ahead of them, as if to catch any words that might still float upon the air around Brunetti.

In the panic of their movement, one of the cameramen caught his foot in a cable and fell forward to the ground, his camera crashing down beside him. The lens popped free from the body of the shattered apparatus and went rolling, like a soda can kicked in a children's game, to the edge of the canal. Everyone stopped, riveted by surprise or other emotions, and watched its progress towards the steps that led to the water. It approached the top step, gently rolled over the lip, touched lightly on the second, then the third and, with a quiet splash, sank into the green waters of the canal.

Brunetti took advantage of the moment of general inattention to resume his way to the front door of the Questura, but the reporters recovered just as quickly and moved to stop him. 'Will you resign from the police?' 'Is it true your wife has a previous record of arrest?' '. . . kept out of court?'

Smiling his most plastic smile, he moved along, not pushing them, but not letting their bodies prevent him from reaching his goal. Just as he got there, the door opened and Vianello and Pucetti emerged, standing on either side of it with their arms extended to prevent the reporters from entering.

Brunetti went in, Vianello and Pucetti following. 'Savage, aren't they?' Vianello said, standing with his back against the glass door. Unlike Orfeo, Brunetti did not look back and did not speak, but started up the stairs to his office. He heard steps behind him and turned to see Vianello, taking the treads two at a time. 'He wants to see you.'

Still wearing his coat, Brunetti went to Patta's office, where he found Signorina Elettra at her desk, the day's *Gazzettino* spread out before her.

He glanced down and saw that the front page of the second section carried a picture of him, one taken some years ago, and the photo of Paola which appeared in her *carta d'identità*. Looking up, Signorina Elettra said, 'If you get much more famous, I'll have to beg for an autograph.'

'Is that what the Vice-Questura wants?' he asked, smiling.

'No, your head, I think.'

'I imagined as much,' he said and knocked at the door.

Patta's voice came through: tones of doom. How much easier it would be if they could simply stop all the melodrama and have done with it, Brunetti found himself thinking. As he entered, a line from Donizetti's *Anna Bolena* flashed through his memory – 'If those who judge me are those who have already condemned me, I have no chance.' Good lord, talk about melodrama.

'You wanted to see me, Vice-Questore?' he asked as he entered.

Patta sat behind his desk, face impassive. All he lacked was the black cap that English judges were said to put on top of their wigs when they condemned a prisoner to death. 'Yes, Brunetti. No, don't bother to sit down. What I have to say is very short. I've spoken about this to the Questore, and we've decided that you should go on administrative leave until it's resolved.'

'What does that mean?'

'That, until this case is settled, there is no need for you to come to the Questura.'

'Settled?'

'Until a judgement is given and your wife pays a fine, or makes restitution to Dottor Mitri for the damage she has caused to his property and business.'

'This is to assume she's charged and convicted,' Brunetti said, knowing how likely both were. Patta didn't deign to answer. 'And that could take years,' Brunetti added, no stranger to the law.

'I doubt that,' Patta said.

'Sir, there are cases in my files that have been open for more than five years, waiting for a trial date to be set. I repeat: it could take years.'

'That depends entirely upon your wife's decision, Commissario. Dottor Mitri was civilized enough, I would even say kind enough, to offer an efficient solution to this problem. But your wife has apparently chosen not to accept it. The consequences, therefore, will be her own.'

'With all respect, sir,' Brunetti said, 'that's not entirely true.' Before Patta could object, Brunetti went on, 'Dottor Mitri offered the solution to me, not to my wife. As I explained, it is a decision I cannot make in my wife's place. If he were to offer it to her directly and if she were to refuse, then what you say would be true.'

'You haven't told her?' Patta asked, no attempt made to disguise his surprise.

'No.'

'Why not?'

'It's Dottor Mitri's business, I think, to do so.'

Again, Patta's surprise was easy to read. He considered this for a while, then said, 'I'll mention it to him.'

Brunetti nodded, whether in thanks or acknowledgement, neither of them knew. 'Will that be all, sir?' he asked.

'Yes. But you're still to consider yourself on administrative leave. Is that clear?'

'Yes, sir,' Brunetti said, though he had no idea what it meant, save that he was no longer to work as a policeman, was not, in fact, to have a job. He didn't bother to say anything to Patta but turned and left his office.

Outside, Signorina Elettra was still at her desk, but she was reading a magazine, having finished with the *Gazzettino*. She looked up at him when he came out.

'Who told the press?'

She shook her head. 'No idea. Probably the lieutenant.' She glanced for an instant towards Patta's door.

'Administrative leave.'

'Never heard of it,' she said. 'It must have been invented to fit the occasion. What will you do, Commissario?'

'Go home and read,' he answered, and with the

answer came the thought, and with the thought came the desire. All he had to do was get through the reporters in front of the building, escape their cameras and repeated questions, and he could go home and read for as long as it took Paola to come to a decision, or for this to be resolved. He could allow his books to carry him out of the Questura, out of Venice, out of this shabby century filled with cheap sentimentality and blood lust, and take him back to worlds where his spirit felt more at ease.

Signorina Elettra smiled, hearing a joke in this answer, and returned her attention to her magazine.

He didn't bother to go back to his office but went directly to the door of the Questura. Strangely enough, the reporters were gone, the only sign of their recent presence some chips of plastic and a broken camera strap.

11

He found the broken pieces of the mob in front of his apartment when he got there, three of them the same men who had tried to interrogate him outside the Questura. He made no attempt to answer their shouted questions, pushed his way through them and raised his key to the lock in the enormous *portone* that led into the entrance hall. A hand shot out from behind him and took his arm, trying to pull his hand away from the door.

Brunetti wheeled to his right, the large bunch of keys clutched in his hand like a weapon. The reporter, seeing not the keys but the expression on Brunetti's face, backed away, one hand raised placatingly between them. 'Excuse me, Commissario,' he said, his smile as false as his words. Something animal in the others heard the naked fear in his tone and responded to it. No one spoke. Brunetti looked around at their faces. No cameras flashed and the video cameras were not raised.

Brunetti turned back to the door and placed the key in the lock. He turned it and let himself into the entrance hall, closed the door, and leaned back against it. His chest, indeed his entire upper body, was covered with the heavy sweat of sudden rage, and his heart pounded uncontrollably. He unbuttoned his coat and pulled it open, letting the chill air of the hallway cool him. With his shoulders, he shoved himself away from the door and started up the stairs.

Paola must have heard him coming because she opened the door when he got to the bottom of the final ramp of stairs. She held it for him and, when he got inside, took his coat and hung it up. He bent and kissed her cheek, liking the smell of her.

'Well?' she asked.

'Something called "administrative leave". Invented for the occasion, I think.'

'Which means?' she asked, walking beside him into the living-room.

He flopped down on to the sofa, his feet splayed out in front of him. 'It means I get to stay home and read until you and Mitri come to some sort of agreement.'

'Agreement?' she asked, sitting on the edge of the sofa beside him.

'Apparently Patta thinks you should pay Mitri for the window and apologize.' He thought about Mitri and corrected himself, 'Or just pay for the window.'

'Once or twice?' she asked.

'Does it make any difference?'

She looked down and, with her foot, straightened the edge of the carpet that ran in front of the sofa. 'No, not really. I can't give him a lira.'

'Can't or won't?'

'Can't.'

'Well, I guess it'll give me a chance, finally, to read Gibbon.'

'Meaning what?'

'That I get to stay home until some sort of resolution, either personal or legal, is made.'

'If they give me a fine, I'll pay it,' she said, her voice so much that of the virtuous citizen that Brunetti was forced to grin.

Still smiling, he said, 'I think it's Voltaire who says somewhere, "I disapprove of what you say, but I will defend to the death your right to say it."'

'He said a lot of things like that, Voltaire. Sounds good. He had a habit of saying things that sounded good.'

'You seem sceptical.'

She shrugged. 'I'm always suspicious of noble sentiments.'

'Especially when they come from men?'

She leaned towards him, covering one of his hands with hers. 'You said that, I didn't.'

'No less true for that.'

She shrugged again. 'You really going to read Gibbon?'

'I've always wanted to. But in translation, I think. His style's a bit too manicured for me.'

'That's the joy of it.'

'I get enough fancy rhetoric in the newspapers; I don't need it in a history book.'

'They're going to love this, aren't they, the newspapers?' she asked.

'No one's tried to arrest Andreotti for ages, so they've got to write about something.'

'I suppose so.' She got to her feet. 'Is there anything I can bring you?'

Brunetti, who had had little lunch and not enjoyed it, said, 'A sandwich and a glass of Dolcetto.' He leaned down and started to untie his shoes. When Paola started towards the door he called after her, 'And the first volume of Gibbon.'

She was back in ten minutes with all three, and he indulged himself shamelessly, stretching out on the sofa, glass on the table beside him, plate balanced on his chest, while he opened the book and began to read. The *panino* contained speck and tomato, with fine slices of an aged Pecorino slipped between them. After a few minutes, Paola came in and spread a cloth napkin under his chin, just in time to catch a piece of damp tomato that fell out of the sandwich. He set his food on the plate, reached for the glass and took a long swallow. Returning to the book, he read the magisterial opening chapter, with its politically incorrect paean to the glory of the Roman Empire.

After some time, just as Gibbon was explaining the tolerance with which the polytheist observes all religions, Paola came in and refilled his glass. She took the empty plate from his chest, picked up the napkin and went back into the kitchen. Gibbon would no doubt have something to say about the submissiveness of the good Roman wife: Brunetti looked forward to reading it.

The next day he alternated his reading of Gibbon with his perusal of the national and local press, brought into the house by the children. *Il Gazzettino*, whose reporter had pulled his arm away from the door, raged about the abuse of power on the part of the authorities, about Brunetti's refusal to co-operate with the press's legitimate right to information, his arrogance, his inclination to violence. Paola's professed motivation, which they had somehow learned about, was made light of, the newspaper fierce in its denunciation of this spirit of vigilante crime, presenting her as a woman in search of publicity, clearly unsuited for her position as a university professor. The fact that she had never been asked for an interview was nowhere mentioned in the article.

The larger papers were less fulminating, though the story was always presented as an example of a dangerous tendency on the part of the private citizen to abrogate the legitimate power of the State in a misguided search for some mistaken idea of 'justice', a word they never failed to include within the quotation marks of their contempt.

After reading the papers Brunetti continued with his book and did not leave the house. Nor did Paola, who spent most of her time in her study, going through the doctoral dissertation of a student who was preparing for his exams under her direction. The children, though alerted by their parents to what was going on, came and went undisturbed, doing the shopping, bringing up the newspapers and in general behaving very well in light of the disruption of their family life.

On the second day, Brunetti treated himself to a long nap after lunch, even going to the trouble of getting into bed and under the covers, not simply stretching out on the sofa to let sleep come upon him accidentally. In the afternoon the phone rang a few times, but he left it to Paola to answer. If Mitri or his lawyer called to speak to her she'd tell him, or maybe she wouldn't.

The phone rang shortly after breakfast on the third day of what Brunetti was coming to think of as purdah. After a few minutes Paola came into the living-room and said it was for him.

He leaned forward on the sofa, not bothering to put his feet on the floor, and picked up the receiver. '*Sì*?'

'It's Vianello, sir. Have they called you?'

'Who?'

'The men on duty last night.'

'No. Why?'

Whatever Vianello started to say was blocked out by the sound of loud voices in the background.

'Where are you, Vianello?'

'Down at the bar near the bridge.'

'What's happened?'

'Mitri was killed last night.'

Brunetti pulled himself up on the sofa, feet on the floor in front of him. 'How? Where?'

'In his home. He was garrotted, or that's what it

looks like. Someone must have got behind him and choked him. Whatever they used, they took it with them. But–' he said and again his voice was drowned out by what seemed like noises coming over a radio.

'What?' Brunetti asked when the sound died down.

'They found a note, next to his body. I haven't seen it, but Pucetti told me it said something about paedophiles and the people who help them. Something about justice.'

'Gesù bambino,' Brunetti whispered under his breath. 'Who found him?'

'Corvi and Alvise.'

'Who called them?'

'His wife. She got home from dinner with friends and discovered him in the kitchen, on the floor.'

'Who was she at dinner with?'

'I don't know, sir. All I know is what the little Pucetti could tell me, and all he knew was what Corvi told him before he went off duty this morning.'

'Who's been given the case?'

'I think Lieutenant Scarpa went to see the body after Corvi called in.'

Brunetti said nothing to this, though he wondered why Patta's personal assistant would be assigned. 'Is the Vice-Questore in yet?'

'He wasn't in when I left to come down here a few minutes ago, but Scarpa called him at home and told him about it.'

'I'll come in,' Brunetti said, searching with his

feet for his shoes.

Vianello was silent for a long time, but then he said, 'Yes. I think you'd better.'

'Twenty minutes.' Brunetti hung up.

He tied his shoes and walked to the back of the apartment. The door to Paola's study was open, an unspoken invitation for him to come in and tell her about the phone call. 'It was Vianello,' he said as he walked in.

She looked up, saw his face, put down the page she was reading and, closing her pen, she placed it on the desk. 'What did he say?'

'Mitri was murdered last night.'

She moved back in her seat, as if someone had waved a menacing hand in her direction. 'No.'

'Pucetti said there was a note, something about paedophiles and justice.'

Her face went rigid, then she raised the back of her right hand to her mouth. 'Oh, *Madonna Santa*.' From behind it she whispered. 'How?'

'He was strangled.'

She shook her head, eyes closed. 'Oh, my God, my God.'

Now was the time to do it, Brunetti knew. 'Paola, before you did it, did you discuss it with anyone else? Or is there anyone who encouraged you?'

'What do you mean?'

'Did you act alone?'

He watched her eyes change, saw the irises grow smaller with shock. 'Are you asking me if someone I know, some fanatic, knew I was going to break the window? And went and killed him?'

'Paola,' he said, careful to keep his voice level, 'I'm trying to ask you a question and to exclude a possibility before anyone else puts things together in the same way and asks you the same thing.'

'There's nothing to put together,' she answered immediately, putting the heavy emphasis of sarcasm on the last two words.

'Then there was no one?'

'No. I never discussed it with anyone. It was a completely independent choice. Not an easy one.'

He nodded. If she had acted alone, then it must have been someone inflamed or encouraged by the press handling of the case. God, we were becoming just like America, where the police go in fear of copy-cat killers, where the mere mention of a crime is enough to encourage imitation. 'I'm going in,' he said. 'I don't know when I'll be back.'

She nodded but stayed at her desk, not speaking.

Brunetti went down the corridor, got his coat and left the apartment. No one was waiting outside, but he knew that the truce would soon end.

12

It ended in front of the Questura, the door of which was blocked by a triple row of reporters. In the front line stood the men and women with their notebooks. At their backs were those with microphones and behind them, closest to the door, the ranks of the video cameras, two of which were mounted on tripods, arc lamps set up behind them.

One of the men saw Brunetti approach and turned the blank eye of his camera in his direction. Brunetti ignored it and also the people who crowded around him. Strangely enough, none of them asked him a question or spoke to him; they did nothing more than turn their microphones in his direction and watch silently as, like Moses, he passed undisturbed between the parted waters of their curiosity and into the Questura.

Inside, Alvise and Riverre saluted him as he came in, Alvise unable to disguise his surprise at seeing him.

'*Buon dì*, Commissario,' Riverre said, a greeting echoed by his partner.

Brunetti nodded to them, knowing it was a waste of time to ask Alvise anything, and started up the steps towards Patta's office. Outside it, at her desk, Signorina Elettra was speaking on the phone when he came in. She nodded in his direction, not at all surprised to see him here, and held up a restraining hand. 'I'd like it by the afternoon,' she said, waited until the other person answered, then said goodbye and hung up. 'Welcome back, Commissario,' she said.

'Am I?'

She gave him a quizzical glance.

'Welcomed?' he explained.

'By me, certainly. I don't know about the Vice-Questore, but he did ask earlier if you'd come in.'

'What did you tell him?'

'That I expected you shortly.'

'And?'

'He seemed relieved.'

'Good.' Brunetti was equally relieved. 'What about Lieutenant Scarpa?'

'He's been with the Vice-Questore since he got back from the murder scene.'

'What time was that?'

'The call from Signora Mitri was logged at ten twenty-seven. Corvi called in at eleven-o-three.'

She glanced down at a piece of paper on her desk. 'Lieutenant Scarpa called in at quarter past eleven and went to the Mitris' immediately. He didn't get back here until one.'

'And he's been there?' Brunetti said, indicating the door to Patta's office with a jerk of his chin.

'Since eight thirty this morning,' Signorina Elettra answered.

'No use waiting,' Brunetti said, as much to himself as to her, and turned to the door. He knocked; Patta's voice called out instantly.

Brunetti pushed open the door and entered. As usual, Patta posed behind his desk, the light streaming in from behind him, reflecting up off the surface and into the eyes of anyone who sat in front of him.

Lieutenant Scarpa stood beside his commander, his posture so straight and his uniform ironed to such perfection that he looked frighteningly like Maximilian Schell in one of his good-Nazi roles.

Patta greeted Brunetti with a nod and gestured to the chair in front of his desk. Brunetti pulled it a bit to the side so that the shadow cast by Scarpa's body blocked some of the light bouncing up from the polished wood. The lieutenant shifted his weight from one foot to the other and moved a small step to his right. Brunetti countered this by shifting to his left and turning a bit more to that side.

'Good-morning, Vice-Questore,' Brunetti said and nodded to Scarpa.

'You've heard, then?' Patta said.

'I heard only that he was killed. Beyond that, I know nothing.'

Patta looked up at Scarpa. 'Tell him about it, Lieutenant.'

Scarpa looked at Brunetti, then back at Patta before he spoke. When he did so, it was with a small bow of his head in Patta's direction. 'With all respect, Vice-Questore, I thought the commissario was on administrative leave.' Patta said nothing, so he went on, 'I didn't know he was going to be brought back to this investigation. And, if I might suggest, the press might find it strange that he is being assigned to it.'

Brunetti found it interesting that, at least in Scarpa's mind, it was all being treated as one investigation. He wondered if this reflected the lieutenant's belief that Paola must somehow be involved in the murder.

'I'll decide who gets assigned to what, Lieutenant,' Patta said in a level voice. 'Tell the commissario what happened. It's his problem now.'

'Yes, sir,' Scarpa answered neutrally. He stood up a bit straighter and began to explain. 'Corvi called me a bit after eleven and I went immediately to the Mitris' home. When I got there, I found his body on the floor of the kitchen. From what I could see of his neck, he appeared to have been strangled, though there was no sign of the murder weapon.' He paused and looked at Brunetti, but when the commissario said nothing, Scarpa continued, 'I examined the body, then called for Dottor Rizzardi, who arrived after about half an hour. He confirmed my opinion about the cause of death.'

'Did he have any suggestion or idea about what could have been used to strangle him?' Brunetti interrupted.

'No.' Brunetti noticed that Scarpa did not address him by his title, but he let that go. He had no need to wonder how the lieutenant must have treated Dr Rizzardi, a man known to be friendly with Brunetti, so he wasn't surprised to learn that Rizzardi hadn't been willing to hazard a guess about what was used to strangle Mitri.

'And the autopsy?' Brunetti asked.

'Today, if it's possible.'

Brunetti would call Rizzardi after this meeting. It would be possible.

'May I continue, sir?' Scarpa asked Patta.

Patta gave Brunetti a long look, as if to ask if he had any other obstructive questions, but when Brunetti ignored the look he turned to Scarpa and said, 'Of course.'

'He was alone in the apartment that evening. His wife was at dinner with friends.'

'Why didn't Mitri go?' Brunetti asked.

Scarpa looked at Patta, as if to ask him if he should answer the commissario's question. When Patta nodded, Scarpa explained, 'His wife said they were old friends of hers, from before she married, and Mitri seldom went out with them when they went to dinner.'

'Children?' Brunetti asked.

'There's a daughter, but she lives in Rome.'

'Servants?'

'All this is in the report,' Scarpa said petulantly, looking at Patta and not at Brunetti.

'Servants?' Brunetti repeated.

Scarpa paused, but then he answered, 'No. At least no live-in help. There's a woman who comes to clean twice a week.'

Brunetti got to his feet. 'Where's the wife?' he asked Scarpa.

'She was still there when I left.'

'Thank you, Lieutenant,' Brunetti said. 'I'd like to see a copy of your report.'

Scarpa nodded but did not speak.

'I'll have to see the wife,' Brunetti said to Patta and, before the Vice-Questore could say it, he added, 'I'll be very careful with her.'

'And your own?' Patta asked.

This could mean many things, but Brunetti chose to answer the most obvious form the question could take. 'She was home all last evening, with me and our children. None of us left after seven thirty, when my son came home from studying at a friend's house.' He paused here to see if Patta would add another question, and, when he chose not to, Brunetti let himself out of the office without saying or asking anything further.

Signorina Elettra looked up from some papers on her desk and, making no attempt to disguise her curiosity, asked, 'Well?'

'It's mine,' Brunetti said.

'But that's crazy.' Signorina Elettra spoke before she could stop herself. Hastily, she added, 'I mean, the press will go wild when they learn.'

Brunetti shrugged. There was little he could do to curb the enthusiasms of the press. Ignoring her remark he asked, 'Have you got those papers I told you not to get?'

He watched while she followed this question to the places it could lead: charges of disobedience and insubordination, failure to obey a direct order from a superior, grounds for dismissal, destruction of her career. 'Of course, sir,' she answered.

'Can you give me a copy?'

'It will take a few minutes. I've got them hidden in here,' she explained, waving a hand at her computer screen.

'Where?'

'In a file I think no one else could find.'

'No one?'

'Oh,' she said loftily, 'if they were as good as I, perhaps.'

'Is that likely?'

'No, not here.'

'Good. Bring them up when you've printed them out, would you?'

'Of course, sir.'

He waved a hand in her direction and went back upstairs.

He called Rizzardi immediately and found the pathologist in his office at the hospital. 'You had time yet?' Brunetti asked as soon as he'd identified himself to the other man.

'No, I'll start in about an hour. I've got a suicide

first. Young girl, only sixteen. Her boyfriend left her, so she took all her mother's sleeping pills.'

Brunetti remembered that Rizzardi had married late and had teenaged children. Two daughters, he thought. 'Poor girl,' Brunetti said.

'Yes.' Rizzardi allowed a pause to establish itself, then went on, 'I don't think there's any doubt. It could have been a thin wire, probably plastic-covered.'

'Like electrical cord?'

'That's the most likely. I'll know once I take a closer look. It might even have been that double wire they use to hook up stereo speakers. There were faint traces of a second impression, parallel to the other, but it might just be that the killer loosened it for a moment to get a better grip. I'll know more once I take a look under the microscope.'

'Man or woman?' Brunetti asked.

'Either, I'd say. That is, either could have done it. If you come from behind with a cord, they don't have a chance; your strength doesn't matter. But it's usually men who strangle: I don't think women are sure they're strong enough.'

'Thank God for that at least,' Brunetti said.

'And it looks like there might be something under the nails of his left hand.'

'Something?'

'If we're lucky, skin. Or material from what the killer was wearing. I'll know after I have a closer look.'

'Would that be enough to identify someone?'

'If you find the someone, yes.'

Brunetti considered that, then asked, 'Time?'

'I won't know until I have a look inside. But his wife saw him at seven thirty when she went out and found him a little after ten when she got back. So there's little doubt and there's nothing I could find that would make it any more certain than that.' Rizzardi stopped for a moment, covered the phone with his hand and spoke to someone in the room with him. 'I've got to go now. They've got her on the table.' Even before Brunetti could thank him, Rizzardi said, 'I'll send it over to you tomorrow,' and hung up.

Though impatient to go and speak to Signora Mitri, Brunetti forced himself to stay at his desk until Signorina Elettra brought him the information about Mitri and Zambino, which she did after about five minutes.

She came in after knocking and placed two folders on his desk, saying nothing. 'How much of this is common knowledge?' Brunetti asked, glancing down at the files.

'Most of it comes from the newspapers,' she answered. 'But some comes from their banks and from incorporation papers held by the various companies.'

Brunetti couldn't contain himself. 'How do you know this?'

Hearing only curiosity, not praise, in his voice she didn't smile. 'I have a number of friends who work in city offices and in banks. I can occasionally ask them to answer queries for me.'

'And what do you do for them in return?' Brunetti asked, finally voicing the question that had teased at him for years.

'Most of the information we have here, Commissario, soon becomes common knowledge or, at least, public knowledge.'

'That's not an answer, Signorina.'

'I've never given police information to anyone without a right to know it.'

'Legal or moral?' Brunetti asked.

She studied his face for a long time, then answered, 'Legal.'

Brunetti knew that the only price high enough for certain information was other information, so he persisted, 'Then how do you get all of this?'

She considered that for a moment. 'I also advise my friends on more efficient methods of information retrieval.'

'What does that mean in real language?'

'I teach them how to snoop and where to look.' Before Brunetti could respond, she continued, 'But I have never, sir, *never* given any unauthorized information of any sort, not to my friends, not to people who are not my friends but with whom I exchange information. I'd like you to believe that.'

He nodded to show that he did, resisting the temptation to ask if she had ever explained to anyone how to get information from the police. Instead, he tapped the folders again. 'Will there be more?'

'Perhaps a longer client list for Zambino, but I don't think there's anything more to learn about Mitri.'

Of course there was, Brunetti told himself: there was the reason someone would put a wire round his throat and pull it tight until he or she choked the life out of him. 'I'll have a look, then,' he said.

'I think it's all clear, but if you have questions, please ask me.'

'Does anyone else know you've given me this?'

'No, of course not,' she said and left the office.

He chose the thinner file first: Zambino. From Modena originally, the lawyer had studied at Cà Foscari and begun to practise in Venice about twenty years ago. He specialized in corporate law and had built a reputation for himself in the city. Signorina Elettra had attached a list of some of his better-known clients; Brunetti recognized more than a few of them. There was no apparent pattern, and certainly Zambino did not work only for the wealthy: the list held as many waiters and salesmen as it did doctors and bankers. Though he accepted a certain number of criminal cases, his chief source of income was the corporate work Vianello had told Brunetti about. Married for twenty-five years to a teacher, he had four children, none of whom had ever been in trouble with the police. Nor, Brunetti observed, was he a wealthy man; at least whatever wealth he might have was not held in Italy.

The fatal travel agency in Campo Manin had belonged to Mitri for six years, though, ironically, he had nothing whatsoever to do with the day-to-day running of the business. A manager who rented the agency licence from him took care of all practical matters; apparently it was he who decided to handle the tours that had provoked Paola's action and appeared to have led to Mitri's murder. Brunetti made a note of the manager's name and read on.

Mitri's wife was also Venetian, two years younger than he. Though there had been only one child, she had never had a career, and Brunetti did not recognize her name as being involved in any of the charitable institutions of the city. Mitri was survived by a brother, a sister and a cousin. The brother, also a chemist, lived near Padova, the sister in Verona, and the cousin in Argentina.

There followed the numbers of three accounts in different banks in the city, a list of government bonds, and stock holdings, all for a total of more than a billion lire. And that was all. Mitri had never been accused of a crime and had never, not once in more than half a century, come to the attention of the police in any way.

Instead, Brunetti reflected, he had probably come to the attention of a person who thought – though he tried to shy away from this, Brunetti could not – as Paola did and who had, like her, decided to use violent means to express his opposition to the tours conducted by the travel agency. Brunetti knew that history was filled with examples of the wrong people dying. Kaiser Wilhelm's good son, Friedrich, had survived his father by only a few months, leaving the path of succession open to his own son, Wilhelm II, and thus leaving the same path open to the first truly global war. And Germanicus's death had put the succession at risk and, ultimately, had led to Nero. But those were cases where fate, or history, had intervened; there had been no figure with a wire to drag the victim down to death; there had been no deliberate selection.

Brunetti called down to Vianello, who answered on the second ring. 'The lab through with the note yet?' he asked him without preamble.

'Probably. Want me to go down and ask them?'

'Yes. And bring it up if you can.'

While he waited for Vianello, Brunetti read again through the short list of Zambino's criminal clients, trying to recall whatever he could about the names he recognized. There was one case of homicide and, though the man was convicted, the sentence had been reduced to only seven years when Zambino brought in a number of women who lived in the same building to testify that the victim had, for years, been abusive to them in the elevator and the halls of the building. Zambino had proceeded to convince the judges that his client had been defending his wife's honour when an argument broke out between them in a bar. Two robbery suspects had been released for lack of evidence: Zambino arguing that they had been arrested only because they were Albanians.

Brunetti was interrupted by a knock at the door and Vianello's entrance. He carried a large transparent plastic envelope in his right hand and held it up as he came in. 'They'd just finished. Nothing at all. *Lavata con Perlana,*' Vianello concluded, using the most successful television slogan of the decade. Nothing could be cleaner than something washed with Perlana. Except, Brunetti thought, a note left at a murder scene that was sure to be found and examined by the police.

Vianello came across the room and placed the envelope on Brunetti's desk. He propped his weight on his hands and leaned over it, studying it again, along with Brunetti.

It looked to Brunetti as if the words had been cut from *La Nuova*, the most sensational and often most vulgar newspaper of the city. He wasn't sure: the technicians would be. They were pasted to half a sheet of lined writing paper. 'Filthy pederasts and baby pornographers. You'll all die like this.'

Brunetti picked up the envelope by a corner and turned it over. All he could see were the same lines and some small patches where the glue had seeped through the paper, staining it grey. He turned it back over and read it again. 'There seem to be some crossed wires, don't there?' he asked.

'To say the least,' Vianello agreed.

Though Paola had told the police who arrested her why she broke the window, she had never spoken to any of the reporters, except briefly and under duress, so whatever stories they carried about her motivation had come from some other source; Lieutenant Scarpa was a good guess. The stories Brunetti had read had done little more than suggest that her motivating force was 'feminism', though the term was never defined. Mention had been made of the tours arranged by the agency, but the accusation that they were sex-tours had been heatedly denied by the manager, who insisted that most of the men who bought tickets to Bangkok at his agency took their wives along. The *Gazzettino*, Brunetti recalled, had carried a long interview with him in which he expressed his shock and disgust at sex-tourism, carefully and repeatedly pointing out that it was illegal in Italy and hence unthinkable for any legitimate agency to play a part in the organizing of it.

Thus the weight of opinion and authority was lined up against Paola, a hysterical 'feminist', and in favour of the law-respecting manager and, behind him, the murdered Dottor Mitri. Whoever had got the idea of 'baby pornographer' had got things wildly wrong.

'I think it's time we talked to a few people,' Brunetti said, getting to his feet. 'Starting with the manager of the agency. I'd like to hear what he has to say about all these married women who want to go to Bangkok.'

Brunetti looked at his watch and saw that it was almost two. 'Is Signorina Elettra still here?' he asked Vianello.

'Yes, sir. She was when I came up.'

'Good. I'd like to have a word with her, then perhaps we could go and get something to eat.'

Confused, Vianello nodded and followed his superior down to Signorina Elettra's office. From the door, he watched Brunetti lean down and speak to her, saw and heard Signorina Elettra's laugh. She nodded and turned towards her computer, then Brunetti joined him and they went down to the bar by Ponte dei Grechi and had wine and tramezzini, talking of this and that. Brunetti seemed in no hurry to leave, so they had more sandwiches and another glass of wine.

After another half hour Signorina Elettra came in, managing to capture a smile from the barman and the offer of coffee from two men who stood at the bar. Though it was less than a block from the office, she had put on a quilted black silk coat that came to her ankles. She shook her head in polite refusal of coffee and came towards the two policemen. She pulled a few sheets of paper from her pocket and held them up. 'Child's play.' She shook her head in false exasperation. 'It's just too easy.'

'Of course.' Brunetti smiled and paid for what had passed as lunch.

13

Brunetti and Vianello turned up at the travel agency just as it was reopening at 3.30 p.m. and asked to speak to Signor Dorandi. Brunetti glanced back into the *campo* and noticed that the glass in the window was so clean as to seem invisible. The blonde woman at the front desk requested their names, pushed a button on her phone, and a moment later the door at the left of her desk opened, revealing Signor Dorandi.

Not quite as tall as Brunetti, he had a full beard already starting to go grey, though he could not have been much into his thirties. When he saw Vianello's uniform, he came forward with his hand outstretched, a smile spreading up from the corners of his mouth. 'Ah, the police. I'm glad you've come.'

Brunetti said good-afternoon but didn't give either of their names, letting Vianello's uniform serve as sufficient introduction. He asked if they might speak in Signor Dorandi's office. Turning, the bearded man held open the door for the other two and paused long enough to enquire if they'd like some coffee. Both refused.

Inside, the walls of the office were filled with the predictable posters of beaches, temples and palaces, sure proof that a bad economy and continuing talk of financial crises were not enough to keep Italians at home. Dorandi took his place behind his desk, pushed some papers to the side, and turned to Brunetti, who folded his coat over the back of one of the chairs facing Dorandi and sat down. Vianello lowered himself into the other.

Dorandi was wearing a suit, but something was wrong with it. Distracted, Brunetti tried to figure out what it was, whether the garment was too big or too small, but neither seemed to be the case. Double-breasted, the jacket was cut of some thick blue material which looked like wool but could as easily have been plasterboard. The jacket fell in a straight line, without a single wrinkle, from his shoulder before disappearing behind the desk. Dorandi's face gave Brunetti the same impression of something being amiss, but he didn't understand what. Then he noticed the moustache. Dorandi had shaved away the top half, leaving that area of his upper lip clean-shaven, so the adornment ran in a thin straight line under his nose and disappeared into his beard on either side. The trimming had been done very carefully and was clearly not the result of a careless hand, but the proportions of the moustache had been destroyed, and the result was a pasted-on rather than a naturally grown appearance.

'What may I do for you, gentlemen?' Dorandi asked, smiling and placing his folded hands in front of him.

'I'd like you to tell me a bit about Dottor Mitri and the agency, if you would,' Brunetti said.

'Ah, yes, gladly.' Dorandi paused for a moment while he thought where to begin. 'I've known him for years, since I first came here to work.'

'When was that exactly?' Brunetti asked.

Vianello took a pad from his pocket, opened it on his lap, and began to take notes.

Dorandi turned his chin to the side and stared at the poster on the far wall, looking for the answer in Rio. He turned back to Brunetti and said, 'It will be exactly six years in January.'

'And what position did you have when you came?' Brunetti enquired.

'The same as I have now: manager.'

'But aren't you also the owner?'

Dorandi smiled as he answered, 'In everything but name, I am. I own the business, but Dottor Mitri still holds the licence.'

'What exactly does that mean?'

Again, Dorandi consulted the helpful city on the far wall. When he'd found the answer, he turned back to Brunetti. 'It means that I decide who gets hired and fired, on what advertising to use, what special offers to make, and I also get to keep the major portion of the earnings.'

'What portion?'

'Seventy-five per cent.'

'And the rest went to Dottor Mitri?'

'Yes. As well as rent.'

'Which was?'

'The rent?' Dorandi asked.

'Yes.'

'Three million lire a month.'

'And the profits?'

'Why is it you need to know this?' Dorandi asked in the same level voice.

'At this point, Signore, I've no idea what I need to know and what not. I am simply trying to accumulate as much information about Dottor Mitri and his affairs as I can.'

'To what purpose?'

'To better understand why he was killed.'

Dorandi's answer was instant. 'I thought that was made very clear by the note you found.'

Brunetti raised a hand as if in concession to this idea. 'I think it's important that we learn as much as we can about him, just the same.'

'There was a note, wasn't there?' Dorandi demanded.

'Where did you hear that, Signor Dorandi?'

'It was in the papers, in two of them.'

Brunetti nodded. 'Yes, there was a note.'

'Did it say what the papers say it did?'

Brunetti, who had seen the papers, nodded.

'But that's absurd,' Dorandi said, voice raised, as if it were Brunetti who had written the words. 'There's no child pornography here. We don't cater for pederasts. The whole thing's ridiculous.'

'Have you any idea why someone might have written that, Signore?'

'Probably because of that madwoman,' Dorandi said, making no attempt to disguise his disgust and rage.

'Which madwoman is that?' Brunetti asked.

Dorandi paused a long time before he answered this, studying Brunetti's face carefully, looking for the trick in the question. Finally he said, 'That woman who threw the stone. She began all this. If she hadn't started with her insane accusations – all lies, all lies – then nothing would have happened.'

'Are they lies, Signor Dorandi?'

'How dare you ask that?' Dorandi bent towards Brunetti, voice raised. 'Of course they're lies. We have nothing to do here with child pornography or with pederasts.'

'That was the note, Signor Dorandi.'

'What difference does it make?'

'They are two different accusations, Signore. I'm trying to understand why the person who wrote the note might have believed that the agency was involved in pederasty and child pornography.'

'And I've told you why,' Dorandi said on a note of rising exasperation. 'Because of that woman. She went to all the papers, libelling me, libelling the agency, saying we arranged sex-tours . . .'

'But nothing about pederasty or child pornography?' Brunetti interrupted.

'What's the difference to a madwoman? Everything's the same to them, anything that has to do with sex.'

'Then do the tours the agency arranged have something to do with sex?'

'I didn't say that,' Dorandi shouted. Then, hearing how loud his voice was, he closed his eyes for a moment, unfolded and carefully refolded his hands, and said in an entirely normal voice, 'I didn't say that.'

'I must have got it wrong.' Brunetti shrugged, then asked, 'But why would this madwoman, as you call her, say those things? Why would anyone, indeed, say those things?'

'Misunderstanding.' Dorandi's smile was back. 'You know how it is with people: they see what they want to see, make things mean what they want them to mean.'

'Specifically?' Brunetti asked with a pleasant expression.

'Specifically I mean what this woman has done. She sees our posters for tours to exotic places – Thailand, Cuba, Sri Lanka – then she reads some hysterical article in some feminist magazine that claims there is child prostitution in those places and that travel agencies arrange tours there, sex-tours, and she puts the two things together in some crazy way, and comes here at night and destroys my window.'

'Doesn't that seem an excessive response? Without proof, I mean.' Brunetti's voice was all sweet reason.

Dorandi answered with more than a touch of sarcasm, 'That's why they're called crazy people: because they do crazy things. Of course it's an excessive reaction. And utterly without cause.'

Brunetti allowed a long pause to spread out between them, and then said, 'In the *Gazzettino* you were quoted as saying that just as many women go to Bangkok as do men. That is, that most of the men who buy tickets to Bangkok take women along with them.'

Dorandi looked down at his joined hands, but didn't answer. Brunetti reached into the pocket of his jacket and took out the sheets of paper Signorina Elettra had given him. 'Would you be willing to be a bit more precise about that, Signor Dorandi?' Brunetti asked, looking down at the papers.

'About what?'

'The number of men who took women with them when they went to Bangkok. Say in the last year.'

'I don't know what you're talking about.'

Brunetti didn't waste a smile on him. 'Signor Dorandi, I'll remind you that this is a murder investigation, which means that we have the right to request, or demand, if we are forced to do so, certain information from the people involved.'

'What do you mean, "involved"?' Dorandi spluttered.

'That should be clear to you,' Brunetti answered in a level voice. 'This is a travel agency, which sells a certain number of tickets and arranges tours to what you call "exotic" locations. An accusation has been made that these are for the purposes of sex-tourism, which I hardly need remind you is now illegal in this country. A man, the owner of this agency, has been murdered and a note left suggesting that these tours might be the motive for that crime. You yourself seem to believe that there is a connection. So it would appear that the agency is involved and so are you as its manager.' Brunetti paused for a moment, before asking, 'Have I made myself clear?'

'Yes.' Dorandi's voice was sullen.

'Then would you mind telling me how accurate your statement – or, if I might speak more plainly – how true your statement was that most of the men who went to Bangkok took women along with them?'

'Of course it's true,' Dorandi insisted, shifting to the left side of his chair, one hand still on the desk in front of him.

'Not according to your ticket sales, Signor Dorandi.'

'My what?'

'The sales of plane tickets made by your agency, all of which, I'm sure you must know, are kept in a centralized computer system.' Brunetti saw this register and went on, 'Most of the tickets to Bangkok that your agency sold, during the last six months at least, were to men travelling alone.'

Almost before he could think, Dorandi blurted out, 'Their wives joined them later. They were travelling on business, the men, and their wives joined them.'

'Did they buy tickets from your agency?'

'How do I know?'

Brunetti placed the papers, face up, on the desk in front of him, leaving them in plain sight, open to Dorandi if he chose to try to read them. He drew a deep breath. 'Signor Dorandi, shall we start again with this? I'll repeat my question and this time I'd like you to consider your answer before you give it to me.' He paused a long time, then asked, 'Did the men who bought tickets to Bangkok through your agency travel with women or not?'

Dorandi took a long time to answer, but finally said 'No' and nothing more.

'And these tours you arrange with "tolerant hotel management" and "convenient location"' – Brunetti's voice was absolutely neutral, not a trace of emotion audible in it – 'are they for the purpose of sex?'

'I don't know what they do when they get there,' Dorandi insisted. 'It's not my business.' He pulled his head down into the too-wide neck of his jacket, rather in the manner of a turtle under attack.

'Do you know anything about the sort of hotels where these particular tourists go?' Before Dorandi could answer, Brunetti put his elbows on the desk, cupped his chin in his palm and looked down at the list.

'They have tolerant managements,' Dorandi said eventually.

'Does that mean they allow prostitutes to work there, perhaps even provide them?'

Dorandi shrugged. 'Perhaps.'

'Girls? Not women, girls?'

Dorandi glared across the desk at him. 'I don't know anything about the hotels except the prices. What my clients do there isn't my business.'

'Girls?' Brunetti repeated.

Dorandi waved a hand angrily in the air. 'I told you, it's none of my business.'

'But it's our business now, Signor Dorandi, so I would prefer an answer.'

Dorandi looked at the wall again, but found no convenient solution there. 'Yes,' he said.

'Is that the reason you choose them?'

'I choose them because they offer me the best price. If the men who go there decide to take prostitutes back to their rooms in those hotels, that's their business.' He tried but could not restrain his anger. 'I sell travel packages. I don't preach morality. I've checked every word of those ads with my lawyer, and there's nothing at all even remotely illegal in them. I'm not breaking any law.'

'I'm sure of that,' Brunetti couldn't stop himself from saying. Suddenly, he didn't want to be here any more. He stood. 'I'm afraid we've taken up rather a lot of your time, Signor Dorandi. I'll leave you now, but we might like to speak to you again.'

Dorandi didn't bother to answer. Nor did he get to his feet when Brunetti and Vianello left the room.

14

As they crossed Campo Manin, Vianello and Brunetti knew without discussing it that they would go and speak to the widow now, while they were still out, rather than go back to the Questura. To get to the Mitris' apartment, which was in Campo del Ghetto Nuovo, they walked back to Rialto and took the number 1 towards the station.

They chose to stand outside, preferring the coldness of the open deck to the damp air trapped inside the passenger cabin. Brunetti waited until they had passed under the Rialto before he asked Vianello, 'Well?'

'He'd sell his mother for a hundred lire, wouldn't he?' Vianello answered, making no attempt to disguise his contempt. He paused for a long time, then demanded, 'Do you think it's television, sir?'

At a loss, Brunetti asked, 'That what's television?'

'That lets us get so distanced from the evil we do.' He saw he had Brunetti's attention and continued, 'That is, if we watch it, there on the screen, it's real, but it isn't actually, is it? I mean, we see so many people getting shot and hit, and we watch us,' here he paused, smiled a little and explained, 'the police, that is. We watch us discovering all sorts of terrible things. But the cops aren't real, nor are the things. So maybe, if we watch enough of them, the true horrors, when they happen or when they happen to other people, don't seem real, either.'

Brunetti was a bit confused by Vianello's language, but he thought he understood what he meant – and that he agreed – so he answered, 'They're how far away, those girls he knows nothing about, fifteen thousand kilometres? Twenty? I'd say it's probably very easy not to see what happens to them as being real, or if it is, it probably isn't very important to him.'

Vianello nodded. 'You think it's getting worse?'

Brunetti shrugged. 'There are days when I think everything's getting worse, then there are days when I know they are. But then the sun comes out and I change my mind.'

Vianello nodded again, this time adding a muffled, 'Uh huh.'

'And you?' Brunetti asked.

'I think it's worse,' the sergeant answered with

no hesitation. 'Like you, though, I have days when everything's fine: the kids jump all over me when I get home or Nadia's happy and it's contagious. But on the whole, I think the world's getting worse as a place to be.'

Hoping to lighten his uncharacteristic mood, Brunetti said, 'Not much other choice, is there?'

Vianello had the grace to laugh at this. 'No, I guess there isn't. For good or bad, this is all we've got.' He paused for a moment, watching the palazzo that held the Casinò draw near. 'Maybe it's different for us because we have kids.'

'Why?' Brunetti asked.

'Because we can see ahead to the world they're going to live in and can look back on the one we grew up in.'

Brunetti, a patient reader of history, recalled the countless times the ancient Romans had fulminated against the various ages in which they lived, always insisting that the generation of their own youth or of their parents' had been far superior in every way to the one in which they now found themselves. He recalled their violent screeds against the insensitivity of the young, their sloth, their ignorance, their lack of respect for and deference to their elders, and he found himself greatly cheered by this memory. If every age thinks this way, then perhaps each is wrong and things aren't getting worse. He didn't know how to explain this to Vianello and felt awkward about quoting Pliny, afraid the sergeant would not recognize the writer or would be embarrassed at being made to show that he did not.

Instead, he tapped him warmly on the shoulder as the boat pulled in to the San Marcuola stop and they both got off, walking single file down the narrow *calle* to make way for the people who hurried towards the *embarcadero*.

'Nothing we're going to solve, is it, sir?' Vianello commented when they got to the wider street behind the church and could walk side by side.

'I doubt it's something anyone can solve,' Brunetti said, aware of how vague a response he had chosen, unsatisfied with it even as he made it.

'May I ask you a question, sir?' The sergeant started walking again. Both of them knew the address, so they had some idea of the location of the house. 'It's about your wife, sir.'

Brunetti knew from the tone of the question what it was bound to be. 'Yes?'

Keeping his eyes straight ahead of them, though no one was any longer coming towards them on the narrow *calle*, Vianello asked, 'Did she tell you why she did it?'

Brunetti walked on, keeping in step with his sergeant. He glanced aside at him and answered, 'I think it's in the arrest report.'

'Ah,' Vianello said. 'I didn't know that.'

'Didn't you read it?'

Again, Vianello stopped and turned to Brunetti. 'As it was about your wife, sir, I didn't think it was right to read it.' Vianello was known to be loyal to Brunetti, so it was unlikely that Landi, a follower of Scarpa, would have spoken to him about it, and it was he who had arrested Paola and taken her statement.

The two men resumed walking before Brunetti replied, 'She said that it was wrong to arrange sextours and that someone had to stop them.' He waited to see if Vianello would question him, but when the sergeant did not, he went on, 'She told me that, since the law wouldn't do anything about it, she would.' He paused again, waiting for Vianello's reaction.

'Was it your wife the first time?'

Without hesitation, Brunetti answered, 'Yes.'

Step and step, feet perfectly in line. Finally the sergeant said, 'Good for her.'

Brunetti turned to stare at Vianello, but all he saw was his heavy profile and long nose. Before he could ask anything, the other stopped and said, 'If it's six-o-seven, it should be right round this corner.' Turning, they found themselves in front of the house.

Mitri's was the top of three bells and Brunetti pressed it, waited, then pushed it again.

A voice, made sepulchral either by grief or a bad connection, came through the speaker phone, asking who they were.

'Commissario Brunetti. I'd like to speak to Signora Mitri.'

For a long time there was no answer, then the voice said, 'Wait a minute' and was gone.

Much more than one minute passed before the door clicked. Brunetti pushed it open and led the way into a large atrium with two large palm trees growing on either side of a round fountain. Light filtered down from the sky above.

They ducked into the passage in front of them and headed for the back of the building and the stairs. Just as in Brunetti's own building, the paint on the walls was flaking off, victim of the salt rising up by absorption from the waters below. Flecks the size of hundred-lire coins lay either swept or kicked to the sides of the staircase, exposing the brick walls below. When they reached the first landing, they could see the horizontal line that marked the point the dampness had reached: above it, the stairs were free of flecks of paint and the walls smooth and white.

Brunetti thought of the estimate an engineering company had given the seven owners of the apartments in his own building to correct the dampness, of the enormity of the sum and, depressed, immediately pushed it from his mind.

At the top the door stood open and a young girl about Chiara's age stood behind it, her body half hidden.

Brunetti stopped and said, not offering his hand, 'I'm Commissario Brunetti and this is Sergeant Vianello. We'd like to speak to Signora Mitri.'

The girl didn't move. 'My grandmother isn't well.' Her voice was uneven with nervousness.

'I'm sorry to hear that,' Brunetti said. 'And I'm sorry about what happened to your grandfather. That's why I'm here, because we'd like to do something about it.'

'My grandmother says there's nothing anyone can do.'

'Perhaps we can find the person who did it.'

The girl considered this. As tall as Chiara, she

had brown hair parted in the middle that fell to her shoulders on either side. She would not grow to be a beauty, Brunetti thought, but that had nothing to do with her features, which were both fine and regular: wide-spaced eyes and a well-defined mouth. Instead, her plainness was made inevitable by a total lack of animation when she spoke or listened. Her placidity and inertness conveyed the sense that she was not concerned with what she was saying or, in a way, not really participating in whatever was said. 'May we come in?' he asked, stepping forward as he spoke, either to make her decision easier or to force her into making it.

She didn't say anything but stepped back and held open the door for them. Both men politely asked permission to enter and followed her into the apartment.

A long central corridor led from the door to a bank of four Gothic windows at the other end. Brunetti's sense of orientation told him that the light must be coming in from Rio di San Girolamo, especially as the distance to the buildings visible through them was so great: the only open space that large must be the expanse of the Rio.

The girl led them into the first room on the right, a large sitting-room with a fireplace flanked by two windows, each more than two metres high. She waved at the sofa that stood facing the fireplace, but neither man sat.

'Would you please tell your grandmother we're here?' Brunetti asked.

She nodded but said, 'I don't think she wants to talk to anyone.'

'Please tell her it's very important,' Brunetti insisted. Thinking it best to make it evident that he intended to stay, he removed his overcoat and put it over the back of a chair, then sat at one end of the sofa. He motioned to Vianello to join him, which he did, first laying his coat on top of Brunetti's, then taking a seat at the other end of the sofa. Vianello removed his notebook from his pocket and clipped his pen to the front cover. Neither man spoke.

The girl left the room and both men used the opportunity to look around. A large gilded mirror sat above a table on which stood an enormous spray of red gladioli, their colour and number reflected by the glass, so that they seemed to multiply and fill the room. A silk carpet, Brunetti thought it a Nain, lay in front of the fireplace, so close to the sofa that whoever sat there would have to put their feet on it. An oak chest stood against the wall opposite the flowers, on its surface a large brass salver gone grey with age. The wealth and opulence, though discreet, were evident.

Before they could say anything, the door to the room opened and a woman in her fifties came in. She was stout-bodied and wore a grey wool dress that came well below her knees. She had thick ankles and small feet in shoes that looked uncomfortably narrow. Her hair and make-up were perfectly arranged and gave evidence of great expenditure of time and effort. Her eyes were lighter than her granddaughter's, her features thicker: in fact, there was little familial resemblance between them save that strange placidity of manner.

Both men got to their feet immediately and Brunetti moved towards her. 'Signora Mitri?' he asked.

She nodded but said nothing.

'I'm Commissario Brunetti and this is Sergeant Vianello. We'd like to speak to you for a few moments about your husband and about this terrible thing that has happened to him.' Hearing this, she closed her eyes but remained silent.

Her face had about it the same absence of animation that was so noticeable on her granddaughter's, and Brunetti found himself wondering if the daughter in Rome, whose child she must be, displayed a similar immobility.

'What do you want to know?' Signora Mitri asked, still standing in front of Brunetti. Her voice had the high pitch that was common among post-menopausal women. Though Brunetti knew she was Venetian, she chose to speak in Italian, as had he.

Before he answered, Brunetti stood away from the sofa and waved his hand towards his former place. She took it automatically and only then did the two men sit, Vianello where he had been and Brunetti in a velvet-covered easy chair that faced the window.

'Signora, I'd like to know if your husband ever spoke to you of enemies or of someone who would wish to do him harm.'

She started to shake her head in denial even before Brunetti had finished asking the question, but she did not speak, letting the gesture serve as response.

'He never mentioned disagreements with other people, business associates? Perhaps of some arrangement or contract that didn't go as planned?'

'No, nothing,' she finally said.

'On the personal level, then. Did he ever have trouble with neighbours, perhaps with a friend?'

She shook her head at this question but again uttered no words.

'Signora, I ask you to excuse my ignorance, but I know almost nothing about your husband.' She didn't respond to this. 'Would you tell me where he worked?' She seemed surprised at this, as if Brunetti had suggested Mitri clocked in for eight hours at a factory, so he explained, 'That is, in which of his factories he had his office or where he spent most of his time.'

'There's a chemical plant in Marghera. He has an office there.'

Brunetti nodded, but didn't ask for the address. He knew they could find it easily. 'Have you any idea of how much he was involved in the various factories and businesses he owned?'

'Involved?'

'Directly, I mean, in the day-to-day running of them.'

'You'd have to ask his secretary,' she said.

'In Marghera?'

She nodded.

As they spoke, however brief her answers, Brunetti watched her for signs of distress or mourning. The impassivity of her face made it difficult to tell, but he thought he detected traces of sadness, though it was more in the way she continually looked down at her own folded hands than anything she said or the tone of her voice.

'How many years were you married, Signora?'

'Thirty-five,' she said without hesitation.

'And is that your granddaughter who let us in?'

'Yes,' she answered, the faintest of smiles breaking the surface of her immobility. 'Giovanna. My daughter lives in Rome, but Giovanna said she wanted to come and stay with me. Now.'

Brunetti nodded his understanding, though the granddaughter's concern for her grandmother made the girl's calm demeanour seem even stranger. 'I'm sure it's a great comfort to have her here,' he said.

'Yes, it is,' Signora Mitri agreed and this time her face softened in a real smile. 'It would be terrible to be here alone.'

Brunetti bowed his head at this and waited a few seconds before looking up and back at her. 'Just a few more questions, Signora, then you can be with your granddaughter again.' He didn't wait for her to respond, but went on without preamble, 'Are you your husband's heir?'

Her surprise was evident in her eyes – the first time anything appeared to have touched her. 'Yes, I think so,' she said without hesitation.

'Has your husband other family?'

'A brother and a sister, and one cousin, but he emigrated to Argentina years ago.'

'No one else?'

'No, no one in the direct family.'

'Is Signor Zambino a friend of your husband's?'

'Who?'

'Avvocato Giuliano Zambino.'

'Not that I know of, no.'

'I believe he was your husband's lawyer.'

'I'm afraid I know very little about my husband's business,' she said and Brunetti was forced to wonder how many women he had heard tell him the same thing over the course of the years. Very few of them turned out to have been telling the truth, so it was an answer he never believed. At times he was uncomfortable about how very much Paola knew about his own business dealings, if that's what one called the identities of suspected rapists, the results of gruesome autopsies, and the surnames of the various suspects who appeared in the newspapers as 'Giovanni S, 39, bus driver, of Mestre' or 'Federico G, 59, mason, of San Dona di Piave'. Few secrets resisted the marriage pillow, Brunetti knew, so he was sceptical about Signora Mitri's professed ignorance. Nevertheless, he let it pass unquestioned.

They already had the names of the people she had been at dinner with the night her husband was murdered, so there was no need to pursue that now. Instead, he asked, 'Had your husband's behaviour changed in any way during the last weeks? Or days?'

She shook her head in strong denial. 'No, he was just the same as always.'

Brunetti wanted to ask her exactly what that was, but he resisted and instead got to his feet.

'Thank you, Signora, for your time and help. I'm afraid I will have to speak to you again when we have more information.' He saw that she took no pleasure in that prospect but thought she wouldn't deny a request for further information. His last words came unsummoned: 'I hope this time is not too painful for you and that you find the courage to bear it.'

She smiled at the audible sincerity of his words, and again he saw sweetness in that smile.

Vianello stood, took his overcoat, and handed Brunetti his. Both men put them on and Brunetti led the way to the door. Signora Mitri got up and followed them to the threshold of the apartment.

There, Brunetti and Vianello took their leave of her and made their way downstairs to the atrium, where the palm trees still flourished.

15

Outside, neither man spoke for some time as they made their way back to the *embarcadero*. Just as they arrived, the 82 from the station was pulling in, so they took that, knowing it would make the wide sweep of the Grand Canal and take them to San Zaccaria, a short walk from the Questura.

The afternoon having grown colder, they went inside and took seats towards the front half of the empty cabin. Ahead of them, two old women sat with their heads together, talking in loud Veneziano about the sudden cold.

'Zambino?' Vianello asked.

Brunetti nodded. 'I'd like to know why Mitri had a lawyer with him when he went to talk to Patta.'

'And one who sometimes takes on criminal defence work,' Vianello added unnecessarily. 'It's not as if he'd done anything, is it?'

'Maybe he wanted advice on what sort of civil case he could bring against my wife if I managed to stop the police from proceeding with criminal charges the second time.'

'There was never any chance of that, was there?' Vianello asked in a voice that made evident his regret.

'No, not once Landi and Scarpa were involved.'

Vianello muttered something under his breath, but Brunetti neither heard it nor asked the sergeant to repeat what he had said. 'I'm not sure what happens now.'

'About what?'

'The case. If Mitri's dead, it's unlikely that his heir will press civil charges against Paola. Although the manager might.'

'What about . . .' Vianello trailed off as he wondered what to call the police. He decided and called them, 'our colleagues?'

'That depends on the examining magistrate.'

'Who is it? Do you know?'

'Pagano, I think.'

Vianello considered this, summoning up years of experience working with and for the magistrate, an elderly man in the last years of his career. 'He's not likely to ask for a prosecution, is he?'

'No, I don't think so. He's never got on well with the Vice-Questore, so he's not likely to be urged into it or to enjoy being cajoled.'

'So what'll happen? A fine?' At Brunetti's shrug,

Vianello abandoned that question and asked instead, 'What now?'

'I'd like to see if anything's come in, then go and talk to Zambino.'

Vianello looked down at his watch. 'Is there time?'

As often happened, Brunetti had lost track entirely of how much time had passed and was surprised to see that it was well past six. 'No, I suppose not. In fact, there's not much sense in going back to the Questura, is there?'

Vianello smiled at this, especially as the boat was still tied up at the Rialto landing. He got up and made for the door. Just as he got to it, he heard the boat's engines shift into a different gear and saw the sailor flip the mooring rope off the stanchion and start to secure it to the boat. 'Wait,' he called out.

The sailor didn't respond, didn't even look back at him, and the engine revved up even higher.

'Wait.' Vianello shouted louder, but still failed to achieve any result.

He pushed his way through the people on deck and placed his hand lightly on the arm of the sailor. 'It's me, Marco,' he said in an entirely normal voice. The other looked at him, saw the uniform, recognized his face and waved a hand at the captain, who was glancing back towards the confusion on deck through the glass window of his cabin.

The sailor waved again and the captain slipped the boat suddenly into reverse. A few people on deck tottered as they tried to keep their balance. A woman fell heavily against Brunetti, who put out an arm and held her upright. He hardly wanted to be involved in a charge of police brutality or whatever would result if she fell, but he had grabbed her before he had time to think about this and, when he released her, was glad to see her grateful smile.

Slowly, the boat reversed itself in the water and headed the half-metre back to the *embarcadero*. The sailor slid the gate open, and Vianello and Brunetti stepped across to the wooden platform of the landing dock. With a wave, Vianello thanked him; the engines surged and the boat pulled forward.

'But why did you get off?' Brunetti asked. It was his stop, but Vianello should have stayed on until he got down to Castello.

'I'll take the next one. What about Zambino?'

'Tomorrow morning,' Brunetti answered. 'But late. I'd like to have Signorina Elettra see if she can find out anything she might have missed so far.'

Vianello nodded in approval of this. 'She's a miracle,' he said. 'If I knew him well, I'd say Lieutenant Scarpa is afraid of her.'

'I do know him well,' Brunetti answered, 'and he is afraid of her. Because she isn't, not in the least, frightened of him. And that makes her one of very few people at the Questura who aren't.' Since he and Vianello were two more among those very few, he could speak like this. 'It also makes him very dangerous. I've tried to say something to her, but she discounts him.'

'She shouldn't,' Vianello said.

Another boat appeared under the bridge and

started towards the landing. When all the passengers had got off, Vianello stepped across the open space on to the deck. '*A domani, capo*,' he said. Brunetti waved in acknowledgement and turned away even before the other passengers started to board the boat.

He stopped at one of the public phones in front of the landing and, from memory, dialled the number of Rizzardi's office at the hospital. Rizzardi had gone for the day but had left a message with his assistant for Commissario Brunetti if he called. Everything was as the doctor had assumed it would be. It was a single cord, plastic-covered and about six millimetres thick. Nothing more. Brunetti thanked the assistant and headed home.

The day had taken all warmth with it. He wished he'd thought to bring his scarf with him that morning but contented himself with pulling up the collar of his coat and hunching his neck down inside it. He walked quickly over the bridge, turning left at the bottom and choosing to walk along the water, drawn to the lights that streamed out from the many restaurants along the *riva*. He ducked right and hurried through the underpass into Campo San Silvestro, then left and up towards his apartment. At Biancat he was tempted by the irises in the window but remembered his anger with Paola and continued past. But then he recalled only Paola, turned back, went into the florist and bought a dozen of the purple ones.

She was in the kitchen when he got home, stuck

her head out to see whether it was he or one of the kids, and saw the package in his arms. She came down the corridor, a damp towel clutched in her hands. 'What's in the paper, Guido?' she asked in real confusion.

'Open it and see,' he said, handing her the flowers.

She flicked the towel across her shoulder and took them. He turned and removed his coat, hung it in the closet and heard the sound of paper rustling. Suddenly there was silence, dead silence, so he turned to look at her, worried he'd done something wrong. 'What is it?' he asked, seeing her stricken look.

She wrapped both arms round the bouquet and pulled it to her breast. Whatever she said was lost in the noise from the crinkling wrapping.

'What?' he asked, bending down a little, for she had lowered her head and pressed her face into the petals.

'I can't stand the thought that something I did led to the death of that man.' A sob choked off her voice, but she continued, 'I'm sorry, Guido. I'm sorry for all the mess I've caused you. I do that to you and you can bring me flowers.' She began to sob, face pressed into the soft petals of the irises, shoulders shaken by the power of her feelings.

He took them from her and looked for a place to put them. There was none, so he lowered them to the floor and put his arms round her. She sobbed against his chest with an abandon his daughter had never shown, even as a small child. He held her protectively, as if afraid she would break apart from the force of her sobs. He bent and kissed the top of her head, drank in her smell, saw the short bits where her hair fell apart into two waves at the base of her skull. He held her and rocked a bit from side to side, saying her name time and again. He had never loved her as much as at this moment. He felt a flash of vindication, then as quickly sensed his face suffuse with a shame stronger than he had ever known. By force of will he pushed back all sense of right, all sense of victory, and found himself in a clean space where there was nothing but pain that his wife, the other half of his spirit, could be in such agony. He bent again and kissed her hair, then, realizing that her sobs were coming to an end, he pushed her away but still held her by the shoulders. 'Are you all right, Paola?'

She nodded, unable to speak, keeping her face turned down so that he couldn't see her.

He reached into the pocket of his trousers and took out his handkerchief. It wasn't freshly laundered, but that hardly seemed to matter. He dabbed her face with it, under each eye, below her nose, then planted it firmly in her hand. She took it and wiped the rest of her face, then blew her nose with a resounding snort. She pressed it against her eyes, hiding from him.

'Paola,' he said in something that came close to his normal voice, though it wasn't, 'what you did is entirely honourable. I don't like the fact that you did it, but you acted with honour.'

For a moment, he thought that was going to set her off again, but it didn't. She took the handkerchief away from her face and looked at him through reddened eyes. 'If I had known . . .' she began.

But he cut her off with a raised palm. 'Not now, Paola. Maybe later, when we both can talk about it. Now let's go into the kitchen and see if we can find something to drink.'

It took her no time at all to add, 'And eat.' She smiled, glad of the reprieve.

16

The next morning Brunetti got to the Questura at his regular time, stopping to buy three newspapers on the way. *Il Gazzettino* continued to devote whole pages to the Mitri murder, lamenting a loss to the city it never made clear, but the national papers appeared to have lost interest in it, only one of them bothering to mention it and then only in a two-paragraph article.

Rizzardi's final report was on his desk. The double mark on Mitri's neck was, he had determined, a 'hesitation mark' on the part of the murderer, who had probably loosened the cord momentarily to tighten his grip, shifting it and thus leaving a second indentation in Mitri's flesh. The material under the nails of Mitri's left hand was indeed human skin, as well as a few fibres of dark-brown wool, probably from a jacket or overcoat and in all likelihood the result of Mitri's wild, and futile, attempt to fight off his attacker. 'Find me a suspect and I'll give you a match,' Rizzardi had pencilled in the margin.

At nine o'clock Brunetti decided it was not too early to call his father-in-law, Count Orazio Falier. He dialled the number of the Count's office, gave his name, and was immediately connected.

'*Buon dì*, Guido,' the Count said. '*Che pasticcio, eh?*'

Yes, it was a mess and more than that. 'That's what I'm calling about.' Brunetti paused, but the Count said nothing, so he went on. 'Have you heard anything or has your lawyer heard anything?' He broke off here for a moment, then continued. 'I don't even know if your lawyer is involved in this.'

'No, not yet,' the Count answered. 'I'm waiting to see what the judge does. Also, I don't know what Paola will want to do. Do you have any idea?'

'We talked about it last night,' Brunetti began and heard his father-in-law's whispered, 'Good.'

Brunetti continued, 'She said she'd pay the fine and whatever it costs to replace the window.'

'What about any other charges?'

'I didn't ask her about that. I thought it was enough to get her to agree to pay the fine and the damages, at least in principle. That way, if it's more than just the window, she might go along and pay that, too.'

'Yes, good. Good. That might work.'

Brunetti was irritated by the Count's assumption that he and Brunetti were united in some plan to outwit or manipulate Paola. However good their motives might be and however strongly both of them might believe they were doing what was best for her, Brunetti didn't like the Count's casual assumption that Brunetti was willing to deceive his wife.

He didn't want to continue with this. 'That's not why I called. I'd like you to tell me anything you might know about Mitri or about Avvocato Zambino.'

'Giuliano?'

'Yes.'

'Zambino's straight as a die.'

'He represented Manolo,' Brunetti shot back, naming a Mafia killer Zambino had successfully defended three years before.

'Manolo was kidnapped in France and brought back illegally for trial.'

Interpretations differed: Manolo had been in a small town just across the French border, living in a hotel, driving each night to Monaco to gamble in the Casinò. A young woman he met at the baccarat table had suggested they drive back into Italy to her place for a drink. Manolo had been arrested as they crossed the border, by the woman herself, who was a colonel of the *Carabinieri*. Zambino had argued, successfully, that his client had been the victim of police entrapment and kidnapping.

Brunetti let it drop. 'Has he ever worked for you?' he asked the Count.

'Once or twice. So I know. And I know from

friends of mine for whom he's handled things. He's good. He'll work like a ferret on a case to defend his client. But he's straight.' The Count paused for a long time, as if debating whether to trust Brunetti with the next piece of information, then added, 'There was a rumour going around last year that he didn't cheat on his taxes. I heard from someone that he declared an income of five hundred million lire or something like that.'

'You think that's what he earned?'

'Yes, I do,' the Count answered in a voice usually reserved for the recounting of miracles.

'What do the other lawyers think of this?'

'Well, you can figure that out, Guido. It makes things hard for all of them, if someone like Zambino declares such an income and the rest of them are saying they earned two hundred million, or even less. It can only cause suspicion about their tax declarations.'

'That must be hard for them.'

'Yes. He's . . .' the Count began, but then his mind registered the tone as well as the words and he stopped. 'About Mitri,' he said with no preamble. 'I think you might take a closer look at him. There could be something there.'

'About what, the travel agencies?'

'I don't know. In fact, I don't know anything at all about him except what a few people have said since he died. You know, the sort of things that get talked about when someone's the victim of a violent crime.'

Brunetti did know. He'd heard rumours of that kind about people killed in the cross-fire during bank robberies and about the victims of kidnap murders. Always, there was someone to raise the question of why they were there at precisely that moment, to ask why it was they died instead of someone else and just what their involvement was with the criminals. Nothing could ever be, here in Italy, simply what it appeared. Always, no matter how innocent the circumstances, how blameless the victim, there was someone to raise the spectre of *dietrologia* and insist that there must be something behind it all, that everyone had his price or got his part and nothing was what it seemed. 'What have you heard?' he asked.

'Nothing outright or specific. Everyone's been very careful to express surprise at what happened. But there's an undertone in what some of them say that suggests they feel differently about it or about him.'

'Who?'

'Guido,' the Count said, his voice going a few degrees cooler, 'if I knew, I wouldn't tell you. But it so happens I don't remember. It was really nothing any one person said, not so much that as an unspoken suggestion that what happened to him wasn't a complete surprise. I can't be any clearer than that.'

'There was the note,' Brunetti said. That could certainly have been enough to lead people to assume Mitri was somehow involved in the violence that had claimed his life.

'Yes, I know.' The Count paused for a moment, then added, 'That might be enough to explain it. What do you think?'

'Why do you ask?'

'Because I don't want my daughter to go through the rest of her life thinking that something she did led to a man's murder.'

This was a hope in which Brunetti joined him with all his spirit.

'What has she said about it?' the Count asked.

'She said last night that she was sorry about it, about starting it all.'

'Do you think she did? Start it, that is?'

'I don't know,' Brunetti admitted. 'There are a lot of crazy people running around today.'

'You'd have to be crazy to kill someone because he owned a travel agency that arranged tours.'

'Sex-tours,' Brunetti clarified.

'Sex-tours. Tours to the pyramids,' the Count fired back. 'People don't go around murdering others because of that, whichever it was.'

Brunetti stopped himself from responding that people normally didn't go around throwing rocks through plate-glass windows, either. Instead, he said, 'People do lots of things for crazy reasons, so I don't think we can exclude it as a possibility.'

'But do you believe it?' the Count insisted and Brunetti could hear from the tension in his voice just how much it cost him to ask this of his son-in-law.

'I told you, I don't want to believe it,' Brunetti said. 'I'm not sure it's the same thing, but it means I'm not prepared to believe it unless we can find very good reasons to do so.'

'What would they be?'

'A suspect.' He was himself married to the only

suspect and he knew she'd been sitting beside him at the time of the murder, so that left either a person who killed because of sex-tourism or someone who did it for some other reason. He was entirely willing to find either, just so long as he could find someone. 'Will you let me know if you hear anything more definite?' he asked. Before the Count could state conditions, he added, 'You don't have to tell me who said it, just tell me what he or she said.'

'All right,' the Count agreed. 'And will you let me know how Paola is?'

'You should call her. Take her out to lunch. Do something that will make her happy.'

'Thanks, Guido. I will.' Brunetti thought the Count had hung up without saying anything else, so long did the silence stretch out, but then the other man's voice was back. 'I hope you find whoever did this. And I'll help you in any way I can.'

'Thank you,' Brunetti said.

This time the Count did cut the connection.

Brunetti opened his drawer and took out the photocopy of the note that had been found with Mitri. Why the accusation of paedophilia? And who was accused, Mitri himself or Mitri as the owner of a travel agency that encouraged it? If the killer was crazy enough to write something like this, then go ahead and murder the man to whom the threats were addressed, would he be someone a man like Mitri would allow into his apartment at night? Though he knew it was an archaic prejudice, Brunetti was of the opinion that flagrantly crazy people usually gave every evidence of being just that. He had only to think of the ones he often saw near Palazzo Boldù in the early morning to be reminded of this truth.

But this person had managed to get into Mitri's apartment. Further, he – or she, Brunetti conceded, but he didn't consider this a real possibility; another one of his prejudices – had managed sufficiently to soothe Mitri that he had allowed his visitor to get behind him and pull out the fatal cord or wire, or whatever it was. And he had come and gone unseen and unremarked: no one in the building – and they'd all been questioned – had seen anything at all strange that evening; most of them had been in their apartments all the time and had realized something was wrong only when Signora Mitri ran screaming into the hall in front of her door.

No, it didn't sound to Brunetti like the behaviour of a madman, nor like that of a person who would write a note as unhinged as this one. Besides, he found it hard to reconcile the paradox that someone who was willing to take a stand against what they perceived as injustice – and here Paola slipped unsummoned into his mind as an example – would commit murder in order to correct that injustice.

He followed these ideas, discarding madmen and madwomen as he went, abandoning fanatics and zealots. That left him at the end asking the same question which was mooted in every murder investigation, *cui bono*? This made even more remote the possibility that Mitri's death and the running of the travel agency were related. His demise changed nothing. The publicity would die down quickly. If anything, Signor Dorandi was bound to profit from it in the end, if only because the name of the agency would have been lodged in people's minds by all the publicity surrounding the murder; and he certainly had made good use of the public forum provided by press coverage to profess his shock and horror at the very idea of sex-tourism.

Something else, then. Brunetti lowered his head and stared at the copy of the message formed by cut-out letters. Something else. 'Sex or money,' he said out loud and heard Signorina Elettra's startled gasp. She had come in unnoticed and stood in front of his desk, a folder in her right hand.

He looked up at her and smiled.

'I beg your pardon, Commissario?'

'That's why he was killed, Signorina. Sex or money.'

She understood instantly. 'Always in good taste, those two,' she said and placed the file on his desk. 'This one is about the second.'

'Whose?'

'Both of theirs.' A look of dissatisfaction crossed her face. 'I can't make any sense out of the numbers there, those for Dottor Mitri.'

'In what way?' Brunetti asked, knowing that if Signorina Elettra found numbers confusing there was little chance that he would have any idea what they meant.

'He was very rich.'

Brunetti, who had been inside his home, nodded.

'But the factories and businesses he owned don't make very much money.'

This was a common enough phenomenon, Brunetti knew. To go by their tax returns, no one in Italy made enough to live on; they were a nation of paupers, scraping by only by turning collars, wearing shoes until they could be worn no more and, for all he knew, surviving on chaff and nettles. And yet the restaurants were full of well-dressed people, everyone seemed to have a new car, and the airports never ceased sending off planeloads of happy tourists. Go figure, as an American friend of his was much in the habit of saying.

'I can't imagine you'd be surprised by that,' Brunetti said.

'No, I'm not. We all cheat on our taxes. But I've studied all the records for his companies, and it looks like they're correct. That is, none of them makes him much more than twenty million or so a year.'

'For a total of what?'

'About two hundred million a year.'

'Profit?'

'That's what he declared,' she answered. 'After his taxes he was left with less than half of that.'

It was considerably more than Brunetti earned per year and hardly meant a life of poverty. 'But why are you so sure?' he asked.

'Because I've also checked his credit card

expenses.' She nodded down at the folder. 'And they are not the expenses of a man who earns that little.'

Not at all sure how to react to that dismissive 'little', Brunetti said, 'How much did he spend?' He waved her to a seat.

She tucked her long skirt under her and sat on the front of the chair, her spine not even flirting with its back, and waved her right hand in front of her. 'I don't remember the exact sum. More than fifty million, I think. So if you add to that the costs of running his home, just running his life, there's no way to explain how he could have almost a billion lire in savings and stocks.'

'Maybe he won the lottery,' Brunetti suggested with a smile.

'No one wins the lottery,' Signorina Elettra answered without one.

'Why would he keep so much money in the bank?' Brunetti asked.

'No one expects to die, I suppose. But he's been moving it around. During the last year, quite a bit of it disappeared.'

'Where?'

She shrugged. 'To the places money disappears to, I suppose: Switzerland, Luxembourg, the Channel Islands.'

'How much?'

'About half a billion.'

Brunetti gazed down at the folder, but didn't open it. He glanced up. 'Can you find out?'

'I haven't really begun to look, Commissario. That is, I've begun, but I've just been glancing around, as it were. I haven't really started to pry open drawers or rifle through his private papers.'

'Do you think you could find time to do that?'

Brunetti could not remember the last time he had offered candy to a baby, but he had a vague memory of a smile much like the one Signorina Elettra gave him. 'There's nothing that would give me greater joy,' she said, surprising him only by her rhetoric, not by her response. She got to her feet, eager to be off.

'And Zambino?'

'Nothing at all. I've never found anyone whose records are so clear and so . . .' She paused here, seeking the proper term. 'So clear and so honest,' she said, unable to restrain her wonder at the sound of the last word. 'Never.'

'Do you know anything about him?'

'Personally?' Brunetti nodded, but instead of answering she enquired, 'Why do you want to know?'

'No reason,' he answered and then, made curious by her apparent reluctance, asked, 'Do you?'

'He's a patient of Barbara's.'

He considered this. He knew Signorina Elettra well enough to be aware that she would never reveal something she thought came under the seal of family, and her sister to realize she would always be bound by her oath as a doctor. He let it drop. 'Professionally?'

'Friends of mine have used him.'

'As a lawyer?'

'Yes.'

'Why? I mean for what sort of cases?'

'Remember when Lily was attacked?' she asked.

Brunetti recalled the case, one that had reduced him to speechless rage. Three years ago, Lily Vitale, an architect, had been attacked on her way home from the opera, in what might have begun as a mugging, but which ended in a much more violent attack, when her face had been repeatedly punched and her nose broken. No attempt had been made to rob her; her bag was found, untouched, beside her by the people who came out from their homes in answer to her screams.

Her attacker was arrested that night and quickly identified as the same man who had attempted to rape at least three other women in the city. But he had never stolen anything and he was actually incapable of rape, so he was given three months of house arrest, but not before his mother and girlfriend had stepped forward at the trial to praise his virtue, loyalty, and integrity.

'Lily brought a civil suit against him for damages. Zambino was her lawyer.'

Brunetti knew nothing of this. 'And?'

'She lost.'

'Why?'

'Because he never tried to rob her. All he did was break her nose, and the judge didn't think that was as serious as stealing her purse. So he didn't even award damages. He said that the house arrest was sufficient punishment.'

'And Lily?'

Signorina Elettra shrugged. 'She doesn't go out alone any more, so she gets around less.'

The young man was currently in jail for having stabbed his girlfriend, but Brunetti didn't think that would matter to Lily, nor would it change anything.

'How did he react to losing the case?'

'I don't know. Lily never said.' She didn't offer anything after this and got to her feet. 'I'll go and have a look,' she said, reminding him that they were here about Mitri and not about a woman whose courage had been broken.

'Yes, thank you. I think I'll have a word with Avvocato Zambino.'

'As you will, Commissario.' She turned to the door. 'But, believe me, if anyone is clean, he is.' As the person named was a lawyer, Brunetti gave this the attention he devoted to the mutterings of the lunatics in front of Palazzo Boldù.

17

He decided not to take Vianello with him, hoping
that his visit to the lawyer would thus appear a
more casual thing, though he hardly believed a
man as exposed to the law in all its workings as
Zambino would be much affected by the sight of a
uniform. A quotation Paola often used slipped into
his mind, the description of one of Chaucer's
pilgrims, the Man of Law: 'He seemed busier than
he was.' Brunetti thus thought it might be wise to
call ahead and let the avvocato know that he was
coming and thus avoid being kept waiting while
he did lawyerly things. His secretary, or whoever
it was that answered the phone, said that he would
be free in about half an hour and would be able
then to speak to the commissario.

The office was in Campo San Polo, so Brunetti

could end his morning close to home and would have plenty of time for lunch. He called Paola to tell her this. Neither of them discussed anything but time and menu.

As soon as he'd finished talking to her, Brunetti went downstairs into the officers' room, where he found Vianello at his desk, reading the morning paper. When he heard Brunetti approach, the sergeant looked up and closed the paper.

'Anything today?' Brunetti asked. 'I haven't had time to read them.'

'No, it's tapering off, probably because there's not much to say. Not until we arrest someone.'

Vianello started to get to his feet, but Brunetti said, 'No, don't bother, Sergeant. I'm going to go and see Zambino. Alone.' Before the other could say anything to this, Brunetti added, 'Signorina Elettra said she's going to take a closer look at Mitri's finances and I thought you might like to see how she does it.'

Recently, Vianello had become absorbed in the manner in which Signorina Elettra discovered things with the help of her computer and the scores of friends, some of whom she'd never met, it linked her to. No barriers of nation or language seemed any longer to impede the free exchange of information, much of it very interesting to the police. Brunetti's attempt to follow along had met with failure, so he was pleased at Vianello's enthusiasm. He wanted someone else to be able to do what Signorina Elettra did, or at least understand how she did it, in case they ever had to work without her. Even as the thought came, he breathed a silent incantation against its possibility.

Vianello finished folding up the paper and let it drop on his desk. 'Gladly. She's shown me a lot, but there's always something she thinks of when the regular paths don't work. The kids are amazed,' he went on. 'They used to kid me about how little I understood of what they brought home from school or what they talked about, but now they come and ask me if they have trouble or can't access someone.' Unconsciously, he used the English verb, the langauge in which he and Signorina Elettra pursued most of their information.

Strangely unsettled by this brief conversation, Brunetti took his leave of the sergeant and left the Questura. A single cameraman stood outside, but his back was to the entrance as he faced away from the wind and lit a cigarette, so Brunetti walked away unnoticed. When he arrived at the Grand Canal, the wind made him decide not to take the *traghetto* and, instead, he crossed the Rialto. As he walked, he ignored the glory that surrounded him on all sides and, instead, thought about what he wanted to ask Avvocato Zambino. He was distracted from this only once when he saw what he was sure were porcini mushrooms on one of the vegetable stalls and was filled with a momentary hope that Paola would see them too and serve them with polenta for lunch.

He walked quickly along Rughetta, past his own *calle*, through the underpass, and out into the *campo*. The leaves had long since fallen from the trees, so the broad expanse seemed curiously naked and exposed.

The lawyer's office was on the first floor of Palazzo Soranzo, and when he arrived Brunetti was surprised to have the door opened by Zambino himself.

'Ah, Commissario Brunetti, this is a pleasure,' the lawyer said, extending his hand and shaking Brunetti's firmly. 'I can't say it's a pleasure to meet you, since we've already met, but it's a pleasure to have you come here to speak to me.' At their first meeting Brunetti had paid most attention to Mitri, so the lawyer had passed all but unobserved. He was short, stocky, with a body that showed signs of a lot of good living and not much exercise. Brunetti thought he was wearing the same suit he'd had on in Patta's office, though he wasn't sure. Thinning hair covered a head that was disconcertingly round; the face was the same and the cheeks as well. His eyes were those of a woman: thick-lashed, almond-shaped, cobalt-blue and strikingly beautiful.

'Thank you,' Brunetti said, looking away from the lawyer and around the office. It was, he saw to his considerable surprise, humble, the sort of room he'd expect to find in the *ambulatorio* of a doctor just graduated from medical school who had recently set up his first practice. The chairs were metal, with seats and backs made from formica that was disguised, badly, to look like wood. A single low table stood in the centre of the room and on it lay a few copies of outdated magazines.

The lawyer led him to an open door and into what must be his office. The walls were covered with books Brunetti recognized instantly as law texts, case studies, and the codes of law, both civil and criminal, of the State of Italy. They filled each wall from floor to ceiling. Four or five of them lay open on Zambino's desk.

As Brunetti took his place in one of the three chairs that faced the lawyer's, Zambino went around to his own chair and closed the books, carefully slipping small pieces of paper into the open pages of all of them, before setting them aside in a little pile.

'I'll waste no time and say that I assume you're here to talk about Dottor Mitri,' Zambino began. Brunetti nodded. 'Good, then if you'll tell me what you'd like to know, I'll try to give you what help I can.'

'That's very kind of you, Avvocato,' Brunetti began with formulaic politeness.

'There's no kindness in it, Commissario. It's my duty as a citizen and my desire as a lawyer to assist you in any way that might in turn help you to find Dottor Mitri's murderer.'

'You don't call him Paolo, Avvocato?'

'Who, Mitri?' the lawyer asked. When Brunetti nodded, he said, 'No. Dottor Mitri was a client, not a friend.'

'Is there any reason why he wasn't a friend?'

Zambino had been a lawyer far too long to show surprise at anything he was asked, so he answered calmly, 'No, no reason at all, except that we never came in contact before he called me for advice about the incident at the travel agency.'

'Do you think he would have become a friend?' Brunetti asked.

'I can't speculate about that, Commissario. I spoke to him on the phone, met him here in the office once, then went to the Vice-Questore's office with him. That is the only contact I had with him, so I have no idea if I would have become a friend of his or not.'

'I see,' Brunetti said. 'Could you tell me what he had decided to do about what you call the incident at the travel agency?'

'About pressing charges?'

'Yes.'

'After speaking to you and then to the Vice-Questore, I suggested he submit a claim for damages for the window and the lost business he thought it would cost the agency – he was entitled to his percentage of that, though the window was entirely his responsibility, as he was the owner of the physical space occupied by the agency.'

'Was it difficult for you to persuade him, Avvocato?'

'No, not at all,' he answered, almost as if he'd been expecting this question. 'In fact, I'd say that he had already made up his mind to this course even before he spoke to me and wanted only to confirm his opinion with a lawyer.'

'Have you any idea why he selected you?' Brunetti asked.

A man less certain of his position would surely have paused here and feigned surprise at anyone's daring to question why he would have been chosen to work as someone's lawyer. Instead, Zambino said, 'No, none at all. There was certainly no need for him to come to someone like me.'

'By that do you mean someone who works primarily in business law or someone who has a reputation as high as your own?'

Zambino smiled here, and Brunetti warmed to it and to the man.

'That's very gracefully put, Commissario. You give me little chance but to sing my own praises.' When he saw Brunetti's answering smile, he continued, 'I've no idea, as I said. I might have been recommended to him by someone he knew. For all I know, he might have picked my name at random out of the phone book.' Before Brunetti could say it, Zambino added, 'Though I hardly think Dottor Mitri was the sort of man to make a decision that way.'

'Did you spend enough time with him to form an opinion about what sort of man he was, Avvocato?'

Zambino considered this for a long time. Finally he answered, 'I got the impression that he was a very sharp businessman and that he was very interested in success.'

'Did you find it surprising that he would so easily abandon the case against my wife?' When Zambino did not answer this immediately, Brunetti continued, 'That is, there's no chance a decision would have gone against him. She admitted her responsibility' – both men noticed that Brunetti did not use the word 'guilt' – 'she said as much to the arresting officer, so he could have claimed virtually any sum he wanted against her – for slander, or suffering, for whatever he chose to claim – and he would probably have won the case.'

'And yet he chose not to,' Zambino said.

'Why do you think that was?'

'It could have been that he had no desire for revenge.'

'Is that what you thought?'

Zambino considered this question. 'No, in fact, I think he would have enjoyed revenge a great deal. He was very, very angry at what happened.' Before Brunetti could say anything, he went on, 'And he was angry not only at your wife but at the manager of the travel agency because he had given him quite specific instructions that he was to avoid that sort of tourism at all costs.'

'Sex-tourism?'

'Yes. He showed me a copy of a letter and contract he'd sent to Signor Dorandi three years ago, telling him quite plainly that he was not to engage in anything of that kind, or he'd cancel his lease and take back the licence. I'm not sure how legally binding the contract would have been had Dorandi contested it – I didn't draw it up – but I think it shows that Mitri was serious.'

'Did he do this for moral reasons, do you think?'

Zambino's answer was long in coming, as if he had to consider his legal obligations to a client who was now dead. 'No. I think he did it because he realized it would be a bad business move. In a city like Venice, publicity like that could be devastating for a travel agency. No, I don't think he considered morality an issue; it was entirely a business decision.'

'Do you, Avvocato, consider it a moral issue?'

'Yes,' said the lawyer shortly and with no need to think before he gave his answer.

Leaving that subject, Brunetti asked, 'Have you any idea what his intentions were regarding Dorandi?'

'I know he wrote a letter, reminding him about the contract and asking him to explain the sort of tours your wife protested against.'

'Did he send this letter?'

'He faxed Signor Dorandi a copy and sent another by registered mail.'

Brunetti thought about this. If Paola's ideals were going to be considered a valid reason for murder, then the loss of the lease on a very lucrative business was just as good. 'I'm still puzzled by the fact that he hired you, Avvocato.'

'People do strange things, Commissario.' The lawyer smiled. 'Especially when they are forced to deal with the law.'

'Businessmen seldom do expensive things, if you will excuse my vulgarity, unnecessarily.' And before Zambino could take exception to that, Brunetti added, 'Because it hardly seems a case where a lawyer would be necessary at all. He merely had to make his conditions known to the Vice-Questore, either with a phone call or a letter. No one opposed those conditions. Yet he hired a lawyer.'

'At considerable expense, I will add,' Zambino offered.

'Exactly. Do you understand it?'

Zambino leaned back in his chair and latched his hands behind his head. In so doing he exposed a considerable breadth of stomach. 'I think it was what the Americans call "overkill".' Still looking at the ceiling, he continued, 'I think he wanted there to be no question that his demands be met, that your wife accept his conditions and the thing be ended there.'

'Ended?'

'Yes.' The lawyer brought his body forward, rested his arms on the desk and said, 'I had a very strong sense that he wanted this episode to cause him absolutely no trouble and no publicity whatsoever. Perhaps the second was even more important than the first. At one point I asked him what he was prepared to do if your wife, who seemed to be acting out of principle, refused to pay the damages; whether he would then consider initiating a civil case. He said no. He was quite insistent on this. I told him there would be no chance of his losing this case, but he still said he wouldn't do it, or even consider it.'

'So if my wife had refused to pay, he would not have taken any legal steps against her?'

'Precisely.'

'You tell me this, knowing that she could still change her mind and refuse to pay?'

Zambino, for the first time, looked surprised. 'Of course.'

'Even knowing that I could tell her what Mitri had decided and thus influence her decision?'

Zambino smiled again. 'Commissario, I imagine

you spent a good deal of time before you came here in finding out all you could about me and about my reputation in the city.' Before Brunetti could admit or deny this, the lawyer went on, 'I did the same thing, as any of us would. And what I learned suggests to me that I am entirely safe in telling you this and that there is no danger of any kind that you would tell your wife or, because of this information, attempt to influence her decision in any way.'

Embarrassment prevented Brunetti from acknowledging the truth of this. He merely nodded and went on to enquire, 'Did you ever ask him why it was so important to avoid bad publicity?'

Zambino shook his head. 'It interested me, I'll admit, but it wasn't part of my responsibility to discover that. There was no way it could be of use to me as his lawyer and that's what he hired me to be.'

'But did you speculate on it?' Brunetti wondered.

Again that smile. 'Of course I speculated, Commissario. It seemed so out of keeping with the man as I understood him to be: wealthy, well-connected, if you will, powerful. Such men can usually get anything at all hushed up, no matter how bad. And this was hardly his responsibility, was it?'

Brunetti shook his head in negative agreement and waited for the lawyer to continue.

'So that meant either that he had a sensibility or sense of ethics which viewed the agency's involvement as wrong – and I'd already excluded that possibility – or there was some reason, personal or business, why he wanted or needed to avoid any sort of bad publicity or the scrutiny it would cause.'

This had been Brunetti's conclusion, and he was glad to have it confirmed by someone who had known Mitri. 'And did you speculate on what that might be?' he asked.

This time Zambino laughed outright, now caught up in the game and enjoying it. 'If we lived in a different century, I'd say he was afraid for his good name. But since that is now a commodity anyone at all can buy on the open market, I'd say it was because that scrutiny might bring to light something he didn't want examined.'

Again his thoughts had mirrored Brunetti's. 'Any ideas?'

Zambino hesitated a long time before he answered. 'I'm afraid this is a complicated point for me, Commissario. Even though the man is dead, I still have a professional responsibility to him, so I cannot allow myself to alert the police to anything I might know or indeed might only suspect about him.'

Immediately curious, Brunetti wondered what Zambino knew and how he could get it from him. But before he could begin to formulate a question, the other proceeded, 'If it will save you time, I will tell you, and this is quite unofficially, that I have no idea at all of what he might have been concerned about. He told me nothing of his other involvements, only about this case. So I've no ideas at all, though I repeat that if I had, I wouldn't tell you about them.'

Brunetti smiled his most open smile while he considered how much of what he had just heard was the truth. Saying, 'You've been very generous with your time, Avvocato, and I'll take no more of it from you,' he got to his feet and made for the door.

Zambino came along behind him. 'I hope you can resolve this, Commissario,' he said on their way out of the office. He extended his hand and Brunetti took it with every sign of warmth, while he contemplated whether the lawyer was an honest man or a very skilled liar.

'As do I, Avvocato,' he said, took his leave and headed back towards his home and his wife.

18

Bubbling in the back of his mind all day had been the knowledge that he and Paola had to go out to dinner that evening. Ever since what Brunetti refused to call her arrest, he and Paola had avoided accepting or issuing any invitations, but this was a date that had been made months ago, the celebration of the twenty-fifth wedding anniversary of Paola's best friend and closest ally at the university, Giovanni Morosini, and there was no way they could gracefully avoid it. It was Giovanni who had, upon two occasions, saved Paola's professional life: once by destroying a letter Paola had written to the Magnifico Rettore in which she called him a power-hungry incompetent, the second time by persuading her not to submit a letter of resignation to the same Rector.

Giovanni taught Italian literature at the university, his wife Art History at the Accademia di Belle Arti, and the four of them had, over the course of years, become close friends. Because the other three lived the major part of their professional lives inside books, Brunetti sometimes found their company unsettling, convinced as he was that they found art more real than everyday life. But there was no question about the Morosinis' affection for Paola, so Brunetti had agreed to accept the invitation, especially when Clara called to make it clear they would not go to a restaurant, but would eat at home. The public eye was not a place where Brunetti wanted to spend any time, at least not until Paola's legal situation was resolved.

Paola saw no reason not to continue teaching her classes at the university, so got home at five. That gave her time to begin to prepare dinner for the children, take a bath, and get ready before Brunetti arrived.

'You're already dressed?' he asked, when he came into the apartment and saw her there, wearing a short dress that looked as though it was made out of gold to airy thinness beat. 'I've never seen that before,' he added, hanging up his coat.

'And?' she asked.

'And I like it,' he finished, 'especially the apron.'

Surprised, she looked down, but before she could register displeasure at having been fooled, he turned and walked down the corridor to their room. She went back into the kitchen, where she did put on the apron and he, in their bedroom, put on his dark-blue suit.

Pulling the collar of his shirt straight under the jacket, he walked into the kitchen. 'What time are we supposed to be there?'

'Eight.'

Brunetti pushed back his sleeve and looked at his watch. 'Leave in ten minutes?' Paola answered with a grunt, head bent over a pot. Brunetti regretted that there was barely time for a glass of wine. 'Any idea who else is going to be there?' he asked.

'No.'

'Hm,' Brunetti said. He opened the refrigerator and pulled out a bottle of Pinot Grigio, poured himself half a glass, and took a sip.

Paola put the lid back on to the pot and turned off the flame. 'That's good enough,' she said. 'They won't starve.' Then, to him, 'Worrying, isn't it?'

'When we don't know who else is invited?'

Instead of answering, she asked, 'Remember the Americans?'

Brunetti sighed and put the glass into the sink. Their eyes met and both laughed. The Americans had been a pair of visiting professors from Harvard the Morosinis had invited to dinner two years before, Assyriologists who had spoken to no one except each other during the entire evening and who had, during the course of the meal, proceeded to get falling-down drunk and thus had to be sent home in a taxi, a bill for which had been put through the Morosinis' mailbox the next morning.

'Did you ask?' Brunetti wanted to know.

'Who'd be there?'

'Yes.'

'I couldn't,' Paola answered and, when she saw that he wasn't convinced, added, 'You can't, Guido. Or I can't. And what am I supposed to do if it's someone dreadful, say I'm sick?'

He shrugged, thinking of the evenings he'd spent, prisoner to the Morosinis' catholic tastes and variegated friendships.

Paola got her coat and put it on before he could help her. Together, they left the apartment and headed down towards San Polo. They crossed the *campo*, went over a bridge, and turned into a narrow *calle* on the right. Just beyond it, they walked right and rang the Morosinis' bell. The door snapped open almost instantly and they ascended to the *piano nobile*, where Giovanni Morosini stood at the open door to their apartment, the sound of voices flowing out and down the steps from behind him.

A large man, Morosini still wore the beard he'd first grown as a student caught up in the violent protests of sixty-eight. It had turned grey and grizzled with the passing of the years, and he often joked that the same thing had happened to his ideals and principles. A bit taller and considerably wider than Brunetti, he seemed to fill up the entire space of the doorway. He greeted Paola with a double kiss and gave Brunetti a warm handshake.

'Welcome, welcome. Come in and have something to drink,' he said as he took their coats and hung them in the cupboard beside the door. 'Clara's in the kitchen, but I have some people I'd like you to meet.' As always, Brunetti was struck by the disparity in the man's size and the softness of his voice, barely more than a whisper, as if he were perpetually afraid of being overheard.

He stepped back to let them enter and preceded them down the central hallway that led to the large *salotto*, off which all the other rooms in the house opened. Four people stood in one corner of the room, and Brunetti was instantly struck by how much two of them appeared to be a couple and how little the other two did.

Hearing them, the people in the room turned and Brunetti saw the eyes of the non-coupled woman light up when she saw Paola. It was not a pleasant sight.

Morosini led them round a low sofa and over to the others. 'Paola and Guido Brunetti,' he began, 'I'd like to present Dottor Klaus Rotgeiger, a friend of ours who lives on the other side of the *campo*, and his wife Bettina.' The two who formed a couple put down their glasses on the table behind them and turned to extend their hands in grips as warm and tight as had been Morosini's. The usual compliments fell from their lips in lightly accented Italian. Brunetti was struck by a shared ranginess of build and clarity of eye.

'And', Morosini continued, 'Dottoressa Filomena Santa Lucia and her husband, Luigi Bernardi.' The second couple placed their glasses next to the others and extended their hands. The same compliments flowed back and forth. This time, Brunetti registered a sort of tactile reluctance on both their parts to allow their hands to be held overlong by strangers. He also noticed that, though they spoke to both him and Paola, they spent far more time observing her. The woman was dark-eyed and had the air of one who believed herself to be far prettier than she was. The man spoke with the elided R of Milano.

Clara's voice called out from behind them, '*A tavola, a tavola, ragazzi*' and Giovanni led them into the next room, where a long oval table stood parallel to a bank of tall windows that looked across at the buildings on the other side of the *campo*.

Clara appeared from the kitchen then, head enveloped in a cloud of vapour rising from a tureen that she carried in front of her like a votive offering. Brunetti could smell broccoli and anchovies, and remembered just how hungry he was.

Conversation during the pasta course was general, the sort of delicate jockeying that always goes on when eight people who really aren't sure of where sympathies lie try to settle what the topics of interest are. Brunetti was struck, as he had been frequently and strongly in recent years, by the absence of talk about politics. He wasn't sure if no one cared any more or if the subject had simply become too inflammable to permit strangers to attempt it. Regardless of the cause, it had joined religion in some sort of conversational gulag where no one any longer dared, or cared, to go.

Dottor Rotgeiger was explaining, in Italian Brunetti thought was quite good, the problems he was having at the Ufficio Stranieri in getting permission to prolong his stay in Venice for another year. Each time he went, he was assailed by self-proclaimed 'agents' who lingered by the long lines and said they could help speed up the paperwork.

Brunetti accepted a second helping of pasta and said nothing.

By the time the fish course began – an enormous boiled branzino that must have been half a metre long – conversation had passed to Dottoressa Santa Lucia, a cultural anthropologist who had just returned from a long research trip to Indonesia, where she had spent a year studying familial power structures.

Though she directed her remarks at the entire table, Brunetti could see that her eyes were most often directed at Paola. 'You have to understand', she said, not quite smiling but with the satisfied look of one who was able to grasp the subtlety of an alien culture, 'that the family structure is based upon the preservation of same. That is, everything must be done to keep the family intact, even if it means the sacrifice of its least important members.'

'As defined by whom?' Paola asked, taking a tiny piece of fish bone from her mouth and placing it with excessive care at the side of her plate.

'That's a very interesting question,' Dottoressa Santa Lucia said in exactly the tone she must have used when explaining the same thing hundreds of times to her students. 'But I think this is one of the few cases where the social judgements of their very complex and sophisticated culture agree with our own more simplistic view.' She paused, waiting for someone to ask for clarification.

Bettina Rotgeiger complied: 'In what way the same?'

'In that we agree on who they are, the least important members of the society.' Having said this, the dottoressa paused and, seeing that she had the full attention of everyone at the table, took a small sip of wine while they awaited her answer.

'Let me guess,' Paola interrupted, smiling, her chin propped in her open palm, her fish forgotten below her. 'Young girls?'

After a brief pause, Dottoressa Santa Lucia said, 'Exactly,' giving no sign that she was disconcerted at having had her thunder stolen. 'Do you find that strange?'

'Not in the least,' Paola answered, smiled again, and returned her attention to her branzino.

'Yes,' the anthropologist continued, 'in a certain sense, societal norms being what they are, they're expendable, given that more of them are born than most families can support and the fact that male children are far more desirable.' She looked around to see how this went down and added with a haste she made obvious was caused by fear that she had somehow offended their rigidly Western sensibilities, 'In their terms, of course, thinking as they do. After all, who else will provide for aged parents?'

Brunetti picked up the bottle of Chardonnay and leaned across the table to fill Paola's glass, then filled his own. Their eyes met; she gave him a small smile and a smaller nod.

'I think it's necessary that we see this issue

through their eyes, that we try to consider it as they do, at least so far as our own cultural prejudices will allow us to do so,' Dottoressa Santa Lucia proclaimed and was gone for some minutes, explaining the need to expand our vision so as to encompass cultural differences and give to them the respect that was earned by having been developed over the course of many millennia to respond to the specific needs of diverse societies.

After a while that Brunetti measured as the time it took him to finish a refill of wine and eat his helping of boiled potatoes, she finished, picked up her glass and smiled, as if waiting for the appreciative members of her class to approach the podium to tell her how illuminating the lecture had been. A lengthening pause stretched out and was at last broken by Paola, who said, 'Clara, let me help you carry these plates into the kitchen.' Brunetti was not the only person who breathed a sigh of relief.

Later, on the way home, Brunetti asked, 'Why did you let her go?'

Beside him Paola shrugged.

'No, why? Tell me.'

'Too easy,' Paola said dismissively. 'It was obvious from the beginning that she wanted to get me to talk about it, about why I did it. Why else would she bring up all that nonsense about girls being expendable?'

Brunetti walked beside her, her elbow tucked into the angle of his arm. He nodded. 'Maybe she believed it.' They walked a few more paces, considering this, then he said, 'I always hate to see women like that.'

'Like what?'

'Who don't like women.' They walked a few more steps. 'Can you imagine what a class of hers must be like?' Before Paola could answer he continued, 'She's so sure of everything she says, so absolutely certain she's found the single truth.' He paused for a moment. 'And imagine what it would be like to have her on your exam committee. Differ from her on anything and there goes your chance for a degree.'

'Not that anyone would want one in cultural anthropology, anyway,' Paola remarked.

He laughed out loud and in complete agreement. As they turned into their *calle* he slowed his steps, then stopped and turned her so that she was facing him. 'Thank you, Paola,' he said.

'For what?' she asked in feigned innocence.

'For avoiding combat.'

'It would have ended up with her asking me why I let myself get arrested and I don't think she's anyone I want to talk about that with.'

'Stupid cow,' Brunetti muttered.

'That's a sexist remark,' Paola observed.

'Yes, isn't it?'

19

Their foray into society left them both wanting no more of it, so they resumed their policy of refusing invitations of any sort. Though both Paola and Brunetti chafed under the restriction of staying home night after night and Raffi seemed to find their continued presence worthy of ironic comment, Chiara loved having them there every evening and insisted on engaging them in card games, watching endless television programmes about animals and initiated a Monopoly tournament that threatened to stretch into the new year.

Each day, Paola went off to the university and Brunetti to his office at the Questura. For the first time in their careers, they were glad of the endless mountains of paperwork created by the Byzantine state which employed them both.

Because of Paola's involvement with the case, Brunetti made up his mind not to attend Mitri's funeral, something he ordinarily would have done. Two days after it, he decided to read again through the lab and scene-of-crime reports of Mitri's murder, as well as Rizzardi's four-page report on the autopsy. It took him a good part of the morning to get through them all, and the process left him wondering why it was that both his professional and his personal life seemed to be so much taken up with going over the same things again and again. During his temporary exile from the Questura he had finished rereading Gibbon and was currently tackling Herodotus, and for when that was finished, he had the *Iliad* ready at hand. All the deaths, all the lives cut short by violence.

He took the autopsy report and went down to Signorina Elettra's office, where he found her looking like the antidote to everything he'd just been thinking about. She wore a jacket redder than any he had ever seen and a white silk-crêpe blouse open to the second button. Strangely enough, she was doing nothing when he came in, simply sitting at her desk, chin lodged in one palm, staring out of the window towards San Lorenzo, a sliver of which was visible in the distance.

'Are you all right, Signorina?' he asked when he saw her.

She sat up and smiled. 'Of course, Commissario. I was just wondering about a painting.'

'A painting?'

'Uh huh,' she said, putting her chin back on her

hand and staring off again.

Brunetti turned to follow her gaze, as if he thought the painting in question might be there, but all he saw was the window and, beyond it, the church. 'Which one?' he asked.

'That one in the Correr, of the courtesans with their little dogs.' He knew it, though he could never remember who had painted it. They sat, as absent and bored as Signorina Elettra had seemed when he came in, looking away to the side, as if uninterested in the thought that life was about to happen to them.

'What about it?'

'I've never been sure if they were courtesans or just wealthy women of those times, so bored with having everything and with nothing at all to do every day that all they could do was sit and stare.'

'What makes you think of that?'

'Oh, I don't know,' she answered with a shrug.

'Are you bored with this?' he asked, encompassing the office and all it signified with a wave of his hand and hoping her answer would be no.

She turned her head and looked up at him. 'Are you joking, Commissario?'

'No, not at all. Why do you ask?'

She studied his face for a long time before saying, 'I'm not at all bored with it. Quite the opposite.' Brunetti was not surprised in the least at how glad he was to hear this. After a moment's pause, she added, 'Though I'm never quite sure just what my position is here.'

Brunetti had no idea what she meant by that.

Her official title was Secretary to the Vice-Questore. She was also meant to be of part-time secretarial help to Brunetti and another commissario, but she had never written a letter or a memo for either of them. 'I suppose you mean your real position, as opposed to your official position,' he suggested.

'Yes, of course.'

Brunetti's hand, the one holding the reports, had fallen to his side during all this. He raised it in front of him, held it a bit towards her and said, 'I think you are our eyes and our nose, and the living spirit of our curiosity, Signorina.'

Her head rose from her hand and she graced him with one of her radiant smiles. 'How nice it would be to read that in a job description, Commissario.'

'I think it would be best', Brunetti said, shaking the folder in the general direction of Patta's office, 'if we left your job description alone, as written.'

'Ah,' was all she said, but the smile grew even warmer.

'And didn't worry about what to call the help you give us.'

Signorina Elettra leaned forward and reached for the folder. Brunetti handed it to her. 'I was wondering if it would be possible to check and see if this method of killing has been used before and, if so, by whom and on whom?'

'The garotte?'

'Yes.'

She shook her head in little angry movements. 'If I hadn't been so busy feeling sorry for myself, I would have thought of that,' she said. Then, quickly, 'All of Europe or only Italy, and how far back?'

'Start with Italy and if you don't come up with anything spread out, beginning with the south.' It seemed to Brunetti a Mediterranean way of killing a person. 'Go back five years. Then ten if you don't find anything.'

She turned and flicked her computer to life, and Brunetti was struck by how completely an extension of her mind he had come to believe it. He smiled and left her office, leaving her to it, wondering if this was more sexist behaviour on his part, or if it degraded her in some way for him to think of her as being somehow part of a computer. On the steps, he found himself laughing, as it were, out loud, aware of what life with a zealot could do to a man and happy to realize he didn't care.

Vianello was standing outside his office when he got back, obviously waiting for him. 'Come in, Sergeant. What is it?'

The sergeant followed Brunetti into the room. 'Iacovantuono, sir.' When Brunetti didn't respond, Vianello went on, 'The people in Treviso have been asking around.'

'Asking around about what?' Brunetti enquired and waved the other man to a chair.

'About his friends.'

'And his wife?' Brunetti asked. There could be no other reason for Vianello's visit.

Vianello nodded.

'And?'

'It seems that woman who called was right, sir, though they still haven't located her. They fought.' He sat quietly and listened. Vianello continued, 'One woman who lives in the next building said that he beat her, that she was in the hospital once.'

'And was she?'

'Yes. She fell down in the bathroom, or at least that's what she said.' Both of them had heard many women say that.

'Did they check the times?' he asked, knowing he didn't have to explain further.

'The man found her on the stairs at twenty to twelve. Iacovantuono arrived at work a little after eleven.' Before Brunetti could say anything, Vianello continued, 'No, no one knows how long she was lying there.'

'Who's been asking?'

'That one we spoke to when we were up there the first time, Negri. When I told him about the phone call we had, he said he'd already begun talking to the neighbours. It's routine for them, too. I told him we thought the call was false.'

'And?'

Vianello shrugged. 'No one saw him leave for work. No one knows exactly when he arrived. No one knows how long she was lying there.'

Though so many things had happened since he'd last seen him, Brunetti still had a clear memory of the face of the *pizzaiolo*, his eyes dark with grief. 'There's nothing we can do,' he finally told Vianello.

'I know. But I thought you'd like to be put in the picture.'

Brunetti nodded his thanks, and Vianello went back down to the officers' room.

Half an hour later, Signorina Elettra knocked on his door. She came in, holding a few sheets of paper in her right hand.

'Is that what I think it is?' he asked.

She nodded. 'There have been three murders similar to this in the last six years. Two were Mafia hits, or appear to have been.' She came over to his desk and placed the first two papers side by side in front of him and pointed to the two names. 'One in Palermo and one in Reggio Calabria.'

Brunetti read the names and the dates. One man had been found on the beach, another in his car. Both had been strangled with a thin piece of what was probably plastic-coated wire: no threads or fibres were found around the neck of either victim.

She put another piece of paper beside the other two. Davide Narduzzi had been killed in Padova a year ago and a Moroccan street vendor had been accused of the crime. He had disappeared, however, before he could be arrested. Brunetti read the details: it looked as if Narduzzi had been taken from the back and strangled before he could react. The same description fitted the two other murders. And that of Mitri.

'The Moroccan?'

'No trace.'

'Why is this name familiar?' Brunetti asked.

'Narduzzi?'

'Yes.'

Signorina Elettra placed the last piece of paper

in front of Brunetti. '"Drugs, armed robbery, assault, association with the Mafia, and suspicion of blackmail,"' she read from the list of the accusations that had been brought against Narduzzi during his brief life. 'Think of the sort of friends a man like this would have. No wonder the Moroccan disappeared.'

Brunetti had been reading quickly to the bottom of the page. 'If he ever existed.'

'What?'

'Look at that,' he said, pointing to one of the names on the list. Two years before, Narduzzi had been involved in a fight with Ruggiero Palmieri, a supposed member of one of the most violent criminal clans in northern Italy. Palmieri had ended up in the hospital, but had refused to press charges. Brunetti knew enough about men like this to be aware that such a matter would be settled privately.

'Palmieri?' Signorina Elettra asked. 'It's a name I don't know.'

'Just as well. He's never worked – if that's the right word – here. Thank God.'

'You know him?'

'I met him once, years ago. Bad. A bad man.'

'Would he do this?' she asked, tapping a finger on the other two papers.

'I think that's his job, eliminating people,' Brunetti answered.

'Then why would this other one, Narduzzi, cause trouble with him?'

Brunetti shook his head. 'I have no idea.' He read through the three brief reports again, then got to his feet. 'Let's see what you can find out about

Palmieri,' he said and went down to her office with her.

It wasn't very much, unfortunately. Palmieri had gone into hiding a year ago, after being identified as one of three men involved in the robbery of an armoured car. Two guards had been wounded, but the thieves had not succeeded in getting the more than eight billion lire being transported in the truck.

Reading between the lines, Brunetti could see that no great expenditure of police energy or resource would have been made to find Palmieri: no one had been killed, nothing had been taken. But now they were dealing with murder.

Brunetti thanked Signorina Elettra and went down to Vianello's office. The sergeant sat with his head lowered over a stack of papers, his forehead resting on his two cupped palms. No one else was in the room, so Brunetti watched him for a while, then approached the desk. Vianello heard him and looked up.

'I think I'd like to call in some favours,' Brunetti said with no introduction.

'From whom?'

'People in Padova.'

'Good people or bad people?'

'Both. How many do we know?'

If Vianello was flattered to be included in the plural, he gave no sign of it. He thought for a while and finally answered, 'A couple. Of both sorts. What are we going to ask them?'

'I'd like to know about Ruggiero Palmieri.' He saw the name register with Vianello and watched as he began to search for the names of anyone, good or bad, who might be able to tell them something about him.

'What sort of information do you want?' Vianello asked.

'I'd like to know where he was when these men died,' said Brunetti, putting the papers Signorina Elettra had given him on Vianello's desk. 'And I'd like to know where he was the night Mitri was murdered.'

Vianello raised his chin in enquiry and Brunetti explained, 'I've heard that he's a paid killer. He had trouble with someone named Narduzzi a few years ago.' Vianello nodded to show that he recognized the name.

'Remember what happened to him?' Brunetti asked.

'Dead. But I forget how.'

'Strangled, perhaps with an electrical cord.'

'And these two?' Vianello asked, nodding down at the documentation.

'The same.'

Vianello put the papers on top of the ones on his own desk and read through them carefully. 'I never heard of either one of these. The Narduzzi murder was about a year ago, wasn't it?'

'Yes. In Padova.' The police there had probably been glad to see the last of Narduzzi. Certainly the investigation had never stretched as far as Venice. 'Can you think of anyone who might know something?'

'There's that man you worked with, the one from Padova.'

'Della Corte,' Brunetti supplied. 'I'd already thought of him. He probably knows some bad people he can ask. But I wondered if you knew anyone.'

'Two,' Vianello stated, offering no explanation.

'All right. Ask them.'

'What can I offer them in return, Commissario?'

Brunetti had to think about this for a while and consider both the favours he might be able to ask of other policemen and the ones he could safely extend himself. Finally he said, 'I'll owe them a favour and if anything happens to them in Padova, so will della Corte.'

'It's not a great deal,' Vianello said, honestly sceptical.

'It's the best they're going to get.'

20

The next hour was filled with phone calls to and from Padova as Brunetti contacted police and *Carabinieri* and engaged in the delicate business of calling in some of the favours he had accumulated during his years in the police. Most of these calls were made from his office to other offices. Della Corte agreed to ask around in Padova and said he'd be willing to match Brunetti's offer of a favour in return for any help they were given. After he was finished with these, he left the Questura, walked out to a bank of public telephones on the Riva degli Schiavoni, and from there used up a small stack of fifteen-thousand-lire telephone cards ringing the *telefonini* of various petty and not so petty criminals with whom he had dealt in the past.

He knew, as did all Italians, that many of these calls could be, perhaps were even now being, intercepted and recorded by various agencies of the State, so he never gave his name and always spoke in the most oblique way, saying only that a certain person in Venice was interested in the whereabouts of Ruggiero Palmieri but no, most decidedly no, he did not want to make contact, nor did he want Signor Palmieri to learn that questions were being asked about him. His sixth call, to a drug dealer whose son Brunetti had not arrested after being attacked by the boy the day after his father's last conviction some years ago, said he would see what he could do.

'And Luigino?' Brunetti asked to show that there were no hard feelings.

'I've sent him to America. To study business,' the father said before he hung up. That probably meant Brunetti would have to arrest him the next time he met him. Or perhaps, empowered by his degree in business management from some prestigious American university, he would rise to great heights in the organization and thus pass into realms where he would hardly be likely to be subject to arrest by a humble *commissario di polizia* from Venice.

Using the last of his phone cards and reading her number from a piece of paper, Brunetti called Mitri's widow and, as he had on the day after Mitri's death, listened to a recorded message saying that the family, burdened with grief, was accepting no messages. He switched the phone to the other ear and searched in his pocket until he found a piece of paper with Mitri's brother's number, but there, too, he heard only a message. On a whim, he decided to pass by Mitri's apartment and see if anyone else from the family was there.

He took the 82 to San Marcuola and easily found his way to the building. He rang the bell and soon heard a man's voice on the intercom, asking who he was. He said he was from the police, gave his rank but not his name, heard nothing for a moment, then was told to come in. The salt was still busy with its corrosive work, and paint and plaster lay in small piles on the stairs as before.

At the top a man in a dark suit stood just inside the open door. He was tall and very thin, with a narrow face and short dark hair just going grey at the temples. When he saw Brunetti, he stepped back to allow him to enter and extended his hand. 'I'm Sandro Bonaventura,' he said, 'Paolo's brother-in-law.' Like his sister, he chose to speak Italian, not Veneziano, though the underlying accent was audible.

Brunetti shook hands and, still not giving his name, entered the apartment. Bonaventura led him into a large room at the end of the short corridor. He noticed that the floor in this room was covered with what looked like the original oak boards, not parquet, and the curtains in front of the double windows appeared to be genuine Fortuny cloth.

Bonaventura motioned to a chair and, when Brunetti was seated, sat opposite him. 'My sister isn't here,' he began. 'She and her granddaughter have gone to stay a few days with my wife.'

'I had hoped to speak to her,' Brunetti said. 'Have you any idea when she'll be back?'

Bonaventura shook his head. 'She and my wife are very close, as close as sisters, so we asked her to come and stay with us when . . . when this happened.' He looked down at his hands and shook his head slowly, then up again and met Brunetti's eyes. 'I can't believe it happened, not to Paolo. There was no reason, none at all.'

'There very often isn't any reason, if a person comes in on a robber and he panics . . .'

'You think it was a robbery? What about the note?' Bonaventura asked.

Brunetti paused before he answered, 'It could be that the robber chose him because of the publicity caused by the travel agency. He could have had the note with him, planned to leave it there after the robbery.'

'But why bother?'

Brunetti had no idea at all and found the suggestion ridiculous. 'To divert us from looking for a professional thief,' he invented.

'That's impossible,' Bonaventura said. 'Paolo was killed by some fanatic who thought he was responsible for something he had no idea was going on. My sister's life has been ruined. It's just crazy. Don't talk to me about thieves who come equipped with notes and don't waste your time going around looking for them. You should be looking for the crazy person who did this.'

'Did your brother-in-law have any enemies?' Brunetti asked.

'No, of course not.'

'I find that strange,' Brunetti said.

'What do you mean?' Bonaventura demanded, leaning forward in his chair, putting himself into Brunetti's space.

'Please, don't be offended, Signor Bonaventura.' Brunetti put a placating palm between them. 'I mean that Dottor Mitri was a businessman, and a successful one. I'm certain that in the course of his years he had to make decisions that displeased people, angered them.'

'People don't kill one another because of a bad business deal,' Bonaventura insisted.

Brunetti, who knew how often they did, said nothing for a while. Then: 'Can you think of anyone he might have had difficulty with?'

'No,' Bonaventura replied instantly and, after a longer period of reflection, added, 'No one.'

'I see. Are you familiar with your brother-in-law's business? Do you work with him?'

'No. I manage our factory in Castelfranco Veneto. Interfar. It's mine, but it's registered under my sister's name.' He saw that Brunetti was not satisfied with this and added, 'For tax reasons.'

Brunetti nodded in what he thought was a very priestlike way. He sometimes believed that a person in Italy could be excused any horror, any enormity, simply by saying that it was done for tax reasons. Wipe out your family, shoot your dog, burn down the neighbour's house: so long as you said you did it for tax reasons, no judge, no jury, would convict. 'Did Dottor Mitri have any involvement in the factory?'

'No, not at all.'

'What kind of factory is it, if I might ask?'

Bonaventura didn't seem to find the question strange. 'Of course you might ask. Pharmaceuticals. Aspirin, insulin, many homeopathic products.'

'And are you a pharmacist, to oversee the operations?'

Bonaventura hesitated before answering, 'No, not at all. I'm just a businessman. I add up the columns of figures, listen to the scientists who prepare the formulas and try to figure out strategies for successful marketing.'

'You don't need a background in pharmacology?' Brunetti asked, thinking of Mitri, who had been a chemist.

'No. It's just a question of making managerial decisions. The product is irrelevant: shoes, ships, sealing wax.'

'I see,' Brunetti said. 'Your brother-in-law was a chemist, wasn't he?'

'Yes, I think so, originally, at the start of his career.'

'But no longer?'

'No, he hasn't worked as one for years.'

'What did he do, then, at his factories?' Brunetti wondered if Mitri had also been a believer in managerial strategies.

Bonaventura got to his feet. 'I'm sorry to be abrupt with you, Commissario, but I've got things to do here and these are questions I really can't answer. I think it would be better if you contacted the directors of Paolo's factories. I truly don't know anything about his businesses or how he ran them. I'm sorry.'

Brunetti stood. It made sense. The fact that Mitri had once been a chemist didn't necessitate his taking a part in the day-to-day running of the factories. In the multifaceted world of business, a man no longer needed to know anything about what a business did in order to run it. Just think of Patta, he told himself, to see how true that was. 'Thank you for your time,' he said, again extending his hand towards Bonaventura. Bonaventura shook it and led him back to the entrance hall, where they parted, leaving Brunetti to walk to the Questura through the back streets of Cannaregio, to him the most beautiful neighbourhood in the city. Which meant, he supposed, in the world.

By the time he got back, most of the staff had gone to lunch, so he contented himself with leaving a note on Signorina Elettra's desk, asking her to see what she could find out about Mitri's brother-in-law, Alessandro Bonaventura. As he straightened up and took the liberty of slipping open her top drawer to replace the pencil he'd used, he thought of how much he'd like to leave a message on her e-mail. He had no idea how it worked or what he'd have to do to send her something, but still he wanted to do it, if only to show her that he was not the technological Neanderthaler she seemed to consider him. After all, Vianello had learned; he saw no reason why he couldn't become computer literate. He had a degree in law; that surely must count for something.

He looked at the computer: silent, toasters

stilled and screen dark. How difficult could it be? But, perhaps, the saving thought came to him, perhaps, like Mitri, he was more suited to be the man behind the scenes than the one who understood the day-to-day workings of the machines. With that salve fresh on his conscience, he went down to the bar at the bridge to have a tramezzino and a glass of wine, and wait for the others to get back from lunch.

That happened closer to four than to three, but Brunetti had long since abandoned any illusions about the level of industry on the part of the people with whom he worked, so it didn't trouble him at all to sit quietly in his office for more than an hour, reading that day's paper, even checking his horoscope, curious about the blonde stranger he was going to meet and happy to learn that he 'was soon going to have some good news'. He could use some.

His intercom rang shortly after four and he picked it up, knowing it would be Patta, interested that things could have happened so quickly, curious to learn what the Vice-Questore wanted.

'Could you come down to my office, Commissario?' his superior asked and Brunetti replied politely that he was already on his way.

Signorina Elettra's jacket hung on the back of her chair, and a list of names and what appeared to be numbers stood in neat lines on her computer screen, but there was no sign of her. He knocked on Patta's door and entered at the sound of his voice.

And found Signorina Elettra seated in front of Patta's desk, legs primly pressed together, a notebook resting on her lap, pencil raised as Patta's last word hung in the air. Because it was only the shouted '*Avanti*' telling Brunetti to enter, she did not take note of it.

Patta barely acknowledged Brunetti's arrival, giving him the slightest of nods, and returned his attention to his dictation. 'And tell them that I do not want . . . No, make that read, "I will not tolerate . . ." I think that has a more forceful sound, don't you, Signorina?'

'Absolutely, Vice-Questore,' she said, eyes on what she was writing.

'I will not tolerate', Patta went on, 'the continued use of police boats and vehicles in unauthorized trips. If a member of the staff . . .' Here he broke off to add in a more casual style, 'Would you look and see what ranks are entitled to use the boats and cars and add it, Signorina?'

'Of course, Vice-Questore.'

'Requires the use of police transportation, he is to . . . excuse me, Signorina?' Patta broke off in response to the confusion on her face as she glanced up at those last words.

'Perhaps it would be better to say "that person", sir,' she suggested, 'to avoid the sound of sexual prejudice, as if only men had the authority to requisition boats.' She lowered her head and turned a page of her notebook.

'Of course, of course, if you think it wisest,' Patta agreed and continued, '. . . that person is to fill out the required forms and see that they are approved by the appropriate authority.' His whole manner changed and his face became less imperious, as though he'd told his chin to stop looking like Mussolini's. 'If you'd be so kind, check and see who it is that's supposed to authorize it and add their name to the memo, would you?'

'Of course, sir,' she said and wrote a few more words. She looked up and smiled. 'Will that be all?'

'Yes, yes,' Patta said. As Brunetti watched, he actually leaned forward in his chair as she rose, as if the sympathetic force of his motion could help her to her feet.

At the door, she turned and smiled at them both. 'I'll have that first thing tomorrow morning, sir,' she said.

'Not before?' Patta asked.

'I'm afraid not, sir. I've got the budget for our office's expenses for next month to calculate.' Her smile blended regret with sternness.

'Of course.'

Without another word, she left, closing the door behind her.

'Brunetti,' Patta said with no preamble, 'what's been happening with the Mitri case?'

'I spoke to his brother-in-law today,' Brunetti began, curious to see if Patta had heard about that yet. The blankness in his face suggested that he had not, so Brunetti continued, 'I've also learned that there have been three other murders in the last few years using what might have been a plastic-coated wire of some sort, perhaps electrical. And all the victims seem to have been taken from behind, the way Mitri was.'

'What sort of crimes were they?' Patta asked. 'Like this?'

'No, sir. It would seem that they were executions, probably Mafia.'

'Then', Patta said, dismissing the possibility out of hand, 'they can have nothing to do with this. This is the work of a lunatic, some sort of fanatic driven to murder by . . .' Here Patta either lost the thread of his argument or recalled to whom he was speaking, for he suddenly stopped.

'I'd like to pursue the possibility that there is some connection between the murders, sir,' Brunetti said, just as if Patta had not spoken.

'Where did they happen?'

'One in Palermo, one in Reggio Calabria and the most recent in Padova.'

'Ah.' Patta sighed audibly. After a moment he explained, 'If they are related, that would make it likely it's not ours, wouldn't it? That it's really the police in those other cities who should be looking at our crime as part of the series?'

'That's entirely possible, sir.' Brunetti did not bother to mention that the same would hold true for the Venetian police: that they also should look into the series.

'Well, then alert them, all of them, to what's happened and let me know when you get an answer from them.'

Brunetti had to admit the genius of the solution. The investigation of the crime had been farmed out, tossed back to the police of those other cities, so Patta had done the officially correct, the bureaucratically efficient, thing: he had passed it on to the next desk and in so doing had fulfilled his own duty or, more important, would be perceived to have done, should his decision ever be questioned. Brunetti got to his feet. 'Of course, sir. I'll contact them immediately.'

Patta bowed his head in polite dismissal. It was seldom that Brunetti, a headstrong, difficult man, would prove so amenable to reason.

21

When Brunetti emerged from Patta's office, he found Signorina Elettra just slipping into her jacket. Her purse and a shopping bag stood side by side on the top of her desk, and her coat lay beside them. 'And the budget?' Brunetti asked when he saw her.

'That,' she said with what sounded like a snort of amusement. 'It's the same every month. Takes me five minutes to print it out. All I do is change the name of the month.'

'Doesn't anyone ever question it?' Brunetti asked, thinking of what the fresh flowers alone must cost them.

'The Vice-Questore did, a while ago,' she said, reaching for her coat.

Brunetti picked it up and held it for her as she

slipped it on. Neither of them saw fit to remark that the office in which she worked would be open for another three hours. 'What did he say?'

'He wanted to know why we were spending more money every month on flowers than on office supplies.'

'And what did you tell him?'

'I apologized and told him I must have exchanged the amounts in each column and that it wouldn't happen again.' She reached down and picked up her handbag, slipping the long leather strap over her shoulder.

'And?' Brunetti couldn't stop himself from asking.

'It hasn't happened again. That's the first thing I do when I make out the report every month. I switch the amounts spent on flowers and office supplies. He's much happier now.' She picked up the shopping bag – Bottega Veneta, he observed – and started towards the door of her office.

'Signorina,' he began, awkward about asking. 'Those names?'

'In the morning, Commissario. It's being taken care of.' So saying, she pointed to her computer with her chin, one hand occupied with the shopping bag and the other busy pushing back a lock of hair.

'But it's off,' Brunetti said.

She closed her eyes for the barest fraction of a second, but he saw her do it. 'Believe me, Commissario. In the morning.' His acquiescence was not immediate, so she added, 'Remember: I'm your eyes and nose, Commissario. Anything that can be found will be here tomorrow first thing.'

Though the door to the office was open, Brunetti went to stand by it, as if to see her safely through. '*Arrivederci, Signorina. E grazie.*'

With a smile she was gone.

For a while, Brunetti stood there and wondered what he should do with the rest of the day. He lacked Signorina Elettra's offhand courage, so he went back up to his office. On his desk he found a scribbled note saying that Conte Orazio Falier wanted him to get in touch.

'It's Guido,' he said when he heard the Count answer with his name.

'I'm glad you called. Can we talk?'

'Is it about Paola?' Brunetti asked.

'No, it's about that other matter you asked me to look into. I spoke to someone with whom I do a certain amount of banking, and he said a large amount of cash flowed into and out of one of Mitri's foreign accounts until about a year ago.' Before Brunetti could respond, the Count said, 'He spoke of a total of five million francs.'

'Francs?' Brunetti enquired. 'As in Switzerland?'

'Not France,' the Count said in a tone that put the French franc on a par with the Latvian lat.

Brunetti knew better than to ask where or how his father-in-law had obtained this information and was wise enough to trust it absolutely. 'Is this the only account?'

'It's the only one I've found out about,' the Count answered. 'But I've asked a few more people and might have something else to tell you later in the week.'

'Did he say where this money came from?'

'He said the deposits came in from a number of countries. Wait a minute and I'll tell you; I've got it written down somewhere.' The phone was put down and Brunetti pulled a piece of paper towards him. He heard footsteps walk away, then return. 'Here it is,' the Count began. 'Nigeria, Egypt, Kenya, Bangladesh, Sri Lanka and the Ivory Coast.' There was a long pause after which he said, 'I tried fitting various things into it: drugs, weapons, women. But there's always something wrong, one of them doesn't·fit.'

'They're too poor, for one thing,' Brunetti mused.

'Exactly. But that's where the money came from. There were other amounts, much smaller, from European countries and some from Brazil, but the bulk of it came from those places. That is, it always came in from those countries in local currencies, then some was sent back there, but in dollars, always dollars.'

'But to the same countries?'

'Yes.'

'How much went back?'

'I don't know.' Before Brunetti could ask, the Count said, 'That's all the information he was willing to give. It's all he owed me.'

Brunetti understood. There would be nothing more; no sense going on about it. 'Thank you,' he said.

'What do you suppose it means?'

'I don't know. I'll have to think about it.' He decided to ask the Count for more help. 'And there's someone I have to find.'

'Who?'

'A man called Palmieri, a professional killer, or as close to one as is possible.'

'What has this got to do with Paola?' the Count wanted to know.

'He might have had something to do with Mitri's murder.'

'Palmieri?'

'Yes, Ruggiero. I think he's originally from Portogruaro. But the last we heard was that he might be in Padova. Why do you ask?'

'I know a lot of people, Guido. I'll see what I can find out.'

For a moment Brunetti wanted to tell the Count to be careful, but a man didn't get to be where he was without having made caution the habit of a lifetime.

'I spoke to Paola yesterday,' the Count said. 'She seems fine.'

'Yes.' Brunetti, suddenly conscious of how miserly that sounded, added, 'If what I'm beginning to suspect is true, she didn't have anything to do with Mitri's death.'

'Of course she didn't have anything to do with his death,' came the instant answer. 'She was with you that night.'

Brunetti quelled his first reaction and spoke calmly: 'I mean in the sense she'd intend, not the way we would – that her actions spurred someone on to kill him.'

'Even if that were true . . .' the Count began, but suddenly lost interest in arguing the hypothetical case and said in his normal tone, 'I'd see what I could find out about what he had to do with those countries.'

'I will.' Brunetti made a polite farewell and put down the phone.

Kenya, Egypt and Sri Lanka all had problems with outbursts of murderous violence, but nothing Brunetti had read suggested there was any common cause there, for all the accused groups seemed to have entirely different goals. Raw materials? Brunetti didn't know enough about them to be able to guess what they had that a voracious West would want.

He looked down at his watch and saw that it was after six; certainly a full commissario, particularly one who was still officially on something called administrative leave, could go home.

On the way, he continued to mull it over, once even stopping to pull out the list of countries and study it again. He went into Antico Dolo and had a glass of white wine and two cuttlefish, but he was so preoccupied that he barely tasted them.

He returned before seven to an empty house. He went into Paola's study and pulled down their atlas of the world, then sat on the shabby old sofa with the book open on his knees, contemplating the multicoloured maps of the various regions. He shifted lower in the sofa and rested his head against the back.

Paola found him like that half an hour later,

deeply asleep. She called his name once, then again, but it wasn't until she went and sat beside him that he woke.

Sleeping during the day always left him dull and stupid, with a strange taste in his mouth.

'What's this?' she said, kissing his ear and pointing down at the book.

'Sri Lanka. And here's Bangladesh, Egypt, Kenya, the Ivory Coast and Nigeria,' he said, turning the pages quietly.

'Let me guess – the itinerary for our second honeymoon tour through the poverty capitals of the world?' she asked with a laugh. Then, seeing his smile, she went on, 'And I get to play Lady Bountiful, bringing along pockets full of small coins to toss to the local population as we visit the sights?'

'That's interesting,' Brunetti said, closing the book but leaving it on his knees. 'That the first thing you think of, too, is poverty.'

'It's either that or civil unrest in most of those places.' She paused for a moment, then added, 'Or cheap Imodium.'

'Huh?'

'Remember when we were in Egypt and had to get Imodium?'

Brunetti remembered the trip to Egypt, a decade ago, when both of them had come down with fierce diarrhoea and had lived for two days on yoghurt, rice, and Imodium. 'Yes,' he answered. He thought he remembered, but he wasn't sure.

'No prescription, no questions and cheap, cheap, cheap. If I'd had a list of the things my neurotic friends take, I could have done my Christmas shopping for the next five years.' She saw that he didn't share the joke, so she returned her attention to the atlas. 'But what about those countries?'

'Mitri received money from them, large amounts. Or his companies did. I don't know which because it all went to Switzerland.'

'Doesn't all money, in the end?' she asked with a tired sigh.

He shook himself free of the thought of those countries and placed the atlas beside him on the sofa. 'Where are the kids?' he asked.

'They're having dinner with my parents.'

'Should we go out, then?' he asked.

'You're willing to take me out again, be seen with me?' she asked lightly.

Brunetti wasn't sure how much she was joking so he answered, 'Yes.'

'Where?'

'Anywhere you like.'

She sprawled against him, pushing her legs out in front of her, beside his longer ones. 'I don't want to go far. How about a pizza at Due Colonne?'

'What time will the kids be back?' he asked, placing his hand on hers.

'Not before ten, I'd say,' she answered, glancing down at her watch.

'Good,' he said, raising her hand to his lips.

22

Neither the next day nor the day after that did Brunetti learn anything about Palmieri. An article appeared in *Il Gazzettino* remarking that there had been no progress in the Mitri case but making no mention of Paola, so Brunetti concluded that his father-in-law had indeed been speaking to people he knew. The national press was similarly silent; then eleven people were burned to death in an oxygen chamber in a hospital in Milan, and the story of Mitri's murder was abandoned in favour of denunciations of the entire national health system.

As good as her word, Signorina Elettra gave him three pages of information about Sandro Bonaventura. He and his wife had two children, both at university; a house in Padova, and an apartment in Castelfranco Veneto. The factory there, Interfar, as Bonaventura had said, was in his sister's name. The money to purchase it, a year and a half ago, was paid over one day after a large withdrawal was made from Mitri's account in a Venetian bank.

Bonaventura had worked as a director of one of Mitri's factories until he had taken over the directorship of the one that his sister owned. And that was all: an *Urtext* of middle-class success.

On the third day, a man was caught robbing the post office in Campo San Polo. After five hours of questioning, he admitted to the robbery of the bank at Campo San Luca. He was the same man whose photo Iacovantuono had identified the first time and whom, after his wife's death, he had failed to recognize. While he was being questioned, Brunetti went down and had a look at him through the one-way glass in the door of the room where the interrogation was taking place. He saw a short, stocky man with thinning brown hair; the man Iacovantuono had described the second time had red hair and was at least twenty kilos lighter.

He went back up to his office and called Negri in Treviso, who was handling the case of Signorina Iacovantuono's death – the case that wasn't a case – and told him they had an arrest for the bank robbery and that he looked nothing like the man Iacovantuono had identified the second time.

After he gave this information, Brunetti asked, 'What's he doing?'

'He goes to work, comes home and feeds his

children, then to the cemetery every other day to put fresh flowers on her grave,' Negri answered.

'Is there another woman?'

'Not yet.'

'If he did it, he's good,' Brunetti stated.

'I found him absolutely convincing when I spoke to him. I even sent a team to protect them, to keep an eye on the house, the day after she died.'

'They see anything?'

'Nothing.'

'Let me know if something turns up,' Brunetti said.

'Not likely, is it?'

'No.'

Usually Brunetti's instinct warned him when someone was lying or trying to hide something, but with Iacovantuono he had had no idea, no sense of warning or suspicion. Brunetti found himself wondering which he wanted to be true: did he want to be right, or did he want the little pizza cook to be a murderer?

His phone rang while his hand was still on it and pulled him away from speculation he knew to be idle.

'Guido, it's della Corte.'

Brunetti's mind flashed to Padova, to Mitri and to Palmieri. 'What is it?' he asked, too excited to dredge up polite formulas and all thought of Iacovantuono driven from his mind.

'We might have found him.'

'Palmieri?'

'Yes.'

'Where?'

'North of here. It looks like he's driving a truck.'

'A truck?' Brunetti repeated stupidly. It seemed too banal for a man who might have killed four people.

'He's using a different name. Michele de Luca.'

'How did you find him?'

'One of our blokes on the drug squad asked around and one of his little people told him. He wasn't sure, so we sent someone up there and he came back with a fairly positive identification.'

'Is there any chance that Palmieri might have seen him?'

'No, this guy's good.' Neither spoke for a while, then della Corte asked, 'Do you want us to bring him in?'

'I'm not sure that's going to be very easy.'

'We know where he's living. We could go in at night.'

'Where is he?'

'Castelfranco Veneto. He's driving a truck for a pharmaceutical factory called Interfar.'

'I'll come out there. I want to get him. Tonight.'

In order to join the Padova police in the raid on Palmieri's apartment, he had to lie to Paola. During lunch he told her that the police in Castelfranco had a suspect in custody and wanted him to go up there to speak to him. When she asked why he had to stay away all night, he explained that the man wouldn't be brought in until quite late and there were no trains back after ten. In fact, there were to be none at all in the Veneto that afternoon. The air-traffic controllers at the airport having declared a wildcat strike at noon, closing the airport and forcing incoming planes to reroute and land at Bologna or Trieste, the railway engineers' union decided to strike in sympathy with their demands, so all train traffic in the Veneto came to a halt.

'Take a car, then.'

'I am, as far as Padova. That's all Patta will authorize.'

'That means he doesn't want you to go up there, doesn't it?' she said, looking at him across the plates and leavings of the meal. The children had already disappeared into their rooms, so they could talk openly. 'Or doesn't know you're going.'

'That's partly it,' he said. He took an apple from the fruit basket and began to peel it. 'Good apples,' he remarked as he tasted the first piece.

'Don't be evasive, Guido. What's the other reason?'

'I might have to talk to him for a long time, so I don't know when I'd get back.'

'And they've got this man and all they're doing is bringing him in so you can grill him?' she asked sceptically.

'I've got to ask him about Mitri,' Brunetti said – an evasion, rather than an outright lie.

'Is this the man who did it?' she enquired.

'It could be. He's wanted for questioning in at least three other murders.'

'Questioning? What does that mean?'

Brunetti had read the files, so he knew there was a witness who had seen him with the second victim on the night of his death. And there was the fight with Narduzzi. And now a job driving a truck for a pharmaceutical factory. In Castelfranco. Bonaventura's company. 'He's implicated.'

'I see,' she said, hearing in his tone his reluctance to be more explicit. 'Then you'll be home tomorrow morning?'

'Yes.'

'What time are you leaving?' she asked in sudden concession.

'Eight.'

'Are you going back to the Questura?'

'Yes.' He was going to add something about needing to hear if the man had been formally charged, but he stopped himself. He didn't like lying, but it seemed better than having her worry about his deliberately putting himself in danger. If she knew, she'd tell him that both his age and his rank ought to spare him that.

He had no idea if he'd get any sleep that night, or where, but he went back into the bedroom and put a few things into a small bag. He opened the left door of the large walnut *armadio*, the one Count Orazio had given them as a wedding present, and pulled out his keys. He used one of them to unlock a drawer, then another for a rectangular metal box. He pulled out his pistol and holster, and slipped them into his pocket, then carefully relocked both the box and the drawer.

He thought of the *Iliad*, then, and of Achilles donning his armour before going into battle with Hector: mighty shield, greaves, spear, sword and helmet. How paltry a thing and how ignoble seemed this little metal object resting against his hip, the gun Paola always referred to as a portable penis. And yet how quickly had gunpowder put an end to chivalry and all those ideas of glory descended from Achilles. He stopped at the door and told himself to pay attention: he was going to Castelfranco on business and he had to say goodbye to his wife.

Though he hadn't seen della Corte for some years, he recognized him the instant he walked into the Padova Questura: same dark eyes and unruly moustache.

Brunetti called to him and the policeman turned towards the sound of his name. 'Guido,' he said and walked over quickly. 'How good to see you again.'

Talking of what they'd done during the last few years, they walked down to della Corte's office. There, the talk of old cases continued over coffee and, when it was finished, they started to discuss the plans for that night. Della Corte suggested they wait until after ten to leave Padova, which would get them to Castelfranco by eleven, when they were supposed to meet the local police, who had been told about Palmieri and had insisted they come along.

When they got to the Castelfranco Questura a few minutes before eleven, they were met by Commissario Bonino and two officers wearing jeans and leather jackets. They had prepared a map of the area surrounding the apartment where Palmieri lived, complete down to every detail: spaces in the parking lot beside the house, location of all of the doors in the building, even a floor plan of his apartment.

'How did you get this?' Brunetti asked, letting his admiration speak in his voice.

Bonino nodded to the younger of the policemen. 'The building is only a few years old,' he explained, 'and I knew the plans would have to be down at the *ufficio catasto*, so I went there this afternoon and asked for a blueprint of the second floor. He's on the third, but the layout is the same.' He stopped talking and looked down at the blueprint, calling their attention back to it.

It appeared simple enough: a single staircase led up to a corridor. Palmieri's apartment was at the end of the hall. All they had to do was place two men below his windows, one at the bottom of the stairs, and that left two to go in and two to work as back-up in the hallway. Brunetti was about to observe that seven seemed excessive, but then he remembered that Palmieri might have killed four men and said nothing.

Two cars parked a few hundred metres beyond the building and they all got out. The two young men in jeans had been chosen to go up to the apartment with Brunetti and della Corte, who would make the actual arrest. Bonino said he'd cover the stairs and the two from Padova moved off to take their places under the three fat pines that stood between the apartment building and the street, one man with a view of the front entrance, the other of the rear.

Brunetti, della Corte, and the two officers took the stairs. At the top they split up. The men in jeans stayed inside the stairwell, one propping open the door with his foot.

Brunetti and della Corte walked to Palmieri's door. Silently, Brunetti tried the handle, but the door was locked. Della Corte knocked twice, not loudly. Silence. He knocked again, louder this time. Then he called, 'Ruggiero, it's me. They sent me to get you. You've got to get out. The police are on the way.'

Inside, something fell over and smashed, probably a light. But none came from under the door. Della Corte banged on it again. 'Ruggiero, *per l'amor di Dio*, would you get out here. Move.'

Inside, there were more noises; something else fell, but this was heavy, a chair or a table. They heard shouts coming from below, probably the other policemen. At the sound of their voices both Brunetti and della Corte moved away from the doorway and stood with their backs against the wall.

And not a moment too soon. One, two more, then two further bullets tore through the thick wood of the door. Brunetti felt something sting his face and when he looked down he saw two drops of blood on the front of his coat. Suddenly the two young officers were kneeling on either side of the door, their pistols in their hands. Like an eel, one of them flipped over on to his back, pulled his legs up to his chest and, with piston-like force, slammed his feet into the door, just where it joined the jamb. The wood gave and his second kick sent it slamming open. Even before the door hit the inside wall, the man on the floor had spun himself like a top into the room.

Brunetti had barely raised his pistol when he heard two shots, then a third, ring out. After that, nothing. Seconds passed, then a man's voice called, 'All right, you can come in.'

Brunetti slipped through the doorway, della Corte following close behind. The policeman knelt behind an overturned sofa, his pistol still in his hand. On the floor, his head visible in a wedge of light that spilled in from the hallway, lay a man Brunetti recognized as Ruggiero Palmieri. One arm was flung ahead of him, fingers aimed at the door and the freedom that once lay behind it; the other was crumpled invisibly under him. Where his left ear should have been was only a red hole, the exit wound from the second of the policeman's bullets.

23

Brunetti had been a policeman too long and had seen too many things go wrong to want to waste time in trying to figure out what had happened or attempting to devise an alternate plan that might have worked. But the others were younger and hadn't learned yet that failure taught very little, so he listened to them for a while, not really paying attention but agreeing with whatever they said while he waited for the lab crew to arrive.

At one point, when the officer who had shot Palmieri lay on the floor to study the angle at which he had entered the apartment, Brunetti went into the bathroom, moistened his handkerchief with cold water, and wiped at the small cut on his cheek where a sliver of wood from the shattering door had sliced off a piece of flesh about the size of one of the buttons on his shirt. Still holding his handkerchief, he opened the small medicine chest, looking for a piece of gauze or something to stop the bleeding, and found that it was full, but not with plasters.

Guests were said to explore the medicine cabinets in the bathrooms they used; Brunetti had never done it. He was amazed at what he saw: three rows of all manner of medicines, at least fifty boxes and bottles, vastly different in packaging and size, but all carrying the distinctive adhesive label with the nine-digit number from the Ministry of Health. But no bandages. He pushed the door closed and went back into the room where Palmieri lay.

During the time Brunetti had been in the bathroom, the other policemen had arrived and now the young ones were gathered at the door, where they replayed the shooting, with, it seemed to a disgusted Brunetti, the same enthusiasm they'd give to rewatching an action video. The older men stood separately and silently in various parts of the room. Brunetti went over to della Corte. 'Can we begin to search the place?'

'Not until their crime crew gets here, I think.'

Brunetti nodded. It didn't make any difference, really. Only in time, and now they had all night to do it. He just wished they would hurry, so that the body would be taken away. He avoided looking at it, but as time passed and the young men ceased their retelling of the tale, that grew harder. Brunetti had just moved over towards the window when he heard footsteps on the stairs and turned to see the familiar uniforms come into the apartment: technicians, photographers, the minions of violent death.

He went back to the window and studied the cars in the parking lot and those few that still drove by at this hour. He wanted to call Paola, but she believed him safely in bed in some small hotel, so he did not. He didn't turn round when the photographer's flash went off repeatedly, nor at the arrival of what must be the *medico legale*. No secrets here.

It wasn't until after he heard the grunts of the two white-jacketed men from the morgue and the thunking noise as one of the handles of their litter hit the door jamb that he turned. He went over to Bonino, who was talking to della Corte, and asked, 'Can we begin?'

He nodded. 'Of course. The only thing on the body was a wallet. With more than twelve million lire in it, in the new five-hundred-thousand-lire notes.' And before Brunetti could enquire, he added, 'It's on the way to the lab to be finger-printed.'

'Good,' Brunetti said, then, turning to della Corte, he asked, 'Shall we take the bedroom?'

Della Corte nodded and together they walked into the other room, leaving the local men to take care of the rest of the apartment.

They had never searched a room together before, but by unspoken consent della Corte went to the cupboard and began going through the pockets of the slacks and jackets hanging there.

Brunetti started on the dresser, not bothering

with plastic gloves, not after he saw the fingerprint powder dusted over its every surface. He opened the first drawer and was surprised to find Palmieri's things lying in neat piles, then wondered why he had assumed that a killer had to be untidy. Underwear was folded into two piles, socks balled and, Brunetti thought, arranged by colour.

The next held sweaters and what looked like gym clothes. The bottom one was empty. He pushed it closed with his foot and turned to look at della Corte. Only a few things hung in the wardrobe: he could see a down parka, some jackets, and what looked like trousers inside the clear plastic wrap of a dry-cleaner's.

A carved wooden box sat on the dresser, its lid left closed by the technician, whose dust fluttered up in a small grey cloud as Brunetti lifted it open. Inside he found a stack of papers, which he took out and placed on the top of the dresser.

Carefully, he began to read through them, laying each one aside as he finished it. He found electric and gas bills, both made out in the name of Michele de Luca. There was no phone bill, but that was explained by the *telefonino* that lay beside the wooden box.

Below that he discovered an envelope addressed to R. P.: the top, where it had been carefully slit open, was grey with much handling. Inside, dated more than five years before, he found a piece of light-blue paper with a message written in a careful hand. 'I'll see you at the restaurant at eight tomorrow. Until then, the beating of my heart will tell me how slowly the minutes are passing.' It was signed with the letter M. Maria? Brunetti wondered. Mariella? Monica?

He folded the letter and slipped it back into the envelope, then placed it on top of the bills. There was nothing else in the box.

He looked round at della Corte. 'You find anything?'

He turned from the cupboard and held up a large set of keys. 'Only these,' della Corte said, holding them up. 'Two of them are for a car.'

'Or a truck?' suggested Brunetti.

Della Corte nodded. 'Let's go and see what's parked outside,' he suggested.

The living-room was empty, but Brunetti noticed two men in the small kitchen angle, where the refrigerator and all the cabinets stood open. Light and noise spilled from the bathroom, but Brunetti doubted that they would find anything.

He and della Corte went downstairs and out into the parking lot. Glancing back, they saw that many of the lights in the building were turned on. At his movement, someone in the apartment above Palmieri's opened the window and shouted down, 'What's going on?'

'Police,' della Corte called back. 'Everything's all right.'

For a moment Brunetti wondered if the man at the window would ask more, demand an explanation for the shots, but the Italian fear of authority manifested itself, and he pulled his head back in and closed the window.

There were seven vehicles parked behind the

building, five cars and two trucks. Della Corte began with the first of these, a grey panel truck with the name of a toy store printed on the side. Below it, a teddy bear rode a hobby-horse off to the left. Neither key fitted. Two spaces along sat a grey Iveco panel truck with no name on it. The key didn't fit, nor did either key fit any of the cars.

As they were turning to go back to the apartment they both noticed a line of garage doors at the far end of the parking lot. It took them a while, testing all the keys on the locks of the first three doors, but finally one of them slid into that of the fourth door.

As he swung it open and saw the white panel truck parked there, della Corte said, 'I guess we'd better call the lab boys back.'

Brunetti glanced down at his watch and saw that it was well after two. Della Corte understood. He took the first car key and tried it on the lock of the driver's door. It turned easily and he pulled it open. He took a pen from the front pocket of his jacket and used it to switch on the light above the seat. Brunetti took the keys from him and went round to the other door. He opened it, selected a smaller key, and opened the glove compartment. From the look of it the clear plastic envelope inside contained nothing but insurance and ownership papers. Brunetti took his own pen and pulled the envelope towards the light, turning it so that he could read the papers. The truck was registered to 'Interfar'.

With the top of the pen he pushed the papers back and closed the glove compartment, then he shut the door. He locked it and went round to the rear doors. The first key opened them. The back compartment of the truck was filled, almost to the roof, with large cardboard boxes bearing what Brunetti recognized as the Interfar logo, the letters I and F, in black, on either side of a red caduceus. Paper labels were pasted to the centre of the boxes and above them, in red, was printed 'Air Freight'.

All were sealed with tape and Brunetti didn't want to cut them open: leave it for the lab boys. He put one foot on to the back bumper and leaned his head into the compartment close enough to read the label on the first box.

'TransLanka', it read, with an address in Colombo.

Brunetti stepped back on to the ground, closed and locked the doors. Together with della Corte he went back into the apartment.

The policemen were standing around inside, obviously finished with their search. As they came in, one of the local officers shook his head and Bonino said, 'Nothing. There was nothing on him and nothing in this place. Never seen anything like it.'

'Do you have any idea how long he's been here?' Brunetti asked.

The taller of the two officers, the one who had not fired, answered, 'I spoke to the people in the next apartment. They said they think he moved in about four months ago. Never gave any trouble, never made any noise.'

'Until tonight,' his partner quipped, but everyone ignored him.

'All right,' Bonino said, 'I think we can go home now.'

They left the apartment and started down the steps. At the bottom, della Corte stopped and asked Brunetti, 'What are you going to do? Do you want us to take you to Venice on our way back?'

It was generous of him, would surely delay them an hour to make the trip to Piazzale Roma, then back out to Padova. 'Thanks, but no,' Brunetti said. 'I want to talk to the people at the factory, so there's no sense in my going with you. I'd just have to come back.'

'What'll you do?'

'I'm sure there's a bed at the Questura,' he answered and walked towards Bonino to ask.

As he lay in that bed, thinking himself too tired to drop off, Brunetti tried to remember the last time he had gone to sleep without Paola beside him. But he could recollect only the time he'd woken without her there, the night all this had been shattered into life. Then he was asleep.

Bonino provided him with a car and driver the next morning and, by nine thirty, he was at the Interfar factory, a large, low building at the centre of an industrial park on one of the many highways that radiated out from Castelfranco. Utterly without concession to beauty, the buildings sat a hundred metres back from the road, besieged on all sides, like a piece of dead meat by ants, by the cars of the people who worked within.

He asked the driver to find a bar and offered him coffee. Though he'd slept deeply, Brunetti had not slept enough, and he felt dull and irritable. A second cup seemed to help; either the caffeine or the sugar would keep him going for the next few hours.

He entered the Interfar office a little after ten and asked if he could speak to Signor Bonaventura. On request, he gave his name and stood by the desk while the secretary called to enquire. Whatever answer she received was immediate and, as soon as she heard it, she set down the phone, got to her feet and led Brunetti through a door and down a corridor covered with light-grey industrial carpeting.

She stopped at the second door on the right, knocked, and opened it, and stood back to allow him to enter. Bonaventura sat behind a desk covered with papers, pamphlets and brochures. He stood when Brunetti came in but remained behind his desk, smiling as he approached, then leaned across it to shake Brunetti's hand. Both sat.

'You're far from home,' Bonaventura said amiably.

'Yes. I came up here on business.'

'Police business, I take it.'

'Yes.'

'Am I part of that police business?' Bonaventura asked.

'I think so.'

'If so, it's the most miraculous thing I've ever known to happen.'

'I'm not sure I understand you,' Brunetti said.

'I spoke to my foreman a few minutes ago and was just about to call the *Carabinieri*.' Bonaventura glanced down at his watch. 'No more than five minutes ago and here you are, a policeman, already on my doorstep, as if you'd read my mind.'

'And may I ask why you were going to call them?'

'To report a theft.'

'Of what?' Brunetti asked, though he was pretty certain he knew.

'One of our trucks is gone, and the driver hasn't reported for work.'

'Is that all?'

'No. My foreman tells me it looks as if a good deal of merchandise is missing, too.'

'About a truckload, would you say?' Brunetti asked in a neutral voice.

'If the truck and the driver are both missing, that would make sense, wouldn't it?' He wasn't angry yet, but Brunetti had plenty of time to push him there.

'Who is this driver?'

'Michele de Luca.'

'How long has he worked for you?'

'I don't know, half a year or so. I don't concern myself with things like that. All I know is that I've seen him around here for months. This morning, the foreman told me his truck wasn't in the lot where it's supposed to be and that he hadn't shown up.'

'And the missing merchandise?'

'De Luca left here yesterday afternoon with a full shipment and was supposed to bring the truck back here before he went home, then be here at seven this morning to pick up another shipment. But he never turned up and the truck wasn't parked where it was supposed to be. The foreman phoned him, but there was no answer on his *telefonino*, so I decided to call the *Carabinieri*.'

It seemed to Brunetti an excessive response to what could well have been no more than an employee being late for work, but then he reflected that Bonaventura actually hadn't made the call, so he kept his surprise to himself, waiting to see how the scene would be played. 'Yes, I can see that you would,' he said. 'What was in the shipment?'

'Pharmaceuticals, of course. That's what we make here.'

'And where were they going?'

'I don't know.' Bonaventura looked down at the papers cluttering his desk. 'I've got the shipping invoices here somewhere.'

'Could you find them?' Brunetti asked, nodding towards the documents.

'What difference does it make where they were going?' Bonaventura demanded. 'The important thing is to find this man and get the shipment back.'

'You don't have to worry about him,' Brunetti said, though he suspected that Bonaventura was also lying about wanting the shipment back.

'What does that mean?'

'He was shot and killed by the police last night.'

'Killed?' Bonaventura repeated, sounding genuinely amazed.

'The police went to question him, and he opened fire on them. He was killed when they entered his

254

apartment.' Then, quickly changing the subject, Brunetti asked, 'Where was he taking this shipment?'

Disconcerted by the sudden switch of topic, Bonaventura hesitated before finally answering, 'To the airport.'

'The airport was closed yesterday. The air-traffic controllers were on strike,' Brunetti told him, but from his expression he could tell Bonaventura already knew. 'What instructions did he have if he couldn't deliver?'

'It's the same for all the drivers: bring the truck back here and put it in the garage.'

'Could he have put it in his own garage?'

'How do I know what he could have done?' Bonaventura exploded. 'The truck's gone and, from what you tell me, the driver's dead.'

'The truck's not gone,' Brunetti said softly and watched Bonaventura's face as he heard the statement. He saw him attempt to hide his shock, then as quickly try to change his expression, but all he achieved was a grotesque parody of relief.

'Where is it?' Bonaventura asked.

'By now, in the police garage.' He waited to see what Bonaventura would ask and, when he remained silent, added, 'The boxes were in the back.'

Bonaventura tried to disguise his shock, tried and failed.

'Not sent to Sri Lanka, either,' Brunetti said, then added, 'Do you think you could help me find those shipping invoices now, Signor Bonaventura?'

'Certainly.' Bonaventura bowed his head to the

task. Idly, aimlessly, he moved papers from one side of his desk to the other, then stacked them all in a pile and went through them one by one. 'That's strange,' he said, looking up at Brunetti after he had gone through the lot, 'I can't find them here.' He got to his feet. 'If you'll wait, I'll ask my secretary to get them for me.'

Before he could take his first step towards the door, Brunetti got to his feet. 'Perhaps you could call her,' he suggested.

Bonaventura turned his mouth up in a smile. 'It's really the foreman who has them, and he's back at the loading dock.'

He started to move past Brunetti, who put out a hand and placed it on his arm. 'I'll come with you, Signor Bonaventura.'

'That's really not necessary,' he said with another motion of his mouth.

'I think it is,' was all Brunetti answered. He had no idea what his legal rights were here, how much authority he had to detain or follow Bonaventura. He was outside Venice, even beyond the borders of the province of Venezia, and no charges had been contemplated, much less brought, against Bonaventura. But none of that mattered to him. He stepped aside and let Bonaventura open the door of his office, then followed him down the corridor, away from the front of the building.

At the back, a door opened out on to a long cement loading dock. Two large trucks were backed up to it, rear doors open, and four men were wheeling dollies filled with cartons from doors further down the dock into the open backs of the trucks. They looked up when they saw the two men emerge from the door but then went back to their work. Below them, between the trucks, two men stood and talked, hands in the pockets of their jackets.

Bonaventura walked over to the edge of the loading dock. When they looked up at him, he called down to one of them, 'De Luca's truck's been found. The shipment's still in it. This policeman wants to see the shipping invoices.'

He had barely finished the word 'policeman', when the taller of the two men sprang away from the other and reached inside his jacket. His hand came out carrying a pistol, but the instant Brunetti saw him move, he ducked back inside the still-open door and pulled his own pistol from its holster.

Nothing happened. There was no noise, no shot, no shouting. He heard footsteps, the slamming of what sounded like a car door and another; then a large motor spring into life. Instead of going out on to the dock again to see what was happening, Brunetti ran back through the corridor and out of the front door of the building, where his driver was waiting, motor running to keep the car warm, while he read *Il Gazzettino dello Sport*.

Brunetti pulled open the passenger door and leaped into the car, seeing the driver's panic disappear when he recognized him. 'A truck, going out of the far gate. Swing round and follow it.' Even before Brunetti's hand reached the car phone, the driver had tossed his paper into the back seat and had the car in gear and spinning round towards the back of the building. As they rounded the corner, the driver pulled the wheel sharply to the left, trying not to hit one of the boxes that had fallen from the open doors of the truck. But he couldn't avoid the next one and their left wheels passed over it, splattering it open and spewing small bottles in a wide wake behind them. Just beyond the gates Brunetti could see the truck moving off down the highway in the direction of Padova, its rear doors flapping open.

The rest was as predictable as it was tragic. Just beyond Resana, two *Carabinieri* vehicles were drawn up across the road, blocking traffic. In an attempt to get past them, the driver of the truck swerved to the right and on to the high shoulder of the road. Just as he did, a small Fiat, driven by a woman on the way to pick up her daughter at the local *asilo*, slowed at the sight of the police block. The truck, as it came back on to the road, swung into the other lane and slammed into her car broadside, killing her instantly. Both men, Bonaventura and the driver, had been wearing their seat-belts, so neither was hurt, though they were severely shaken by the crash.

Before they could free themselves from their seat-belts, they were surrounded by *Carabinieri*, who pulled them down from the truck and flung them face forward against its doors. They were quickly surrounded by four *Carabinieri* carrying machine-guns. Two others ran to the Fiat but saw there was nothing to be done.

Brunetti's car pulled up and he got out. The scene was absolutely silent, unnaturally so. He heard his own footsteps approaching the two men, both of whom were breathing heavily. Something metal clanged to the ground from the direction of the truck.

He turned to the sergeant. 'Put them in the car,' was all he said.

24

There was some discussion about where the men should be taken for questioning, whether back to Castelfranco, which had territorial jurisdiction over the scene of their capture, or back to Venice, from which city the investigation had begun. Brunetti listened to the police discuss this for a few moments, then cut into the conversation with a voice of iron: 'I said put them in the car. We're taking them back to Castelfranco.' The other policemen exchanged glances, but no one contradicted him and it was done.

Standing in Bonino's office, Bonaventura was told he could call his lawyer, and when the other identified himself as Roberto Sandi, the foreman of the factory, he was told the same. Bonaventura named a lawyer in Venice with a large criminal practice and asked that he be allowed to call him. He ignored Sandi.

'And what about me?' Sandi asked, turning to Bonaventura.

Bonaventura refused to answer him.

'What about me?' Sandi said again.

Still, Bonaventura remained silent.

Sandi, who spoke with a pronounced Piedmontese accent, turned to the uniformed officer next to him and demanded, 'Where's your boss? I want to talk to your boss.'

Before the officer could respond, Brunetti stepped forward and said, 'I'll be in charge of this,' even though he wasn't sure of that at all.

'Then it's you I want to talk to,' Sandi stated, looking at him with eyes that glimmered with malice.

'Come now, Roberto,' Bonaventura suddenly broke in, placing his hand on Sandi's arm. 'You know you can use my lawyer. As soon as he gets here we can talk to him.'

Sandi shook off his hand with a muttered curse. 'No lawyer. Not yours. I want to talk to the cop.' He addressed Brunetti: 'Well? Where can we talk?'

'Roberto,' Bonaventura said in a voice he tried to make menacing, 'you don't want to talk to him.'

'You don't tell me what to do any more,' Sandi spat. Brunetti turned, opened the door to the office, and took Sandi into the hall. One of the uniformed officers followed them outside and led them down the corridor. Opening a door to a small interview room, he said, 'In here, sir,' and waited for them to enter.

Brunetti saw a small desk and four chairs. He sat down, waiting for Sandi. When the latter was seated, Brunetti glanced across at him and said, 'Well?'

'Well what?' Sandi asked, still filled with the anger Bonaventura had provoked.

'What do you want to tell me about the shipments?'

'How much do you already know?' Sandi demanded.

Ignoring the question, Brunetti enquired, 'How many of you are involved in it?'

'In what?'

Instead of answering immediately, Brunetti propped his elbows on the table, folded his hands, and rested his mouth on the backs of his knuckles. He remained like that for almost a minute, staring across at Sandi, then repeated, 'How many of you are involved in it?'

'In what?' Sandi asked again, this time allowing himself a small smile, the sort children use when they ask a question they think will embarrass the teacher.

Brunetti raised his head, placed his hands on the desk, and pushed himself to his feet. Saying nothing, he went to the door and knocked on it. A face appeared beyond the wire-mesh screen. The door opened and Brunetti left the room, closing the door behind him. He signalled the guard to remain there and went back up the corridor. He peered into the room where Bonaventura was being held and saw that he was still there, though no one was with him. Brunetti stood at the one-way window for ten minutes, watching the man inside. Bonaventura sat sideways to the door, trying not to look at it or to respond to the sound of footsteps when people walked by.

Finally Brunetti opened the door without knocking and went in. Bonaventura's head shot round. 'What do you want?' he asked when he saw Brunetti.

'I want to talk to you about the shipments.'

'What shipments?'

'Of drugs. To Sri Lanka. And Kenya. And Bangladesh.'

'What about them? They're perfectly legitimate. We've got all the documents at the office.'

Brunetti had no doubt of that. He stayed by the door, leaning back against it, one foot propped up behind him, arms folded over his chest. 'Signor Bonaventura, do you want to talk about this or do you want me to go back and have a word with your foreman again?' Brunetti made his voice sound very tired, almost bored.

'What's he been saying?' Bonaventura asked before he could stop himself.

Brunetti stood and watched him for a time, then said again, 'I want to talk about those shipments.'

Bonaventura decided. He folded his arms in imitation of Brunetti. 'I'm not saying anything until I see my lawyer.'

Brunetti left and went back to the other room, where the same officer was standing outside. He stepped away from the door when he saw the commissario and opened it for him.

Sandi looked up at Brunetti when he came in.

Without preamble he said, 'All right. What do you want to know?'

'The shipments, Signor Sandi?' Brunetti asked, naming him for the microphones hidden in the ceiling, and came to sit opposite him. 'Where do they go?'

'To Sri Lanka, like the one last night. And Kenya, and Nigeria. Lots of other places.'

'Always medicines?'

'Yes, just like you'll find in that truck.'

'What kind of medicines are they?'

'A lot of it's for hypertension. There's some cough syrup. And mood elevators. They're very popular in the Third World. I think they can buy them without a prescription. And antibiotics.'

'How much of it is good?'

Sandi shrugged this away, uninterested in such details. 'I don't have any idea. Most of it is outdated or discontinued, things we can't sell in Europe any more, at least not here in the West.'

'What do you do? Change the labels?'

'I'm not sure. No one told me about that. All I did was ship it.' Sandi's voice had the calm assurance of the practised liar.

'But surely you must have some idea,' Brunetti urged, softening his voice as if to suggest that a man as clever as Sandi would have figured it out. When Sandi didn't respond to this, Brunetti made his voice less soft: 'Signor Sandi, I think it's time you started telling me the truth.'

Sandi considered this, staring at an implacable Brunetti. 'I suppose that's what they do,' he finally said. With a toss of his head in the direction of the room where Bonaventura sat, he added, 'He also owns a company that collects expired medicines from pharmacies. For disposal or destruction. They're supposed to be burned.'

'What happens?'

'Boxes get burned.'

'Boxes of what?'

'Old papers. Some are just empty boxes. Enough to get the weight right. No one much cares what's inside, so long as the weight's right.'

'Isn't someone supposed to watch what they do?'

Sandi nodded. 'There's a man from the Ministry of Health.'

'And?'

'He's been taken care of.'

'So these things, these drugs, that don't get burned, they're taken to the airport and sent to the Third World?'

Sandi nodded.

'It gets sent?' Brunetti repeated, needing a recording to be made of Sandi's answers.

'Yes.'

'And paid for?'

'Of course.'

'But it's already outdated or expired?'

Sandi seemed offended by the question. 'A lot of those things last much longer than the Ministry of Health says. A great deal of it's still good. Probably lasts longer than what's written on the package.'

'What else gets shipped?'

Sandi watched him with clever eyes but said nothing.

'The more you tell me now, the better it will be for you in the future.'

'Better how?'

'The judges will know that you were willing to help us and that will count in your favour.'

'What guarantee do I have?'

Brunetti shrugged.

Neither man spoke for a long time, then Brunetti asked, 'What else did you ship?'

'Will you tell them I helped you?' Sandi asked, not content until he could cut a deal.

'Yes.'

'What guarantee do I have of that?'

Brunetti shrugged again.

Sandi lowered his head for a moment, traced a figure on the surface of the desk with his finger, then looked up. 'Some of the stuff in the shipments is useless. Nothing. Flour, or sugar, or whatever it is they use when they make placebos. And coloured water or oil in the ampoules.'

'I see,' Brunetti said. 'Where is all this made?'

'There.' Sandi raised a hand to point into the distance, towards where Bonaventura's factory might or might not be. 'There's a crew that comes in at night and works. They make the stuff up, label it, and box it. Then it gets taken to the airport.'

'Why?' Brunetti asked and, when he saw that Sandi didn't understand his question, added, 'Why placebos? Why not the real medicine?'

'The hypertension medicine – especially that – is very expensive. The raw material or chemical or whatever it is. And some of the stuff for diabetes, or at least I think it's that. So to cut costs they use the placebos. Ask him about it,' he said, pointing in the direction where he had left Bonaventura.

'And at the airport?'

'Nothing. Everything's just as it should be. We put it on planes and it gets delivered at the other end. There's never any trouble there. Everything's been taken care of.'

'Is all this commercial?' Brunetti asked, possessed of a new idea. 'Or is some of it given away?'

'We sell a lot of it to the charity agencies, if that's what you're asking. The UN, things like that. We give them a discount and take the rest off taxes. As charity.'

Brunetti stopped himself from showing any reaction to what he was hearing. It sounded as though Sandi knew far more than how to drive a truck to the airport. 'Does anyone from the UN check the contents?'

Sandi gave a snort of disbelief. 'All they care about is getting their picture taken when they deliver the stuff to the refugee camps.'

'Do you send the same things to the camps that you send in the regular shipments?'

'No, most of that's for diarrhoea and amoebic dysentery. And a lot of cough syrup. When they're so thin, that's what they have to worry about, those things.'

'I see,' Brunetti ventured. 'How long have you been doing this?'

'A year.'

'In what capacity?'

'Foreman. I used to work for Mitri, in his

factory. But then I came up here.' He grimaced at this, as if the memory caused him pain or regret.

'Did Mitri do the same thing?'

Sandi nodded. 'He did until he sold his factory.'

'Why would he sell it?'

Sandi shrugged. 'I heard that he had an offer he couldn't refuse. That is, that wasn't safe to refuse. That some big people wanted to buy it.'

Brunetti understood perfectly what he meant and was surprised to see that, even here, Sandi was afraid to name directly the organization these 'big people' represented. 'So he sold it?'

Sandi nodded. 'But he recommended me to his brother-in-law.' Mention of Bonaventura called him back from the realms of memory. 'And I damn the day I started to work for him.'

'Because of this?' Brunetti asked, waving a hand at the bleak sterility of the room in which they sat and all it represented.

Sandi nodded.

'What about Mitri?' Brunetti asked.

Sandi contracted his eyebrows in an expression of feigned confusion.

'Was he involved in the factory?'

'Which one?'

Brunetti raised his hand and brought his fist smashing down on the table just in front of Sandi, who jumped as if Brunetti had struck him. 'Don't waste my time, Signor Sandi,' Brunetti shouted. 'Don't waste my time with stupid questions.' When Sandi didn't answer, he leaned towards him and demanded, 'Do you understand me?'

Sandi nodded.

'Good,' Brunetti said. 'What about the factory? Did Mitri have a part in it?'

'He must have.'

'Why?'

'He came up here sometimes to prepare a formula or to tell his brother-in-law how something had to look. He'd have to make sure that what went into the packages looked right.' He glanced up at Brunetti and added, 'I didn't understand all of that, but I think that's why he came.'

'How often?'

'Maybe once a month, sometimes more often than that.'

'How did they get on?' Brunetti asked, then, to prevent Sandi from asking who, he added, 'Bonaventura and Mitri?'

Sandi considered this for a while before he answered, 'Not well. Mitri was married to his sister, so they had to get along somehow, but I don't think either of them liked it.'

'What about Mitri's murder? What do you know?'

Sandi shook his head repeatedly. 'Nothing. Nothing at all.'

Brunetti let a long moment pass before he asked, 'And here at the factory, was there any talk?'

'There's always talk.'

'About the murder, Signor Sandi. Was there talk about the murder?'

Sandi remained silent, either trying to remember or weighing possibilities. Finally he mumbled, 'There was talk that Mitri wanted to buy the factory.'

'Why?'

'Why was there talk or why did he want to buy it?'

Brunetti took a deep breath and spoke calmly. 'Why did he want to buy it?'

'Because he was much better at it than Bonaventura. It was a mess with him running it. No one ever got paid on time. The records were hopeless. I never knew when the shipments were going to be ready to go out.' As Brunetti watched him, Sandi shook his head in tight-lipped disapproval, the perfect picture of a conscientious accountant, pushed beyond all patience by fiscal irresponsibility.

'You say you're foreman of the factory, Signor Sandi.' Sandi nodded. 'It sounds like you knew more about the running of it than the owner did.'

Sandi nodded again, as if not at all displeased to hear that someone would recognize this.

Suddenly there was a knock on the door and when it opened a crack Brunetti saw della Corte in the hall, signalling to him to come outside. As he stepped into the corridor, della Corte said, 'His wife's here.'

'Bonaventura's?' Brunetti asked.

'No, Mitri's.'

25

'How did she get here?' Brunetti asked. Seeing the confusion his question caused della Corte, he explained, 'I mean, how did she know to come here?'

'She said she was staying with his wife – Bonaventura's – and came up here when she heard he had been arrested.'

Brunetti's sense of time had been distorted by the events of the morning, and he was surprised when he glanced down at his watch and saw that it was almost two o'clock in the afternoon; hours had passed since they'd brought the two men to the police station, but he'd been too intent to notice. Suddenly he was overcome with hunger and felt a faint ringing through his entire body, as though he had been plugged into a mild electric current.

His impulse was to go and talk to her immediately, but he knew nothing good would come of it until he had eaten something or somehow stopped the tremors in his body. Was it age or stress that was doing this to him and should he be alarmed at the possibility that it might mean something else, some sickness that was looming over him? 'I have to eat something,' he said to della Corte, who was too surprised at what he heard to hide it.

'There's a bar on the corner. You can get a sandwich there.' He led Brunetti to the door of the building and pointed it out, then, saying he had to call Padova, he went back inside. Brunetti walked the half-block to the bar, where he had a sandwich he didn't taste and two glasses of mineral water that left him still feeling thirsty. At least it put an end to the tremors and he felt more in control of himself, but still worried that his physical response to the morning should have been so strong.

He walked back to the Questura, where he asked to be given the number of Palmieri's *telefonino*. When he had it, he rang Signorina Elettra, told her to drop whatever she was doing and get a list of all the calls made to and from Palmieri's phone in the last two weeks, as well as for the offices and homes of both Mitri and Bonaventura. He requested her to hold the line and asked the officer whose phone he was using where Palmieri's body had been taken. When he was told it was in the morgue of the local hospital, he instructed Signorina Elettra to tell Rizzardi and to get someone up there immediately to take tissue samples. He wanted them checked with the traces found under Mitri's nails.

When he had finished, he asked to be taken to Signora Mitri. After speaking to her that one time, Brunetti's instinct had been to believe that she knew nothing about her husband's death, so he had not sought to question her again. The fact that she had turned up here made him doubt the wisdom of that decision.

A uniformed officer met him at the door and took him down a corridor. He stopped in front of the room next to the one where Bonaventura was being held. 'His lawyer's in there with him,' he said to Brunetti, pointing towards the adjacent door. 'The woman's in here,' he added.

'Did they come together?' Brunetti asked.

'No, sir. He came in a little after she did, but they didn't recognize one another.'

Brunetti thanked him and stepped over to take a look through the one-way glass. A man sat facing Bonaventura, but all Brunetti could see was the back of his head and shoulders. He moved to the next door and stood a moment, studying the woman sitting inside.

He was struck, again, by her stoutness. Today she wore a woollen suit with a box-cut skirt that made no concession to fashion or style. It was the sort of suit women of her size, age and class had worn for decades, and it would probably be worn by them, or women like them, for decades to come. She wore little make-up and whatever lipstick she might have applied had been chewed away during the day. Her cheeks were rounded, as though she were puffing them up to make a funny face at a child.

She sat with her hands folded in her lap, knees tightly together, looking across at the window in the top of the door. She looked older than she had the last time, but Brunetti didn't know why that was so. His eyes met hers and he was disconcerted by the feeling that she was looking at him, though he knew very well that all she could see was a pane of seemingly black glass. Her eyes did not waver from his and he turned his away first.

He opened the door and went in. 'Good-afternoon, Signora.' He approached her and held out his hand.

She studied him, face neutral, eyes busy. She did not stand but extended her hand and shook his, neither lightly nor limply.

Brunetti sat opposite her. 'You've come to see your brother, Signora?'

Her eyes were childlike and filled with a confusion Brunetti believed was genuine. Her mouth opened and her tongue protruded nervously, licked at her lips, then retreated. 'I wanted to ask him . . .' she began, but did not complete the sentence.

'Ask him what, Signora?' Brunetti prompted.

'I don't know if I should be saying this to a policeman.'

'And why is that?' Brunetti leaned towards her a bit.

'Because,' she began, then paused for a moment. Then, as if she'd explained something and he'd understood, she said, 'I need to know.'

'What is it you need to know, Signora?' Brunetti nudged.

She pulled her lips tightly together and, as Brunetti watched, she turned herself into a toothless old woman. 'I need to know if he did it,' she finally said. Then, considering other possibilities, she added, 'Or had it done.'

'Are you speaking of your husband's death, Signora?'

She nodded.

For the hidden microphones and the tape that was recording all that was said in this room, Brunetti asked again, 'Do you think he might be responsible for his death?'

'I don't . . .' she began, then changed her mind and whispered, 'Yes,' so low that the microphones might not have caught it.

'Why do you think he was involved?' Brunetti asked.

She moved awkwardly in her chair and he saw her make a motion that he'd been watching women make for more than four decades: she half stood and pulled at the underside of her skirt, yanking out the wrinkles. Then she sat down again and pressed her ankles and knees together.

It seemed for a moment as though she hoped the gesture would suffice by way of answer, so Brunetti repeated, 'Why do you think he's involved, Signora?'

'They fought,' she measured out by way of response.

'About what?'

'Business.'

'Can you be more specific than that, Signora? What business?'

She shook her head a few times, insistent on displaying her ignorance. Finally she said, 'My husband never told me anything about his businesses. He said I didn't need to know.'

Again, Brunetti asked himself how many times he had heard this, and how many times it had been an answer structured to turn away guilt. But he believed this heavy-set woman was telling him the truth, found it entirely credible that her husband had not seen fit to share his professional life with her. He recalled the man he'd met in Patta's office: elegant, well-spoken, one might even say sleek. How odd to pair him with this little woman with her dyed hair and tight-fitting suit. He glanced down at her feet and saw that she was wearing a pair of stout-heeled pumps, their toes narrowed to a painful point. On her left foot, a large bunion had pushed its way into the leather and sat there like a section of an egg, the leather stretched tight across it. Was marriage the ultimate mystery?

'When did they fight, Signora?'

'All the time. Especially during the last month. I think something happened that made Paolo angry. They'd never got on well, not really, but because of the family and because of business, well, they rubbed along somehow.'

'Did anything particular happen during the last month?' he asked.

'I think there was an argument,' she said, her voice so soft that Brunetti again thought of future listeners to the tape.

'An argument between them, between your husband and your brother?'

'Yes.' She nodded repeatedly as she spoke.

'Why do you think that, Signora?'

'Paolo and he had a meeting at our apartment. It was two nights before it happened.'

'Before what happened, Signora?'

'Before my husband was . . . before he was killed.'

'I see. And why do you think there was an argument? Did you hear them?'

'Oh, no,' she answered quickly, looking up at him as if surprised at the suggestion that there could ever be raised voices in the house of Mitri. 'I could tell it from the way Paolo behaved when he came upstairs after they had talked.'

'Did he say anything?'

'Only that he was incompetent.'

'Was he talking about your brother?'

'Yes.'

'Anything else?'

'He said that Sandro was ruining the factory, ruining the business.'

'Do you know what factory he was talking about, Signora?'

'I thought he was talking about the one up here, in Castelfranco.'

'And why would your husband be interested in that?'

'There was money invested in it.'

'His money?'

She shook her head. 'No.'

'Whose money, Signora?'

She paused, considering how best to answer this. 'It was my money,' she finally said.

'Yours, Signora?'

'Yes. I brought a lot of money to the marriage. But it remained in my name, you see. Our father's will,' she added, gesturing vaguely with her right hand. 'Paolo always helped me decide what to do with it. And when Sandro said he wanted to buy the factory, they both suggested I invest in it. This was a year ago. Or perhaps two.' She broke off when she saw Brunetti's response to her vagueness. 'I'm sorry, but I don't pay much attention to these things. Paolo asked me to sign papers and the man at the bank told me what was happening. But I don't think I ever understood, not really, what the money was for.' She stopped and brushed at her skirt. 'It went to Sandro's factory, but because it was mine, Paolo always thought it belonged to him as well.'

'Do you have any idea of how much you invested in this factory, Signora?' She looked to Brunetti like a schoolgirl about to burst into tears because she couldn't remember the capital of Canada, so he added, 'If you have an idea, that is. We really don't need to know the exact amount.' This was true; it would all be found out later.

'I think it was three or four hundred million lire,' she answered.

'I see. Thank you,' Brunetti said, then asked, 'Did your husband say anything else that night, after he spoke to your brother?'

'Well.' She paused and, Brunetti thought, tried to remember. 'He said the factory was losing money. From the way he spoke, I think Paolo might have had money invested in it privately.'

'Aside from yours?'

'Yes. With just a note from Paolo. Nothing official.' When Brunetti was silent, she continued, 'I think Paolo wanted to have more control over the way they did things.'

'Did your husband give you any idea of what he was going to do?'

'Oh, no.' She was clearly surprised by the question. 'He never told me about things like that.' Brunetti wondered what sort of things he did tell her about but thought it best not to ask. 'Afterwards he went to his room and the next day he didn't mention it, so I thought, or I hoped, that he and Sandro had settled things.'

Brunetti responded instantly to her reference to 'his room', surely not the stuff of happy marriages. He worked his voice into a lower tone: 'Please forgive me for asking you this, Signora, but could you tell me what sort of terms you and your husband were on?'

'Terms?'

'You said he went to "his room", Signora,' Brunetti replied in a soft voice.

'Ah.' The quiet sound escaped her entirely involuntarily.

Brunetti waited. Finally he said, 'He's gone now, Signora, so I think you can tell me.'

She looked across at him and he saw the tears form in her eyes. 'There were other women,' she whispered. 'For years, other women. Once I followed him and waited outside her house, in the rain, for him to come out.' Tears flowed down her face, but she ignored them. They began to drop on to the front of her blouse, leaving long oval marks on the fabric. 'Once I had him followed by a detective. And I started to listen to his phone calls. Sometimes I'd play them back, hear him talking to other women. The same things he used to say to me.' Tears cut her off and she paused a long time, but Brunetti forced himself not to speak. Finally she went on, 'I loved him with my whole heart. From the first day I saw him. If Sandro did this . . .' Her eyes filled with tears again, but she brushed them away with both palms. 'Then I want you to know it and I want him to be punished. That's why I want to talk to Sandro.' She stopped, looking down.

'Will you come and tell me what he says?' she asked, eyes still on her hands, which lay quite still in her lap.

'I don't think I can do that until it's all over, Signora. But then I will.'

'Thank you,' she said, looking up, then down again. Suddenly she got to her feet and walked towards the door. Brunetti was there before her and opened it. He stepped back to allow her to pass through ahead of him. 'I'll go home, then,' she said and, before he could say anything, she walked out of the door, down the corridor and towards the entrance hall of the police station.

26

He went back to the desk of the officer whose phone he had used and, without bothering to ask permission, called Signorina Elettra again. As soon as she heard his voice, she told him the technician was already on the way to the Castelfranco morgue to take tissue samples, then asked him to give her a fax number. He put down the phone and went to the front desk, where he had the sergeant in charge write down the number. After giving it to Signorina Elettra, he remembered he had not called Paola that morning, so he dialled his home number. When no one answered, he left a message, saying that he was delayed in Castelfranco, but would be back later in the afternoon.

He sat down after that and lowered his head into his hands. A few minutes later he heard someone say, 'Excuse me, Commissario, but these just came in for you.'

He looked up and saw a young officer standing in front of the desk he had requisitioned. In his left hand he held the distinctive curling papers of a fax, quite a few of them.

Brunetti tried to smile at him and extended his hand to take the proffered papers. He set them on the desk and smoothed them as best he could with the edge of his hand. He read through the columns, glad to discover that Signorina Elettra had put an asterisk next to any call made between any of the numbers, then put the papers into three separate piles: Palmieri, Bonaventura, Mitri.

In the ten days before Mitri's murder, there had been repeated calls back and forth between Palmieri's *telefonino* and the Interfar phone, one of them lasting seven minutes. The day before the crime, at nine twenty-seven at night, a call was made from Bonaventura's home phone to Mitri's. This conversation went on for two minutes. On the night of the murder, at almost the same time, a call lasting fifteen seconds had been made from Mitri's phone to Bonaventura's. After that, there had been three from the factory to Palmieri's *telefonino* and a number between Bonaventura's and Mitri's homes.

He stacked the papers and went back down the hall. When he was let into the small room where he had last talked to Bonaventura, he found him sitting opposite a dark-haired man who had a small leather briefcase on the table beside him and a notebook in matching leather open in front of him. He turned round and Brunetti recognized Piero Candiani, a criminal lawyer from Padova. Candiani wore rimless glasses; behind them Brunetti saw a pair of dark eyes which combined in startling fashion, particularly in a lawyer, both intelligence and candour.

Candiani got to his feet and extended his hand. 'Commissario Brunetti,' he acknowledged and shook hands.

'Avvocato.' Brunetti nodded in the direction of Bonaventura, who hadn't bothered to get to his feet.

Candiani pulled out the remaining chair and waited for Brunetti to sit before resuming his own. Without preamble he said, flicking a negligent hand towards the ceiling, 'I assume our conversation is now being recorded.'

'Yes,' Brunetti acknowledged. Then, to save time, he recited the date and time, and gave their three names in a loud voice.

'I understand you've already spoken to my client,' Candiani began.

'Yes. I asked him about certain shipments of medicines which Interfar has been making to foreign countries.'

'Is this about EEC regulations?' Candiani asked.

'No.'

'Then what?'

Brunetti glanced across at Bonaventura, who now sat with his legs crossed, one arm draped over the back of his chair.

'It's about shipments to Third World countries.'

Candiani wrote something in his notebook.

Without raising his head he asked, 'And what interest do the police have in these shipments?'

'It would seem that many of them contained medicines which are no longer good. That is, they've expired or, in some cases, they contain useless substances which have been camouflaged to look like real medicines.'

'I see.' Candiani turned a page. 'And what evidence do you have in support of these accusations?'

'An accomplice.'

'Accomplice?' Candiani asked with barely disguised scepticism. 'And may I ask who this accomplice is?' The second time he pronounced the word, he gave it the heavy emphasis of doubt.

'The foreman of the factory.'

Candiani glanced across at his client, and Bonaventura shrugged his shoulders in confusion or ignorance. He pressed his lips together and, with a quick flickering of his eyes, blinked away the possibility. 'And you'd like to ask Signor Bonaventura about this?'

'Yes.'

'Is that all you want?' Candiani glanced up from his notebook.

'No. I'd also like to ask Signor Bonaventura what he knows about the murder of his brother-in-law.'

At this, Bonaventura's expression progressed to something akin to astonishment, but still he didn't speak.

'Why?' Candiani's head was bent once more over his notebook.

'Because we've begun to examine the possibility that he might somehow be implicated in Signor Mitri's death.'

'Implicated how?'

'That's exactly what I'd like Signor Bonaventura to tell me,' Brunetti replied.

Candiani looked up and across at his client. 'Would you like to answer the Commissario's questions?'

'I'm not sure I could,' Bonaventura said, 'but certainly I'm perfectly willing to give him any help I can.'

Candiani turned towards Brunetti. 'If you'd like to question my client, then, Commissario, I suggest you do it.'

'I'd like to know', Brunetti began, addressing Bonaventura directly, 'what involvement you had with Ruggiero Palmieri or, as he was known when he worked for your company, Michele de Luca.'

'The driver?'

'Yes.'

'As I told you before, Commissario, I saw him occasionally around the factory. But he was only a driver. I might have spoken to him once or twice, but nothing more than that.' Bonaventura did not enquire why Brunetti had asked.

'So you didn't have any dealings with him beyond the occasional contact you had there at work?'

'No,' Bonaventura said. 'I told you: he was a driver.'

'You never gave him any money?' Brunetti asked, hoping that Bonaventura's fingerprints would turn up on the bills in Palmieri's wallet.

'Of course not.'

'So the only time you saw him or spoke to him was when you met him in the factory?'

'That's what I just told you.' Bonaventura made no attempt to disguise his irritation.

Brunetti turned his attention to Candiani. 'I think that's all I want from your client for the moment.'

Both men were obviously surprised by this, but Candiani reacted first, got to his feet and flipped his notebook closed. 'Then may we leave?' he asked, reaching across the table and pulling the briefcase towards him.

Gucci, Brunetti noted. 'I think not.'

'I beg your pardon,' Candiani said, putting decades of courtroom astonishment into the words. 'And why not?'

'I imagine the Castelfranco police are going to have a number of charges to place against Signor Bonaventura.'

'Such as?' Candiani demanded.

'Fleeing from arrest, conspiracy to obstruct a police investigation, vehicular homicide, to name a few.'

'I wasn't driving,' Bonaventura broke in, his outrage audible in both words and tone.

Brunetti was looking at Candiani when the other man spoke, and he saw the flesh under the lawyer's eyes contract minimally, either in surprise or something harsher, he wasn't sure.

Candiani pushed the notebook into the brief-case and flipped it closed. 'I'd like to be sure that the Castelfranco police have decided this, Commissario.' Then, as if to remove any lack of faith those words might imply, he added, 'As a mere formality, of course.'

'Of course,' Brunetti repeated, also getting to his feet.

Brunetti knocked on the glass of the window to summon the officer who waited in the hall. Leaving Bonaventura inside, the two men left the interview room and went to speak to Bonino, who confirmed Brunetti's judgement that the Castelfranco police would indeed be pressing various serious charges against Bonaventura.

An officer accompanied Candiani back to the interview room to inform and say farewell to his client, leaving Brunetti with Bonino.

'Did you get it all?' Brunetti asked.

Bonino nodded. 'It's all new, the sound equipment. It'll pick up the smallest whisper, even heavy breathing. So yes, we've got it all.'

'And before I got there?'

'No. We can't turn it on until there's a police officer in the room. Lawyer–client privilege.'

'Really?' Brunetti asked, unable to mask his amazement.

'Really,' Bonino repeated. 'We lost a case last year because the defence could prove we listened to what the suspect said to his lawyer. So the Questore has ordered that there will be no exceptions. Nothing gets turned on until there's an officer in the room.'

Brunetti nodded at this, then asked, 'As soon as his lawyer's gone, can you fingerprint him?'

'For the money?'

Brunetti nodded.

'It's already done,' Bonino said with a small smile. 'Completely unofficially. He had a glass of mineral water earlier this morning and we lifted three good prints from it when he was finished.'

'And?' Brunetti asked.

'And our lab man says it's a fit, that at least two of the prints appear on some of the bills in Palmieri's wallet.'

'I'll check his bank, too,' Brunetti said. 'Those five-hundred-thousand-lire notes are still new. Most people won't even take them: too hard to change. I don't know if they keep a record of the numbers, but if they do . . .'

'He's got Candiani, remember,' Bonino said.

'You know him?'

'Everyone in the Veneto knows him.'

'But we've got the phone calls to a man he denies knowing well and we've got the prints,' Brunetti insisted.

'He's still got Candiani.'

27

And never had prophecy proven more true. The bank in Venice had a record of the numbers of the five-hundred-thousand-lire notes distributed on the day that Bonaventura withdrew fifteen million in cash from the bank, and the numbers of the notes found in Palmieri's wallet were among them. Any doubt that they were the same notes was removed by the presence of Bonaventura's fingerprints.

Candiani, speaking for Bonaventura, insisted that there was nothing at all strange in this. His client had withdrawn the money in order to pay back a personal loan his brother-in-law, Paolo Mitri, had made to him and had done so in cash, handing the money to Mitri the day after he made the withdrawal, the day he was murdered. The fragments of Palmieri's skin under Mitri's nails made it all perfectly clear: Palmieri had robbed Mitri and had prepared the note in advance in order to pull suspicion away from himself. He had killed Mitri, either by accident or by design, in the course of the robbery.

As to the phone calls, Candiani made short work of them by pointing out that the Interfar factory had a central number, so calls made from any extension would register as having come from that central number. Hence anyone, anywhere in the factory, could have made the calls to Palmieri's *telefonino*, just as he could have been calling the factory to do no more than report a delay in shipment.

Told of the phone call made to his number from Mitri's apartment on the night of the murder, Bonaventura remembered that Mitri had called that evening to invite him and his wife to dinner the following week. When it was pointed out that the call had lasted only fifteen seconds, Bonaventura recalled that Mitri had cut it short, saying someone had just rung the doorbell. He expressed horror at the realization that it must have been Mitri's killer.

Each man had had time to construct a story to explain their flight from the Interfar factory. Sandi said he'd taken Bonaventura's sudden warning that the police were there as a command to flee and that Bonaventura had run ahead of him to the truck. Bonaventura, for his part, insisted that Sandi had pointed the pistol at him and thus forced him into the truck. The third man said he'd seen nothing.

In the matter of the shipments of drugs, Candiani proved far less able to turn away the suspicions of the forces of justice. Sandi repeated and expanded his testimony and provided the names and addresses of the night-time crew that was brought in to fill and pack the false medicines. Because they were paid in cash, there were no bank records of their salaries, but Sandi produced time sheets with their names and signatures. He also gave the police an extensive list of past shipments: dates, contents, and destinations.

The Ministry of Health stepped in at this point. The Interfar factory was closed, the premises sealed, while inspectors opened and examined boxes, bottles and tubes. All the medicines in the central part of the factory were determined to be exactly what their labels stated them to be, but an entire section of the warehouse contained shipping crates filled with packages of substances which proved, upon examination, to have no medicinal value whatsoever. Three crates were filled with plastic bottles labelled as cough medicine. Upon examination, they were discovered to be made up of a mixture of sugar water and antifreeze, a combination which would prove harmful, perhaps lethal, to anyone who took it.

Other crates contained hundreds of boxes of medicines long past their expiry date; still others packages of gauze and sutures whose wrappings crumbled at a touch, so long had they been sitting unused in warehouses somewhere. Sandi provided the bills of loading and invoices which were to accompany these crates to their final destinations in lands racked by famine, war and pestilence, as well as a list of the prices to be paid for them by the international aid agencies so willing to distribute them to the suffering poor.

Removed from involvement in the case by a direct order from Patta, himself obeying one from the Minister of Health, Brunetti followed the investigation in the newspapers. Bonaventura admitted to some involvement in the sale of false medicines, though he insisted that the original plan and instigation had been Mitri's. When he'd bought Interfar, he'd hired much of his staff from the factory Mitri had been forced to sell: they had brought the rot and corruption with them, and Bonaventura had found himself helpless to stop them. When he had protested to Mitri, his brother-in-law had threatened to call in his personal loan and withdraw his wife's money from the factory, actions which would surely have led Bonaventura to financial ruin. Victim of his own weakness, then, and helpless in the face of Mitri's superior financial strength, Bonaventura had had no choice but to continue with the production and sale of these false medicines. To have protested would have caused bankruptcy and disgrace.

From all that he read, Brunetti inferred that, should Bonaventura's case ever reach trial, he would be subjected to a fine, not a particularly heavy one, for the labels of the Ministry of Health had never actually been changed or tampered with. Brunetti had no idea what law was broken by the sale of expired medicines, especially if that sale took place in some other country. The law was clearer on the falsification of medicines, but again the issue grew complicated by the fact that the medicines were not sold or distributed in Italy. All of this, however, he dismissed as worthless speculation. Bonaventura's crime was murder, not tampering with packages: the murder of Mitri and the murder of anyone who died as a result of the medicines he sold.

In this belief Brunetti stood alone. The papers were now fully convinced that Palmieri had killed Mitri, though nowhere was a retraction made of the original theory that his killer was a fanatic inflamed and encouraged to murder by Paola's action. The presiding magistrate decided not to press criminal charges against Paola, so the case was filed in the archives of the State.

A few days after Bonaventura was sent home, where he was to remain under house arrest, Brunetti sat in the living-room of his home, engrossed in Arrian's account of the campaigns of Alexander, when the phone rang. He lifted his head, listening to see if Paola would pick it up in her study. When it stopped after the third ring, he went back to his book and to Alexander's evident desire that his friends prostrate themselves before him as though he were a god. The charm of the book quickly tugged Brunetti back to that far-away place, that distant time.

'It's for you,' Paola said from behind him. 'A woman.'

'Hm?' Brunetti asked, looking up from the pages, but not yet fully there either in the room or in the present.

'A woman,' Paola repeated, standing by the door.

'Who?' Brunetti asked, slipping a used boat ticket into his book and setting it beside him on the sofa.

He was just pushing himself to his feet when Paola said, 'I've no idea. I don't listen to your calls.'

He froze, bent over like an old man with a bad back. '*Madre di Dio*,' Brunetti exclaimed. He stood and stared across at Paola, who remained at the door, giving him a strange look.

'What is it, Guido? Did you hurt your back?'

'No, no. I'm fine. But I think I've got it. I think I've got him.' He walked to the *armadio* and took out his coat.

When she saw him, Paola asked, 'What are you doing?'

'I'm going out,' he said, offering no explanation.

'What'll I tell this woman?'

'Tell her I'm not here,' he answered and, a moment after he spoke, that was true.

Signora Mitri let him in. She wore no make-up and the roots of her hair showed grey at the parting. She wore a shapeless brown dress and seemed to have grown even stouter in the time since he had last seen her. As he came close to shake her hand, he caught a faint whiff of something sweet, vermouth or Marsala.

'You've come to tell me?' she said when they were seated in the sitting-room, facing one another across a low table on which stood three soiled glasses and an empty bottle of vermouth.

'No, Signora, I'm afraid I can't tell you anything.'

Her disappointment pulled her eyes closed and drew her hands towards one another. After a moment, she glanced across at him and whispered, 'I'd hoped . . .'

'Have you read the papers, Signora?'

She didn't have to ask him what he meant. She shook her head.

'I need to know something, Signora,' Brunetti said. 'I need you to explain something to me.'

'What?' she asked neutrally, not really interested.

'You said, when we last spoke, that you listened to your husband's conversations.' When she made no acknowledgement that he had spoken he added, 'With other women.'

As he had feared, her tears started, trailing down her cheeks and dropping on to the thick fabric of her dress. She nodded.

'Signora, could you tell me how you did this?'

She looked up at him, her eyes pulled together in complete confusion.

'How did you listen to the calls?'

She shook her head.

'How did you do it, Signora?' She didn't answer and he went on. 'It's important, Signora. I need to know this.'

As he watched, her face blushed red with embarrassment. He'd told too many people that he was like a priest, that all secrets were safe with him, but he knew this to be the lie it was, so he didn't try to convince her. Instead, he waited.

Finally she said, 'The detective. He attached something to the phone in my room.'

'A tape-recorder?' Brunetti asked.

She nodded, her face growing even redder.

'Is it still there, Signora?'

Again, she nodded.

'Could you get it for me, Signora?' She didn't acknowledge having heard him, so he repeated, 'Could you get it for me? Or tell me where it is?'

She put one hand over her eyes, but the tears continued to spill out from under it.

Brunetti waited. Finally, with her other hand, she pointed over her left shoulder, towards the back of the apartment. Quickly, before she had time to change her mind, Brunetti got up and went out into the hall. He walked down the corridor, past a kitchen on one side, a dining-room on the other. At the back, he glanced into one room and saw a man's suit rack standing against the wall. He opened the door opposite and found himself in a teenager's dream room: white chiffon flounces surrounded the lower part of the bed and dressing-table; one wall was entirely covered with mirrors.

Beside the bed stood an elaborate brass phone, its receiver resting on top of a large square box, the round dial a memento from an earlier time. He approached it, knelt and pushed aside the billows of chiffon. Two wires led from the base, one to the phone jack and the other to a small black recorder no larger than a Walkman. He recognized it as one he'd used in the past, when speaking to suspects: voice-activated, its clarity of sound was remarkable for something so small.

He detached the recorder and went back into the sitting-room. When he entered she still had her hand over her eyes, but she looked up when she heard him coming in.

He set the machine on the table in front of her. 'Is this the tape recorder, Signora?' he asked.

She nodded.

'May I listen to what's on here?' he asked.

He'd once watched a television programme, one that showed the way snakes could mesmerize their prey. As her head moved back and forth, following him as he leaned down towards the recorder, he thought of it and the thought made him uncomfortable.

She nodded in agreement and, her head again following his gesture, he leaned down and pressed the 'Rewind' button and, when that clicked to show the tape was rewound, he pushed 'Play'.

Together they listened, as other voices, one of them that of a dead man, filled the room. Mitri spoke to an old school friend and made a date for dinner; Signora Mitri ordered new drapes; Signor Mitri called a woman and told her how eager he was to see her again. At this, Signora Mitri turned away her face in shame and the tears came again.

There followed minutes of the same mixture of calls, all equal in their banality and inconsequence. And nothing, now that he had embraced death, seemed more inconsequential than the vocal expression of Mitri's lust. Then he heard Bonaventura's voice, asking Mitri if he would have time to look at some papers the next evening. When Mitri agreed, Bonaventura said he'd stop by at about nine or perhaps send one of the drivers over with the documents he wanted Mitri to see. Then he heard it, the call he had prayed would be there. The phone rang twice, Bonaventura answered with a nervous '*sì*?' and the voice of another dead man was heard in the room. 'It's me. It's done.'

'Are you sure?'

'Yes. I'm still here.'

The pause that followed this was evidence of Bonaventura's shock at this rashness. 'Get out. Now.'

'When can I see you?'

'Tomorrow. In my office. I'll give you the rest.' Then they both heard the phone put down.

The next thing they listened to was the shaken voice of a man asking for the police. Brunetti reached over to the recorder and pressed 'Stop'. When he looked across at her, all emotion had been blasted from her face, all tears forgotten. 'Your brother?'

Like the victim of a bombing, she could do nothing but nod, eyes wide and staring.

Brunetti got to his feet and reached down to pick up the recorder. He slipped it into his pocket. 'I have no words to tell you how sorry I am, Signora,' he said.

28

He walked home, the small tape-recorder heavier in his pocket than any pistol or other instrument of death had ever been. It pulled him down, and the messages it contained weighed on his spirit. So easily had Bonaventura been able to prepare his brother-in-law to meet his death: no more than a phone call and the message that the driver would pass by with some papers he wanted him to read. Mitri, unsuspecting, had let his killer in, had perhaps taken papers from him, turned away to put them on a table or desk. Thus had he given Palmieri the opportunity he needed to slip the fatal wire over his head and draw it tight around his neck.

To a man as strong and practised as Palmieri, it would have been the work of an instant, and then perhaps another minute, even less, to pull the ends tight and hold them until Mitri's life was choked out of him. The traces of skin under Mitri's fingernails proved that he had tried to resist, but it had been hopeless from the moment Bonaventura called to talk about delivering the papers, from the instant, whenever that was and for whatever reason, Bonaventura decided to free himself of the man who endangered his factory and its squalid business.

Brunetti had no idea how many times he'd said that there was little in human evil that could surprise him, yet each time he stumbled or pounced upon it, it did. He'd seen men killed for a few thousand lire and for a few million dollars, but it never made any sense to him, regardless of the amount, for it still put a price on human life and said that the acquisition of wealth was a greater good – a first principle he could not grasp. Nor, he realized, could he ever fully comprehend how anyone could do it. He could understand why they did it. That was easy enough and the motives were as clear as they were varied: greed, lust, jealousy. But how bring themselves actually to do the deed? His imagination failed him; the action seemed too profound, its consequences utterly beyond his powers to know.

He arrived back at his apartment with this confusion filling his mind. When she heard him, Paola left her study and came down the corridor towards him. She saw the expression on his face and said, 'I'll make us some tisane.'

He hung up his coat and went into the

bathroom, where he washed his hands and face, and looked at himself in the mirror. How could he know such things, he wondered, and not see some sign of them in his face? He remembered a poem Paola had once read to him, something about the way the world looked on disaster and was not shaken by it. The dogs, he thought he remembered the poet writing, continued to go about their doggy business. He went about his.

In the kitchen, his grandmother's teapot stood on a raffia mat in the centre of the table, two mugs beside it, a large jar of honey to the left. He sat down and Paola poured out the aromatic tea.

'Is linden all right?' she asked as she opened the honey and spooned some into his mug. He nodded and she slid it across the table, leaving the spoon inside. He stirred it round and round, glad of the scent and the steam that rose to his nostrils.

With no introduction he said, 'He sent someone to kill him and, after it was done, the killer phoned him from Mitri's house.' Paola said nothing, but went through the same ritual of adding honey, this time a bit less, to her own tisane. As she stirred it Brunetti continued, 'His wife – Mitri's – was taping his calls from other women. And to them.' He blew across the top of the mug and sipped. Having set it down he went on, 'There's a tape of the call. From the killer to Bonaventura. He says he'll give him the rest of the money the next day.'

Paola continued stirring, as if she'd quite forgotten she was meant to drink it. When she sensed that Brunetti had nothing else to say she asked, 'Is this enough? Enough to convict him?'

Brunetti nodded. 'I hope so. I think so. They should be able to get a voice print from the tape. The machine's very sophisticated.'

'And the conversation?'

'There's no mistaking what they mean.'

'I hope so,' she said, still stirring her tea.

Brunetti wondered which of them would say it first. He looked across at her, saw the bright wings of her hair falling to either side of her face and, touched by that, said, 'So you had nothing to do with it.'

She was silent.

'Nothing at all,' he repeated.

This time she shrugged, but still she didn't speak.

He reached across the table and eased the spoon from her fingers. He placed it on the raffia mat and took her hand in his. When she made no response he insisted, 'Paola, you had nothing at all to do with it. He would have killed him anyway.'

'But I gave him a way to make it easier.'

'You mean the note?'

'Yes.'

'He would have used something else, done something else.'

'But he did that.' Her voice was firm. 'If I hadn't given them the opportunity, perhaps he wouldn't have died.'

'You don't know that.'

'No and I never will. That's what I can't stand, that I'll never know. So I'll always feel responsible.'

He pasued a long time before he found the

courage to ask, 'Would you still do it?' She didn't answer, so he added, needing to know, 'Would you still throw the stone?'

She considered this for a long time, her hand motionless beneath his. Finally she said, 'If I knew only what I knew then, yes. I'd still do it.'

When he made no answer, she turned her hand over and gave his an interrogative squeeze. He looked down, then up at her. 'Well?' she finally asked.

His voice was level when he said, 'Do you need me to approve?'

She shook her head.

'I can't, you know,' he said, not without sadness. 'But I can tell you that you weren't responsible for what happened to him.'

She considered this for a while. 'Ah, Guido, you want so much to take the trouble from the world, don't you?'

He picked up his mug with his free hand and took another sip. 'I can't do that.'

'But you want to, don't you?'

He thought about that for a long time and finally said, as though confessing to a weakness, 'Yes.'

She smiled then and squeezed his hand again. 'The wanting's enough, I think.'

For more of Donna Leon's elegant mystery series, look for the

Acqua Alta

As Venice braces for a winter tempest and the onslaught of *acqua alta*—the rising waters from torrential rain—Commissario Guido Brunetti finds out that an old friend has been savagely beaten at the palazzo home of reigning diva Flavia Petrelli.   *ISBN 978-0-14-200496-8*

Blood from a Stone

Shortly before Christmas a man is killed in Venice's Campo Santo Stefano. An illegal immigrant from Senegal, he is one of the *vu cumprà* who sell fake fashion accessories while trying to stay ahead of the law. At first the crime seems like a simple clash between rival vendors, but as Commissario Guido Brunetti probes more deeply, he begins to suspect that this murder was the work of a professional. And why does his boss want him off the case?

ISBN 978-0-14-303698-2

Death and Judgment

A truck crashes on one of the treacherous mountain roads in the Italian Dolomites, spilling a terrible cargo. Meanwhile, a prominent international lawyer is found dead in the carriage of an intercity train at Santa Lucia. Can the two tragedies possibly be connected? Commissario Guido Brunetti digs deep into the secret lives of Italy's elite classes to find the answer.   *ISBN 978-0-14-303582-4*

Death in a Strange Country

Brunetti confronts a grisly sight when the body of a young American is fished out of a fetid Venetian canal. Though all the signs point to a violent mugging, something incriminating turns up in the victim's apartment that suggests the existence of a high level conspiracy.

ISBN 978-0-14-303482-7

Doctored Evidence
After a wealthy elderly woman is found brutally murdered in her apartment, the authorities suspect her maid. But when the maid meets an untimely end trying to escape from border police, and it appears that the money she carried may not have been stolen, Commissario Guido Brunetti decides—unofficially—to take the case on himself.
ISBN 978-0-14-303563-3

Dressed for Death
Brunetti's hopes of a refreshing family holiday in the mountains are dashed when a gruesome discovery is made in Marghera—a body so badly beaten that the face is completely unrecognizable. But when the victim's identity is revealed the investigation takes a very unexpected turn.
ISBN 978-0-14-303584-8

A Noble Radiance
The new owner of a farmhouse at the foot of the Italian Dolomites is summoned to the house when his workmen disturb a macabre grave. Once on the job, Brunetti uncovers a clue that reignites an infamous cold case of kidnapping and disappearance involving one of Venice's oldest, most aristocratic families.
ISBN 978-0-14-200319-0

Through a Glass, Darkly
When the body of a night watchman is found in front of a blazing furnace at De Cal's glass factory along with an annotated copy of Dante's *Inferno,* Brunetti must investigate. Does the book contain the clues Brunetti needs to solve the murder and uncover who is ruining the waters of Venice's lagoon?
ISBN 978-0-14-303806-1

Uniform Justice
Brunetti faces an unsettling case when a young cadet has been found hanged, a presumed suicide, in Venice's elite military academy. As he pursues his inquiry, he is faced with a wall of silence and finds himself caught up in the strange and stormy politics of his country's powerful elite.
ISBN 978-0-14-200422-7